SUNRISE AT ARMAGEDDON

THE FOURTH DOCTOR SIX NOVEL

James Rozhon

Gotham Books

30 N Gould St.
Ste. 20820, Sheridan, WY 82801
https://gothambooksinc.com/

Phone: 1 (307) 464-7800

© 2023 James Rozhon. All rights reserved.

No part of this book may be reproduced, stored in a retrieval system, or transmitted by any means without the written permission of the author.

Published by Gotham Books (May 3, 2023)

ISBN: 979-8-88775-191-7 (sc)
ISBN: 979-8-88775-192-4 (e)

Because of the dynamic nature of the Internet, any web addresses or links contained in this book may have changed since publication and may no longer be valid.

The views expressed in this work are solely those of the author and do not necessarily reflect the views of the publisher, and the publisher hereby disclaims any responsibility for them.

Table of Contents

Chapter 1 6
Chapter 2 14
Chapter 3 23
Chapter 4 32
Chapter 5 41
Chapter 6 50
Chapter 7 58
Chapter 8 67
Chapter 9 76
Chapter 10 85
Chapter 11 94
Chapter 12 103
Chapter 13 112
Chapter 14 121
Chapter 15 130
Chapter 16 139
Chapter 17 148
Chapter 18 157
Chapter 19 166
Chapter 20 175
Chapter 21 184
Chapter 22 193
Chapter 23 202
Chapter 24 211
Chapter 25 220

Chapter 1

I believe in God, but probably not the way you do. Normally, I wouldn't even talk about a subject like this because I feel that faith is personal and should be kept that way. Why do I bring this up then? Because of what was about to happen to me. Someone was about to inflict – and I use that word intentionally – *inflict* their theology, faith and beliefs on me in a way that I wasn't going to like.

I am Doctor Evangeline Monica Sixkiller-Collins Collins. Doctor Six. I practice medicine in Kalispell, Montana after being born in Portland, Maine and having done an internship in Los Angeles. All that is little but introductory piffle. I don't care if you like me, agree with me or even if you think I'm a saint. I'm a doctor and as such I will treat you to the best of my abilities. I will even treat certifiable looney tunes such as Rebecca Ruth Seer. Well, crap. Someone had to do it. It might as well have been the crazy doctor from Montana. And, yes, I regret calling her a looney tune. She's crazy. And I have the certificates that allow me to say that.

It was high summer in Montana, the end of June, school was out and my perfectly idyllic life was about to get a dose of insanity. It was the end of the day in my office, my medical practice. Norma Young, my not-quite-a-doctor physician's assistant and I were closing our files for the day. Everyone had gone home. I couldn't wait to see my kids, especially my six-month-old son, Alex. Oh, stop. I love Travis and Madison, my two oldest kids just as much, but Alex is my last baby and I'm going to enjoy every moment I can with him.

Norma is my age and we've really hit it off these past three years. She'd like to finish her medical degree, do an internship across the parking lot at Kalispell Regional Medical Center and I'm encouraging her to do that. She has all the tools to be a very good doctor, but I'm the thing that's preventing her from pursuing all her goals. I know, what?

For her to go back to medical school and get all her legalities out of the way, she'd have to quit as my physician's assistant and *she doesn't want to do that.* "I'd leave you here alone and I will not allow that to happen," she said the last time we talked about it, which was yesterday.

My argument was really simple: "You ain't the only PA in the country, girlfriend." Then I added, "Norma? Just go back to school and do this. You'll make a great doctor."

Well, she's thinking about it – and was still thinking about it when the outside door opened. A man with a full dark beard entered and with his hand still on the doorknob, looked at the waiting room as though to make sure it was empty. When he was satisfied, he stood aside and a woman entered the office and came straight to the waiting room counter.

My first thought was uncomplimentary and involved an act between two people who were doing something that should be fun for both of them but was probably only fun for one of them. Okay, *fuck.* Satisfied? Why that thought? Easy. I'd just entered into the company of Rebecca Ruth Seer – because I knew who she was. As an aside? While my first thought upon seeing RRS – sorry, I just can't use her whole name because she leans on the "Seer" part of her name and that tends to intimidate people

- was to myself, Norma's first thought was aloud, albeit just barely. "What does that bitch want?" I smiled because Norma is usually a lot more tactful than that.

RRS is a short woman with an absolutely round Charlie Brown face. She makes it worse by wearing her dark brown hair short. Thus, her face looks like a bowling ball with fringe. She was wearing a dark brown shirt that looked at least two sizes too big for her. She could have been a double for Anne Hathaway in life, but that shirt hid *everything* and made me wonder if she wasn't being *just a tad* self-conscious.

Still, I smiled and said, "Can I help you?" Look, I *am* a doctor. If you're sick? I'll help regardless of your particular situation. Her? Even though I knew who she was and what she preached, I was going to be straight with her because –

I assumed – she was here because she had a medical condition that I might be able to help her with. Well, she had a problem, but its resolution was going to be difficult to cure and that had *almost* nothing to do with her brand of religion.

She looked at Norma and said, "I wish to speak you speak you alone." She might have looked like a bowling ball with fringe, but her voice was rich, powerful and the type the public swallows like vitamins.

"My office then," I said moving away from the counter and toward it.

She paused and looked back at the bearded man as though considering something. After a moment, she looked back at me and said, "No, I wish your colleague to leave."

"Evie?" Norma said. "I can finish tomorrow early."

"You sure?" I said.

"Yeah," she said. Then she hugged me with her back toward RRS and said softly, "She's a bigot not a murderer."

I laughed and said, "Okay. You go home."

Left unsaid was an item that would have caused RRS to go…well…biblical on us. Norma was going home to Doctor Kris Tice. Yeah, they're lesbians and have the union card to prove it. No, really. They do. Kris had a bunch of cards printed that proclaim her as being in good standing with local 69 of the Lady Eats Sluts Bunches Organization. Yeah, LESBO 69. Had Kris been here, RRS would have gotten one of her cards. I'm glad she wasn't because I like both of them and their sexual orientation doesn't matter to me. To RRS? Well, I'll leave that to you.

This seems to be the perfect place to drop some information about exactly who Rebecca Ruth Seer is and what she espouses.

The first time I ever heard her name was when she bought about one hundred acres in the foothills adjacent to Lolo National Forest west of Arlee, Montana. That's about sixty-five miles south of here. That was nearly five years ago and was at least two years before I moved to Kalispell. She gets national attention sporadically, but doesn't seem to seek it like a lot of folks do. The attention she gets just sort of happens. My guess is that when you preach the stuff she does, *someone* is going to look at it, try to be objective and then laugh his ass off. Maybe an example of the type of stuff she says is warranted.

I was living in Compton, California, and working in an ER there the first time I heard her name. One of the cable news outfits interviewed her in relation to an apocalyptic zealot from the Middle East somewhere who said that God was coming that April. He gave an exact date and everything. He said that God would come to Megiddo in Israel, throw The Beast into a vast pit and the world would be ruled by the righteous at that point. I don't remember the prophet's name, but I remembered Becky, um RRS. Someone stuck a microphone in her face and asked her about the end of the world that was coming that April and her reply was short, succinct and to the point. She said, "God hasn't reveal His plans for the end of the world to me as yet. When he does, I'll let you know." After April came and went and God was still somewhere else, no one heard from that particular zealot again. She made occasional appearances on television after that time and each time she repeated. "God hasn't revealed His plans as yet. Don't worry. I'll let you."

I knew she was married, did not have children and claimed she was still a virgin. I wondered about Mr. Seer, a guy named Albert, and how he handled a celibate wife.

All this was preliminary to seeing RRS in person. After Norma left and it was just her and the guy with the beard, I asked her, "Where would you like to talk?"

"Right here," she said.

The bearded man stood at the door looking for all the world like a goalie. And, No. I have no idea what that is. I'm a doctor, so maybe he looked like a white blood cell guarding against bacteria.

"That's fine by me," I said and headed toward the waiting room door.

She stopped me by putting up her hand and saying, "No. Stay on that side of the counter."

I smiled and returned to where she stood. "So, this isn't a medical visit?"

I thought I was going to get one of those brimstone speeches about how I married my uncle and that my children were, therefore, mongoloids or some such. While it's true that Mario is my uncle because he is my mother's brother, there is no genetic material between us because both my mother and my husband were adopted by my grandfather, Jack Collins.

That's not what happened.

This was a medical visit, a most unusual medical visit.

And as it turned out, most of what she told me was at best a lie and at least misinformation.

My job was to determine which was which.

And if I could help her because, as it turned out again, someone was going to have to help her and why not me, why not someone who knew nothing about anything but medicine? Well, and my husband and kids. In their case? I came late to the party. As Mario says, "Better late than never."

***

I was born Rebecca Ruth Teller. God didn't talk to me until I was fourteen. The first thing He told me was, "There are Others here with me. You will meet them." Then He told me who they were. "Guinevere is at my right hand. You will listen to her. Anne Frank is with me. Sappho is with me. You will listen to them as you would listen to me." Sappho was a test for me. I was to learn who she was and what she did. I tried to rebel against God when I found out who she was. My punishment was a week in bed and a night in the hospital. I caught pneumonia and almost died. I listened after that.

God told me obey after that. I did. Then He told me to date a boy named William. I did. William was a goober. He could recite Pi to thirty-two places. William died. He was fifteen. I never found out what killed him. Then God said, "Date Samuel." I did. Samuel was sixteen. He died, too. I never found out what killed him. I wasn't curious either. If I needed to know, God would tell me.

Mother said I needed a job when I turned eighteen. She wanted me to work in her restaurant. It burned down. They said it was arson. They didn't know who did it. I didn't care. I didn't like the job anyway. I went to a religious school in Amarillo after that.. Mom opened another restaurant with insurance money.

School was interesting. God told me that most of what they taught there was heresy. I made a friend there. Albert Seer. I liked him. Sometimes we talked and didn't go to class. Sometimes we walked across the plains and talk. God told me that Albert was special. He told me that I should tell Albert a secret. I did. I told him that Pastor Kennedy was a fraud. Albert believed me. He said, "I knew it."

Pastor Kennedy taught Bible classes at the school. He said that the Bible was decided at The Council of Nicaea in 325 AD. God said that the Bible Always Was. I believed Him. God doesn't lie. Pastor Kennedy was fired from his position. Someone sent pictures of him and a female student together. They were together in the Biblical sense of that word. They were filmed entering a motel room. The photographer took pictures of them while outside their room. He filmed them through a gap in the curtains. She was doing obscene things to him with her mouth. Pastor Kennedy eventually received divorce papers from his wife.

Albert and I did not graduate from the school in Amarillo. We went to another school in Lawton, Oklahoma. I was twenty and Albert was twenty-seven. His father died and left Albert money. I never asked Albert how much money it was. He told me. Then he proved it by showing me a check for seven million, three hundred-twenty-eight thousand twenty-nine dollars and fifty-six cents. He said, "That's a lot of money." Albert said, "Want to see a movie?"

I said, "Which one?"

He said, "The Greatest Story Ever Told," It was playing at a theater in town.

We went.

I did not like it. John Wayne should have had a bigger role. Max von Sydow is Swedish. Neither of them were used correctly. I told Albert how I felt. God told me he would agree. He did. I hugged him. I liked hugging him. It made me good. I like feeling good.

He asked me if I wanted to see another movie. I said yes. "I want to see 'The Passion Of The Christ'. Mel Gibson knows things." We went. I cried with heartfelt tears when Jesus was scourged. All that blood. God told me that Mel Gibson was going to Heaven when he died. I agreed with God. Respectfully, of course. I've learned my lesson. Be humble. I am.

Albert asked me to marry him. I didn't mind marrying him, but I had reservations. Albert asked me what they were. I told him, "God said I must be a virgin or I won't enter Heaven." Albert said that was okay with him. I told him we could be married. I did the naughty thing with my mouth with him on our wedding night. I didn't like it. God told me that I should. "Albert Seer is your husband. You should be docile to him." I told God I didn't know what that word meant. God told me to look it up. I did. I am docile to Albert. I believe I always have been.

A man named David Koresh said he was The Final Prophet. God told me, "No. You are The Final Prophet." I told Albert not to listen to him. Albert didn't. I did the naughty thing to him and he smiled. David Koresh was killed by the government. God's Kingdom did not come. God said it would not. God told me that I would establish His Kingdom but not yet. God said I was to wait. God said I had to build His temple first. God told me where it was to be built. I listened. He told me. I told Albert where we were going. Albert said, "You need to write this stuff down. A book will attract the righteous." I agreed.

One of the businesses that Albert's mother owned was a small publishing Company. Albert wanted to tell his mother about my book. I told him to wait until I'd written it. He agreed and I did the nasty thing with him. I still didn't like the taste. God said I would get used to it. I will. It hasn't happened yet. It will.

I told Albert we needed to move to Arlee, Montana. God's Temple would be built there. We would build it. I did the nasty thing with him and we moved to Arlee, Montana.

His mother died and Albert inherited her estate. Her name was Deborah. A good, Godly name. He showed me the bottom line. Just under three hundred million dollars.

It took little more than six months to buy land near Arlee. It cost only twenty-seven thousand dollars to buy five acres. The land was along the foothills of a mountain. God said, "Remember Mt. Ararat and why it was important." I didn't have to read the Bible to know. It was where the Noah's Ark came to rest when the waters receded. I wondered what God meant by that, but he said, "All will become clear in My Time."

The first thing we did was build our home. It took longer to accomplish than I thought it might. We had all the permits needed to build it, but workers were difficult to find. God told me, "Post a sign." It was ingenious. It was God. I posted a sign. It read, "Unless the Lord builds the house, those who build it labor in vain." Psalms 127:1. Simple.

Albert and I had the plans for the house. Albert had an architect draw up plans. God told me that there needed to be a room that looked at the mountains and was made of glass. Albert said it would be done. Then he asked, "Which mountain?" I pointed at the one behind our future home. "That one. That is where The End will start."

He looked nervous.

I did the nasty thing.

Albert was okay after that.

Then I wrote my book.

I wrote The Book.

Chapter 2

Every behavior is a symptom. I learned that from my mother when I was seven and I thought she was dying from aspirin poisoning. Then followed orange juice poisoning, symptoms of epilepsy, symptoms of an aneurysm and so many other false flags that Mom arranged for me to spend two hours with my grandfather, Doctor Albert Morganstern. He showed me text books, anatomical drawing – and yes, they were anatomically accurate because Mom wanted them to be so – and let me listen to his heart beat through his stethoscope, take his blood pressure and his heart rate. When I was done, I said, "Doctor Grandpa? You have a heart murmur." He laughed so hard that I really did think he was going to burst a blood vessel and die. Mom got me my own copy of Gray's Anatomy and I don't mean the stupid TV show either. Sometimes I got so absorbed in it that I forgot to go to school. Mom was cool with that because I was always a good student.

All that means is that when Rebecca Ruth Seer stood in front of me over my counter in my office that every single twitch, turn and movement became symptoms against which I would base a diagnosis of whatever was wrong with her. I folded my hands on the countertop and asked, "So, how I can help you otherwise?"

She turned and said to the man at the door, "Please step outside."

Okay. Insurance. You might note that I hadn't asked her anything like that. I don't. Almost never. Well, my staff does because they're trained to ask for it and I trained them. But me? I never ask because it never dawns on me that your illness and my ability to help you might depend on your insurance. I'm a doctor, a rich one. I won't be able to spend all my money, my husband won't be able to spend all of his and my kids – even if they turn out to be throw-money-to-the-wild types – will need at least one more generation beyond them to spend it all. I *never* think about money. I have an accountant and I pay him to think about my money. Once, about two years ago, I had to talk to him about something, but I couldn't find his business card and couldn't remember his name or the company that had all my money. It took Mario to call him and front my question. That's what I think about money.

After I asked RRS the question, I waited and observed. *Pupils aren't dilated, so that means she's not on any pupil-dilating drugs.* Okay, okay. It was a doctor joke and I've learned not to tell them out loud around people who aren't doctors and even around some who are. Look, I think they're funny.

Anyway.

"I think I have a problem and I want you to tell me what it is," she said and then raised her head a bit as though expecting something, but not from me.

"And I can't touch you or examine you any closer than this?" I said.

"That's right," she said with her head still tilted upwards a bit.

Dammit. I wanted to tell her to find another doctor, but that old itch was still there just like it always had been with my mother. I'd see all these phantom symptoms and she wouldn't let me touch her. She'd just smile and say something like, "Well, what do you *think* is wrong with me this time?" Christ, it was anything from head lice to muscular dystrophy. She'd always give me a gentle laugh and then say, "Nope. Try again tomorrow." And I'd try, too. She gave me one diagnosis per day during the summer when I was thirteen. My copy of Gray's Anatomy was already dog-eared and that summer just made them worse. My first real diagnosis was the morning I woke up and found my mother euphorically dancing around the kitchen. "You're bi-polar," I said feeling as though I'd nailed it.

"Well, no, I'm not, but there are others that would disagree." Then she looked at me as sternly as she could and said, "And Doctor Morganstern agrees with that, so don't call him." Then she danced to where I stood in the doorway and said, "But that's very good, Evie. You keep it up and you'll figure it out."

Well, encouragement. The next morning, I walked in just as she dropped a butter knife and I said as I stabbed my finger at her and screamed horrifically, "You have a brain tumor!"

She fell into such deep laughter that I stood ready to administer first aide whenever she collapsed. She didn't, but she hugged me and said, "No, Evie. Your mother is just clumsy, but thank you ever so much for worrying about me. Keep trying."

All that – and I never diagnosed my mother with anything more serious than her love for her family – led to this. Rebecca Ruth Seer was playing the same game that my mother allowed me to play with her over twenty years ago. I got lots of practice with her and never got it right one single time. Thankfully. My mother is still healthy and is now a junior Senator from Maine. Her next goal is to be elected the first female President of The United States and given her past, I would not bet against her.

But Becky.

She was still in that stance that suggested she was listening to someone, or expecting something to happen. What did that suggest? A muscle spasm? No, I didn't think so because she was holding the pose too rigidly and hadn't elicited any signs of either discomfort or unease. So, I asked, "Are you expecting something to happen?"

Oddly enough, she said, "Yes. I expect God to talk to me and tell me what I should do in this case."

"So, God gave you free will and you don't plan to use it?"

Bystanders would say I was arguing theology with her, but all I was doing was trying to get another set of symptoms upon which to base a diagnosis. I like to say that she had either high or low blood pressure but neither of those conditions has any overt signs that you can see. Well, a heart attack might signify something, but I hoped this diagnosis didn't come to that.

She looked at me with a cool demeanor and said, "Correct. God tells me what to do and I listen to Him."

"Did he tell you to come to see me?"

She inclined her head, winced – and that was her first overt emotional outburst – and said, "Yes. I only hope He doesn't come to disagree with my decision."

Delusional? Okay, that was tentative. "What sort of things does that leave you to decide?"

She frowned and said, "I didn't come here to debate with you. I want you to tell me what's wrong with me so I can get better."

Hmm.

"Well," I said for no other reason than to keep her talking and thus giving me more symptoms upon which to base a diagnosis, "You could always just ask God. He tells you everything else, so why not this?"

"God has been silent on these issues. I don't know why."

"Can you tell me more of your symptoms so that I can maybe help you decide what to do about this?"

Okay, okay. I should have started with that question. You have to admit, though, that this entire scene was a bit out of the ordinary. I can count on one hand and have three fingers and a thumb left over from the number of times a patient has asked me to diagnose him or her without touching him – and medical school doesn't count and neither do reruns of House.

What she was going to do was omit the one symptom that might have ended this long before it started. Stupid me, I saw it with my own two eyes right there and then and never counted it as a symptom of anything but delusion. But delusion is a symptom that I didn't see or didn't use as a diagnosis as to what was really wrong with her. I was watching for overt physical signs of something like head trauma or concussion. Hell, my own troubles with her might have been allayed if I had only been able to do a test on either her saliva or her blood. One or the other would have given me the tool to start treatment with her.

She looked around the room as though making certain there was no one there but her and I. Then she said, "It hurts when I...urinate."

Wow. A real symptom. Okay, there were any number of reasons why that would present itself. A kidney stone, a urinary tract infection, a bladder infection, cystitis and several others popped into my mind at that point.

"Anything else?" I asked.

She looked like she wanted to bash my head in with the stone tablets Moses brought down from Sinai. "Isn't that enough?" she said, her chin showing signs of turning to stone.

"Nope," I said cheerfully because despite the circumstances, I thought I was making progress. "That could be a sign of anything from adenocarcinoma to vaginal candidiasis." Okay, that neatly ran the spectrum of possible causes of her condition. Then I smiled and said, "Or anything in between."

Her head tilted up again and she said, "Okay. I hear and obey."

Then she turned around and left the office.

There it was again. The symptom that led all the others.

And there were others. Hell, there was at least one other that was she hiding and that was going to cause Hell to pay.

All those religious signs. Hell, God, Obey and so many others that by the time this was done, I'd feel like becoming a hermit in the desert.

Yep. See?

***

God told me to write The Book. He instructed me to call it "The Universal Word of God". People would call it "The Universal". It would be the reference to all things Godly. It was going to transcend every other book. It was going to be coherent. There would be no contradictions. I started writing The Book when I was twenty-six.

All I did for the first six months we lived in Arlee was write. No one read it. No one needed to read it. It was the direct Word of God. The first thing God told me about the book was, "It will be brief". God doesn't like questions, so I accepted it. Even had I not known that, I would have. During this time, I ate did little beside transcribe His words and eat. I never had the desire to socialize with others. Albert didn't mind. God told me that. "Your husband will allow you to finish this." He did. I did, too.

It took two years to write. Just over one hundred thousand words. The first sentence was simple and direct. "This is God's Testament." Everything that followed, flowed from that point. I was God's tool and He used me. It was a glorious feeling to know that I was doing His work.

Albert agreed to publish The Universal through our publishing company. He opened an office in Kalispell and he commutes there daily. I spend my time communing with God. Servants bring me food and I thank them. Having an earthly body is tedious. However, God wants me here to do His work. I will do it and long as He want to me here to do His will.

I am healthy. I have always been healthy. God would not choose an unhealthy person to do His work. One day, I went to cleanse myself in the bathroom. It burned when I relived myself. That was okay. I must have disobeyed God in some way. He was admonishing me to be a stronger moral force. I reapplied myself and fired all my servants. They were at fault for my transgressions. The burning continued, however.

God said, "Child? I can cure you, but I will not. You must prove yourself to me. Find another that is strong enough to do this."

The pain began to interfere with my ability to communicate with God. It got worse when I started to bleed from my special place. I told Albert to find a doctor. He came to me the next day and said he found one. It was a woman. Doctor Collins. The Heavenly Signs were excellent. Her name was Doctor Eve Collins.

We went there the next day. God hadn't spoken to me since the bleeding began. He was testing me again. He was testing me like He tested Jesus. I understood. Still, I missed His voice. It was only during this time that I wondered why He spoke to me with the voice of a female. I asked Him, "Why do You speak to me as a female?" He did not answer. It bothered me so much that I snapped at Albert. He loves me. He smiled and said, "Don't worry, Rebecca. You'll be fine again in no time."

The sign on Doctor Collins's door showed her real name to be Doctor Evangeline Sixkiller-Collins Collins. I began to get nervous and suspicious of her because her name wasn't Eve. It was Evangeline. I didn't know what that meant. I asked God and He did not reply. I was in the desert alone. I had only my faith to sustain me.

My own personal dictate was only Doctor Collins. No one else. There was another lovely woman with her. Still, I asked her to leave. God gave His blessing to me preference. Doctor Collins asked her to leave and she did. I was going to be fine. God had brought me to this place.

I know about doctors. I know that they mean well, but they completely miss the mark on why people get sick. Illnesses are a sign that God is displeased with you. Period. There are no exceptions. Once in a moment of weakness, Albert asked about babies who were born sick. I conferred with God and told him why they are born sick. "It is a punishment on the parents." He asked what that meant. Albert is more intelligent than that. I wouldn't have married him otherwise. I told him that sick newborns are a sign that the parents have committed a sin. If they repent, their baby will be healthy. He nodded and went away. He knows I will not do the nasty thing with him when he acts obtuse. He isn't and I didn't.

God has already told me that I will not have children. I will not adopt any either. That was another commandment from God. My place in the world was to transcribe His words. Then I was to guide as many of them to His Temple as I could. I was to have a long life. I was ready for it. There was much to do.

I felt as though I was wasting my time with Doctor Collins. She asked me how she could help me if she couldn't touch me. I thought it was a stupid question. I told her that I wanted her to tell me what was wrong with me. It seemed simple. It clouded me impression of her. She played Devil's advocate and I wondered if this God or The Devil. It could have been either. I decided that God was speaking through her mouth when she asked me to describe a few symptoms. The only one I could talk about was the pain I had when urinating.

She nodded knowingly. Maybe this was God's Way after all. It seemed that she already had an idea of what was wrong. Still, I was impatient. I wanted the pain to stop. I know God could cure me, but He wasn't. I believe He was telling me that I was a child of the world. In that case, I would take her medicine.

Things began to feel wrong when she asked for additional symptoms. There were others, but none that I could tell her. They were intensely personal. I looked to Heaven and implored God to tell me what to do. He didn't. He was still silent. It was unnerving to grow up with God's voice and then be denied it. However, I had promised never to argue with Him again,. I wouldn't. I didn't. Instead, I left.

There were other doctors.

Albert seemed distressed when I went to our car. I know he worries about me. Husbands do. I told him I would do the nasty thing with him. He seemed compliant at that point. We went home and I did it. I still did not like the taste. I loved it when he hugged my head. It was his sign that he loved me. I wanted to do it again. He laughed and said that he loved that. It took time to accomplish it. I still didn't like the taste.

I went to bed that night and had the same signs of illness. God was still upset with me. That could be the only reason I saw. I listened for His voice and did not hear it. God was still there, but was testing me and punishing me for something. I do not like being punished. I decided to cleanse myself.

The next day I asked Albert to drive me to the Flathead River. I told him where. It was a place upstream from Dixon. There was an island there. We parked in the dirt along the river and I said, "Help me. I need to cleanse myself." He asked me what sort of help I needed. I told him. He said he could do that.

We went down to the river. He removed my clothes and I waded out until I was waist-deep in water. It was cold. I knelt in it until it cover me. I stayed under until my lungs were bursting. Then I stood, threw my arms wide and said, "I am clean, Lord!"

We went home and God spoke to me.

At least that's how I interpreted it.

It still hurt to urinate.

I wasn't clean.

That doctor knows something.

She is The Devil's voice.

The Devil's vice.

Chapter 3

I forgot to go home that night. I mean, completely. After Becky walked out, I went back to my office and did an internet search for her. Oh, don't get me wrong. I knew *exactly* who she was and where she lived Well, within limits. I knew she owned a large tract of land to the west of Arlee. She built a huge church there, called it God's Temple and didn't advertise it at all for several years. I read where someone asked her why she built it in such an out-of-the-way place and said – predictably, I might add – "God told me to build it here." I mean, what else could she say?

Well, stupid me. My phone rang and I noticed that it was after nine o'clock. I moaned because my monomania had struck again. I had a patient – no, I had a person that I thought should be a patient – and they left without giving me a chance to figure out what was wrong with them. Well, her. Well, to be honest, that shirt she was wearing hid all traces of her femininity, so I left her as a generic patient. The patient got away from me before I could diagnose whatever condition was present. I think that succinctly summed up my medical opinion of Rebecca Ruth Seer.

"I'm sorry, Mario," I said and wondered for maybe the millionth time if he ever got tired of my apologies. "I kind of had a patient."

"Kind of?" he said, his voice full of good humor.

"Yeah. I'll tell you about it when I get home."

"You won't forget where you live, will you?" he chided me.

"No, you fool," I said happily. "Hell, it's a kind of puzzle that you might be able to help me with."

"Then by all means, come home and we'll talk."

"We will," I said.

My office is no more than a couple of miles from my home on Stillwater Loop north of the city. It's so close that by the time I get comfortable in my car, I'm home. My routine is always the same. I pulled into the driveway, hit my garage door remote, park my car and go into the house. This time was a bit different. I hit the garage door remote, the door slid up and I saw Travis and Madison, my oldest kids, standing where I was going to park my car. They had their arms crossed and both were tapping their left foot impatiently. Both of them looked at their wrists as though checking an invisible watch for the time. It was too cute. I put my face in my hands and started to giggle.

They backed up to the wall that would put them at my door when I parked in the garage. Then, in complete synchronicity, they waved their left arms and bade me park my Honda Pilot. This had Mario written all over it. I pulled into the garage. Travis and Madison resumed their perturbed arms-folded stance right where I'd open my door.

Once I had it open, Travis looked as stern as he could and said, "And where have you been, young lady?" He's eleven. Madison is nine.

I stumbled through, "Um, I was working and…um…time sort…um…got away from me and …um…I'm sorry." I tried hard not to laugh.

Madison pointed to the house and said, "Inside, young lady! No dinner for you!"

Travis pointed the same way and said, "Straight to your room and be ass-end-up over your bed!" Then he looked nervously at his sister and said, "Did I say it right?"

Oh, Mario,. You are so going to get it. I got out of my car and Travis looked absolutely scared to death. Maddy said, "I think so."

Travis replied with a squeaky voice, "I don't even know what it means."

Maddy rallied and said, "Upstairs, young lady!"

I tried on my best apologetic look and practically cried, "I'm really sorry. I won't do it again."

Maddy started to giggle and Travis elbowed her and said, "Stop it. We're being serious." She put on her most ferocious frown, pointed at the house and said, "Get!"

Like a convicted felon, I hung my head and walked with the slow steps of doom to my home. Maddy giggled again from behind me and Travis did it again. "Stop it," he said like every big brother ever born. Then he giggled.

Mario was waiting for me in the living room. He was slapping a belt against his thigh and looking as fierce as I ever saw him. Travis took a position to his left and Maddy one to his right. "Explain this," he said gravely.

With my head held low, I said, "I forgot the time. Sorry."

Alex was there, too. He was sleeping in a swing setup in the living room.

Still smacking his belt against his thigh, he said, "Go to your room and do what your son told you to do."

"Yes, sir," I said and suppressed a giggle when I headed for the second floor to my bedroom. Violet, our...um...house person, was in the hallway with her son, David. Their bedroom is on the third floor. Yeah, I have a big house. It's smaller when Vee's family and friends show up from the reservation. She's a Blackfoot Indian. She sing-songed, "Someone's in trouble." People think we're sisters when we're together. My hair, if anything, is darker than hers. David put his face into his mother's stomach and laughed. I tried to look scared. Mario, trailed by Travis and Maddy, followed me into the bedroom. I heard the sounded of Mario and Vee high-fiving each other behind me. I knew Vee would go downstairs and get Alex.

Once in the bedroom, he said sternly to his kids, "This is between your mother and I."

"Yes, sir," they said as though rehearsed. Well, duh.

With the door closed, he hugged me and whispered, "Thank you for playing along. We have one more act in our play."

"Sure," I said reveling in his hug.

"Ass end up over the bed," he said loud enough for the kids to hear.

We took a spot just inside the door so that when he blew open, our kids would see us.

"This is for being late," Mario said slapping the belt against his thigh.

Right on cue, the door opened and Travis screamed, "Stop it! You promised..." and came face-to-face with his parents hugging each other.

We had a group hug that included Vee, David, and Alex. Mario thanked his kids for playing along and said to them, "Maybe this will help get her home on time for dinner a bit more often."

"Daddy made spaghetti and you missed it!" Maddy said, her voice breaking as she tried to be stern.

Mario nodded toward the balcony and said, "Well, not exactly."

There was a candle-lit table there. Our balcony is enclosed because, well, this *is* Montana. We can have dinner out there no matter what type of weather we're having. While, I never expect it because I've never managed to be the one who prepares it, I'm always grateful to him and them because they tend to collaborate.

"Someone has a boyfriend," Vee sing-songed.

Everyone wound up in our bedroom, but that's not unusual. I put my purse and my doctor's bag next to the my side of the bed and went out to the balcony. It was decorated like I would assume an Italian restaurant would do it. A green tablecloth, an ornate candleholder and silverware that looked positively Florentine – if I knew what that meant. I expected a violin to start playing somewhere.

What followed was a complete spaghetti dinner that was delivered to my table by everyone else in the family. Even Alex got to deliver my bright red napkin. Of course, he'd been teething on it before he gave it to me. He squawked when Mario took it from him and gave it to me. I almost gave it back when Mario pulled a pacifier from his pocket and gave it to him. Everyone was happy.

Maddy had that Mommy-can –I-sit-in-your-lap look and I let her. She's going to be a tall girl like her mother and her grandmother, maybe even taller than Mom. All that means is that it's getting tougher to get her seated. Given that Mom sat in Grandpa's lap when he was in his sixties, I think I can manage despite how much my lap disagrees.

She chattered for ten straight minutes about someone named Bruno and seemed to be having a serious case of puppy love toward him until I realized he was a singer. All that meant was that she was at the age when she began noticing them. I wondered how much else I'd missed of her childhood. It made me sad until she hugged me and said, "I love you, Mommy." Even better, Travis did it, too, and said the same thing. David looked at his mother and she nodded. He came up to me, hugged me and said, "I love my mom, but I really like you." Alex took that moment to make a mess in his diapers. I think that meant it was unanimous.

All too soon, they were gone and it was just us. "I can't apologize enough," I said to him as I stood and hugged him.

"No need. We'll always be cool."

"Right up until you find a blond with big tits," I said, my arms around him.

He could have been as clever as he always is, but instead he said, "Evie? Don't worry. No one will ever tempt me. It's been you ever since I was five. There won't be anyone else."

Then he kissed me and I completely forgot about Rebecca Ruth Seer.

Hell, it wasn't going to matter anyway because I wasn't going to see her again until it was her idea.

And, Lord, I could wait forever for that to happen.

***

I kept waiting for God to say, "Rebecca? Kill that woman." He did. He said nothing. I was beginning to think I'd sinned somehow. I knelt in front of the altar in the Temple and prayed fervently. I asked Him to punish me. I asked Him to give me a penance. I asked Him if I should scourge myself. I'd never done that. It frightened me that He might tell me to do that. He didn't. He remained silent. I felt as though I was in the desert for forty days.

Albert came and whispered to me, "Rebecca, dear. It's nearly one o'clock in the morning. You need some rest."

His voice forced me back into this world. I realized my knees were sore. So was my back and thighs. I'd been kneeling for...three hours? I had no memory of the intervening time. That happened a lot to me. I'd fall into prayer and forget everything that happened. It was almost always Albert that woke me from my reverie with God. I stood wearily and gave him a Godly Hug. Our bodies did not touch. Just our arms.

I went to the bathroom and the pain was worse than before. I leaned over, my arms around my stomach and withheld a moan. It took a Biblical effort to remain silent. When I finished, the pain had spread to my stomach. It doubled me over as I sat on the toilet.

Albert said from the other side of the door, "Are you okay?"

God wants me to be strong. He told me that many times in the past month or so. I don't keep track of time. God does that for me. Well, and Albert. Albert loves me in a way God approves. I do not lay down and spread myself for him. I give myself to God and no other. God approves of the nasty thing. That's my gift to Albert. He approves of it as well. He told me once he wanted to hug after I did it. I knelt and asked God for a decision. He approved a single hug. I hugged Albert and he was very happy.

But was I okay? No. I was in pain. I could not tell Albert, however. Instead, I answered, "Yes. Just a moment." I was bleeding again from my special place. It hurt. The insides of my special place hurt. I thought about going back to that heathen doctor. Would God approve? I got on my knees and prayed for an answer. God remained silent. He was punishing me. I did not know why. I was scared.

I stood and pulled up my underwear and pants. My hands were shaking. Albert would be worried. I decided to calm myself. I said a quiet prayer. Then another. It helped but I was still in pain.

I opened the bathroom door. Albert was there. "Are you really okay?" he said.

"Yes," I said with a small smile. God does not like loud celebrations that are not directed at Him. We did a Godly hug and I said, "Please. Do not worry about me."

"I do and I will," he said. I was happy that he was acting as a supplicant. God spoke to me and I deserved respect.

"I will decide tomorrow if I need to see a doctor."

"That doctor, Sixkiller. She's very good. You should give her another chance."

Doctor SixSixSix is not a good doctor. God didn't say that, so it might not be true. Albert might be right. He is a good man and we are happy. I must take his counsel seriously. "In the morning," I said. "I will decide then."

I sleep on my back. I hold a crucifix in my hands at my chest. Sometimes I wish I did not have breasts. They are an unnecessary nuisance. Were I to have children, I could suckle them. I will not have children. I will remain chaste throughout my life. Albert sleeps to my right because I am always at God's right hand. With my left hand, I can touch Him. It has never happened, but I am positive it will. With all my strength, I know that one day I will touch God. Only then will my life be complete. It already has meaning.

I am a terrible sinner. Once in a moment of madness, I considered pleasuring myself with my fingers. It was so disgusting that I cried. Albert became very agitated. I said to him, "It is nothing, husband. I merely want to please God. I know that sometimes I fail. This is one of those times." He looked nervous and I had to give him a Godly Hug to calm him.

Sleep came hard that night. I slept maybe three or four hours. I spent the rest of the time with my teeth and fists clenched because I was in pain. I clutched the crucifix tighter to my chest. I held it closely over my heart. I'd given my heart to Him Who Is Most Just. If I was in pain, I deserved it.

God's Temple has begun to attract attention. Albert was talking to people from a tour bus. They were pilgrims seeking God's Word. Despite my pain, I went to where Albert was speaking to them. There were maybe twenty souls. Albert was saying, "God has spoken to Rebecca and she has responded by building His Temple." He saw me and smiled. "This is Rebecca Ruth Seer, God's Messenger. God told her to build it and she did. She is God's servant. You should listen to her."

They were all holding The Universal, God's complete plan for us, his servants. Upon seeing me, the group chanted, "The world was unshaped. God shaped it. Man was primitive. God stood him upright." Those were the first four sentences God told me to write. I clasped my hands together in front me and bowed to them.

When they finished chanting those verses, I said aloud, "Please, enter into God's Temple." It felt wonderful that people knew those words. It felt even better that I was God's secretary.

I escorted them to God's Temple. Albert took charge of building it. I don't know where the paintings that glorified God came from. I don't care either. They are as magnificent as He is. I led them down the center aisle and they spread themselves through the pews. I walked to the pulpit and stood before them.

God spoke to me.

His voice hit me so hard that my entire body began to tingle and shudder with a rhapsody that caused me to grasp the edges of the speaker's platform. Otherwise, I might have fallen. I think I screamed, "Oh, God." His revelation was that intense. As His power swept through me, I lost sight of those who came to see me. Slowly, I regained a sense of myself. I looked at them and they were wide-eyed with reverent awe.

"God has spoken to me," I said. "He tells me that He is coming."

Someone from the small crowd asked, "When, your reverence?"

I listened to Him. He said one word. I repeated it to them. "Soon."

The supplicants began to sing, a chorus sounded. They were standing and singing. "God in the highest!" Their faces were rapturous. A woman in the front pew had her hands gripping her blouse. She fell to her knees and sang with them. I was a witness to the power of God.

Then a spasm of pain ripped across my stomach. I bent over the lectern. I screamed, "God! Help me!"

All of them began to chorus it. "God help us!"

Despite the pain, I stood taller and threw my arms toward Heaven. Then I cried, "It will all be over soon! All of our suffering! All of our pain! No one will hurt anymore!"

Still, I wondered why He had chosen me.

It hurt to be His chosen one.

Chapter 4

Norma was already in the office when I got there at six-forty-five. Norma has beautiful blond hair and should the one who is mistaken for being a California airhead instead of me. She wears it in a bun while working, but you'd have to be blind not to see how beautiful she is. Me? Well, I've pushed three kids into a doctor's hands so my ass counts as deadweight if not downright fat. Okay, okay. Mario doesn't agree, but then he's my husband and he's supposed to feel that way. All that means is that his opinion doesn't count. Neither does Norma's because she giggles every time I tell her I have a fat ass. "Yeah, and your mother says that shit, too," she responds every time.

Then, I got lost inside my day, just like always. Norma caught me in my office and said, "Um, lunch? Don't you ever get hungry?" Then she looked at her watch and said, "It's only three-thirty and you've been here since six-forty-five. Either go willingly or I'll throw you into the parking lot and lock the door." Cindy and Hannah were right behind her and their arms were crossed defiantly. I looked like I was going to lunch whether I liked it or not. Norma added, "Your next client isn't scheduled for another half hour. That means you have at least forty-five minutes."

I stood, hugged all of them and said, "No, it means I have at most twenty minutes and that means I'll be eating in my car while I drive back here."

"Evie?" Norma said. "I'll lock the door. Go get something to eat and don't come back until you're done. I mean it." She even stomped her foot for good measure.

I threw up my hands and said, "Okay, I surrender. I'll go eat tacos over at Joe's."

Cindy rolled her eyes and said, "Oh, great. We get her to go out and she's going to eat all that high cholesterol food Joe serves."

I smiled at her and said, "So? Am I going or are you going to play food critic to all my choices?"

"Just go," she said as Hannah and Norma stared daggers at her.

Our office is on Sunset Boulevard. Highway 93 by any other name. Sunnyview Lane is a cross street of it. While Joe's Mexican Food's address is on Sunset, all I had to do was cross Sunnyview to get to it. It's operated by a guy named Hector Ramirez who came here from...wait for it...England. Yep, an Hispanic who speaks with a right proper English accent. Better than that? His wife looks like Princess Di and she speaks with...wait for it...an Hispanic accent because she's from Mexico. Her name is Isabella. I get culture shock every time I go in there. This time was no exception.

Bella – because that's what she wants to be called, said upon seeing me, "Late lunch again, Doc?"

"Early dinner," I said smiling.

"Let me guess. "Two chicken tacos, fried rice and a glass of water."

"To go," I added.

"Naturally," she said. "All that means is that you'll be eating them as you cross the street back to your office."

Joe came out from the grill with a Styrofoam container in one hand and cup with a lid on it. He handed them to me and said, "Norma called it in as soon as you left the office. And it's Sprite and not water because she wants you to have a spurt of energy that will last the day."

It used to make me furious that Norma would do stuff like this. I tried to ask her to stop and she put her face in mine and screamed, "My job depends on you being at your best and a doctor that doesn't eat is headed for so many physical problems that I can't list them all! Evie! You're going to eat if I have to tie you to the chair and force feed you!" Then she spat, "Do. I. Make. Myself. Clear!"

I crossed my arms a bit too petulantly for her taste and said, "Yes, Mommy."

She mashed her nose against mine and screamed, "I'll call your mother!"

It was too much. I started to laugh and it turned into a fit of giggles. Flo, Liz, Cindy and Hannah held up pieces of paper that read 8, 10, 9 and 5.

I looked at Hannah and said, "5?"

She looked serious when she said, "I think you need to wear a shock collar."

All that led me to crossing the street, talking with abject surrender to Bella as Joe hands me a container with food that Norma ordered for me. I took the container back to my Honda Pilot, sat in the driver's seat and my mind immediately went to Rebecca Ruth Seer. I didn't even fight it. She was sick, came to me and I considered that her abrupt exit of my office was a symptom of whatever was wrong with her. The only thing she told me was that, "It hurts when I urinate." I even considered the way she said it. She paused before she used the word "urinate". Most people would have used the word "pee". Then I closed my eyes, took a bite of a chicken taco and tried to recreate the scene as closely as I could. *She turned and raised her head as she spoke the words. It was as though she was listening to someone tell her what to say.* Was that another symptom? If so, of what? Also, another potential symptom was her insistence that I wouldn't touch her, that I would diagnose her illness from across the counter.

There were, like I told her, a lot of things that could cause that condition. Could I eliminate any of them from the other signs that I saw? I didn't see how? As I continued to sit there and consider RRS and what she allowed me to see, a knocking came at my window. I turned my head and saw a very unhappy Cindy Brown standing there and looking at her watch. I looked at the dashboard clock and saw that nearly forty-five minutes had elapsed since I went to lunch. I put my head on the steering wheel and said an old Blackfoot curse that I learned from one of the Indians on the reservation near Browning.

Cindy said, "I swear, you're worse than a five-year old. I suppose we should be grateful that you aren't wandering around in traffic."

"Does this mean that Fred Thomas is here?"

"And Maxine Redmon and Larry Andrews," she said.

What made this situation even worse? I hadn't eaten my second taco, touched my rice or even sipped my drink. One taco was my entire lunch. Even worse than that? I shunted RRS's problem aside and began considering why Fred Thomas was here to see me. He had a chronic cough, was at least a hundred pounds overweight and thought he had the flu. Oh, and smokes, too. My preliminary diagnosis was emphysema. I was going to start at that point and work with his symptoms until I knew exactly what it was.

As soon as I entered the office, Maxine stuck out her hand to Fred and said, "Pay up. I win." Then she looked at Larry and repeated. Both men gave her a five dollar bill. She stuck them inside her bra and looked proud of herself. To me, she said, "Thank you, Doctor Six for being so predictable." She was in the office to have a cast removed. She'd broken her arm trying climb onto her roof to change the position of her satellite dish.

"You're up, Fred," I said to him.

He coughed as though on cue. One of the reasons I don't think he has the flu is that he's been coughing like this for at least three months. He's a realtor in town and Kalispell isn't so big that others who saw him didn't remark on Fred's hacking cough. Even Mario commented on it because Fred has two kids going to his school. Cayn Wyatt is his partner and they call it The Other Place. Fred showed up at the school, dropped off his two kids, made some small talk with Mario that included a couple of bouts of hacking that sounded like he was trying to cough up his lungs and Mario told me about it. Yep, Fred didn't make an appointment. I called him and scheduled one for him. The wonder was that Laura, his wife, didn't drag him down to my office.

I can't say that I didn't concentrate on Fred's condition because I did. I thought from my initial exam of him that he did indeed have emphysema. A complete blood test would confirm it, but there were other signs as well. While there is no point in listing them, I thought one of the best indicators was his wheezing upon exhaling. I asked Cindy to give him a form that he could take over to the hospital. They would perform the test, send the results to me and I'd make another call to him. I cautioned him to stop smoking or risk further to his lungs.

It was while I was getting ready for Maxine that a thought regarding RRS hit me. *Was she having an auditory hallucination? Was that why she turned her head up and acted as though she was listening to someone?*

I had to admit that I wanted to talk to her.

While that was going to happen, it was going to be a diagnosis unlike any I have ever performed before.

While I've been called a degenerate for lots of reasons – and Mario being my nominal uncle isn't the only reason that I have been so called – this was going to be the first time someone tried to throw me into Hell.

Literally, I mean.

I'd say it was boiling oil, but it was going to fire and brimstone.

And I don't even know what brimstone is much less why it's associated with Hell.

Well, at least I was going to have interesting company.

Very interesting company.

***

It happened again. No, not the pain I was experiencing, but lost time. It was like blinking my eyes and waking up somewhere else. One moment I was there and the next moment I was in bed with a foul taste in my mouth. I wanted God to tell me what was wrong with me. He didn't. He was still punishing me. I wish He would tell me why. Then I could do penance and correct my wrongdoings. As much as I want to scream at God, I cannot. He is all-powerful. He will tell me what I have done wrong when it suits Him.

Albert was there and he saw my uneasiness. "Are you okay?" he said.

"It matters not whether I am or not. God will take care of me one way or another," I said. That is true for all of us. God will weigh our souls and make a decision about us.

He sat on the bed with me. Then he said, "We could talk to that doctor again. Doctor Six. She seemed willing to treat you."

"Doctor SixSixSix is evil."

"Did God say that?" he asked.

"I said that," I answered.

I allow him to hold my hand. That is the extent of our physical relationship. He took it and said, "Rebecca? Please consider that it seems the pain is getting worse. How much longer before you cannot hear Him at all?"

That was stupid. At least that was my first reaction. A voice sounded, *Yes.* God was telling me that Albert was right. However, I am weak and tried to find a way to argue with Albert. But who am I to argue with God? Whatever anger I had inside me dissipated. Maybe the doctor could also tell me what the bad taste was and suggest treatment. It also suggested a way to find out about the missing time. I could tell the doctor about it.

"I will call her," I said.

"Good. That's good, Rebecca," Albert said.

I don't worry about dying. God will make a decision on my soul. He will decide if I go to Heaven or Hell. There is no purgatory. That is something I know. God told me. Someone asked me recently in The Temple, "What about people who don't know Jesus? You know, pagans who never got the Word?"

The answer is simple. God doesn't care if you've read the Bible. God doesn't care if you've never heard of it. God wants obedience. If you live a good life, it will get you into Heaven. Otherwise, your soul will burn forever. It isn't as complicated as two thousand years of history would suggest. I once read the six-hundred thirteen Jewish commandments. They are all interesting. However, they can be summarized with one commandment. Obey. If you are obedient, you will go to Heaven. If not, I should not have to repeat myself. However, I will. You will go to Hell if you are not obedient.

That was why I decided to call Doctor SixSix...Doctor Sixkiller-Collins Collins. God did not tell me she was a heathen. It was something I decided. That means I could be wrong about her. Still, I decided that anyone with that word in her name – six – should be handled warily.

Albert left the bedroom. He said he was going to The Temple to work on the ceiling.

It was shortly after he left that I heard the mumbling. Sappho was arguing with Guinevere. Anne Frank was laughing. Guinevere was saying that Sappho was a pagan and Sappho replied that it didn't matter. Specifically, she said, "We are all God's children." They are among the Elder Souls. There are others but those three are mine. Sometimes I hear others. Joan of Arc is one. She told me, "I am above your level. You must listen, obey and only then will I teach you." Anne Frank said one thing that I remembered that day. "You must prepare the fire." I was going to ask, "What fire?" Then I saw that this was my trial. It was my penance.

I went to The Temple. I found Albert fixing a light above the pulpit. I said, "I have something that needs to be done."

He was on a ladder. He turned to me and said, "What is that?"

"I have been instructed to prepare the fire. God is telling me to make a lake of fire. Those that are not obedient will burn in it."

He came down and said, "Please. Do not misunderstand. But how will I do that?"

Translating God's word was not going to be as easy as I thought. I closed my eyes, listened and heard nothing. God did not tell me what to do. Then I heard Anne Frank. She said, "Ovens." It confused me. I listened more and she said, "Gas fires." I know what happened to her. I know how she died. She did not die in the ovens. Disease killed her. God was being lenient.

I opened my eyes and said, "Can you use natural gas to make a fire?" I had no idea what that meant. All I knew was that our heat was provided by natural gas.

"Yes," he said. "Why?"

I wanted to scream at him. He was arguing against the word of God. Then, *he is asking you to translate My word.* God was speaking to me again! It was a glorious feeling!

While I don't know how sex feels, I believe that the feelings I got from God far surpasses anything a man can do for me. It reinforced God's word to me. I will be celibate. My joy will come from Him.

"A flaming pit right here in The Temple will be a warning to all those who defy God."

He looked a bit confused. Well, I wasn't. I put myself in front of him. Then I said, "Is it possible, Albert? Can you do it? God commands it."

"It will take time," he said.

"God has time. I do not. Please hurry."

Albert has been my greatest disciple. Were the world to continue to another generation, I would erect a monument to him. It will not last that long. God only needs to tell me when He is returning and I will call his true believers to this place. When that day comes, Albert will be at my side. We will ascend into Heaven together. The chosen will accompany us. The rest will burn. The fire that Albert will build will preview their everlasting agony

"It will done as quickly as I can manage it," he said.

"Thank you for being as Godly as me," I said.

We shook hands.

I went back to my room. It is a simple place. I can rest comfortably forever in Heaven. My bed is not as comfortable as Heaven will be. My phone is an old-fashioned one. There is a phone line attached to it. Other types of phone debase us. Other types of phones encourage us to ignore God. My phone does not. I picked up the receiver and dialed Doctor Sixkiller-Collins-Collins's office. A woman named Cindy answered. She asked how she could help me. "By loving God and allowing me to talk to the doctor," I said.

"Your name?"

"Rebecca Ruth Seer."

"One moment," she said.

I have patience for God. I do not have patience for those who make me wait. I am trying to become healthy enough to help others who will be here for The Ascension. Guinevere said, *Patience is a virtue.* I became more patient.

The phone was answered by a woman who said, "Ms. Seer? This is Doctor Six. How can I help you?"

"By making the pain stop," I said.

"Will you allow me to give you an examination?"

My stomach lurched. Sappho said, *she is trying to help.* I said with great distaste, "Yes. But I won't like it."

I didn't. Not even a little.

Anything for God.

Chapter 5

I was in my office at the end of the day when my phone rang. It was Cindy. My first impulse was to ask, "Why are you still here?" She beat me to it by saying, "Rebecca Ruth Seer on line one, doc."

I resisted the impulse to say, "Seriously?" Instead, I said, "This is Doctor Six. How can I help you?"

Nothing happened for several long seconds. There was static on the line; that's all. I was going to ask once more how I could help her when she said with a faraway voice, "By making the pain stop."

The way patients respond to me are symptoms, too. It's rare for someone who is ill to scream it loudly. Sure, some do, but that's a symptom of something else. Thanks, Mom, for letting me use you as a bagful of symptoms for all those years when I was a kid. Looking back? It actually helped that you let me. But this? Sure, I could diagnose RRS without touching her, but that would make me guilty of being a witch doctor. I prefer the hands-on approach. That led me to say, "Will you allow me to give you an examination?" As soon as I asked the question, I listened closely to the manner of her reply.

Her voice got a bit stronger, but still sounded faraway and weak. All I could read into it was that she felt stronger about me not touching her than she did about actually seeing me. She said, "Yes. But I won't like it." In fact, it dawned on me that every spoken word of conversation between us that referred back to her and not God was spoken with a sort of assumed humility. The few references to God were spoken loud, strong and passionately. Okay, she was telling everyone that God spoke to her, so that just figured.

"When can you be here?" I asked as upbeat as I could.

"In an hour?" she replied with the same detached voice. "Is that okay with you?"

Crap. Another dinner with Mario and the kids down the drain. My fear – and one I have been living with since I was four and that damn kid named Mario walked into my life – was that he would discover my basic fraud and leave. Every now and again, I ask him with fear splitting my voice if this is it, if this time was one time too many. He *always* reassures me that he'll never leave, that he's in it for the long haul. Then he kisses me and I can't remember my own name. Sometimes Travis and Maddy giggle in the background. How much longer before Alex joins them?

"Yes," I said hoping that RRS didn't listen to my voice with the same critical ear that I listened to hers. "I'll wait for you." If she did, she'd hear the long-standing fear that this was the last time I'd ever stand-up my husband and kids for dinner. She'd hear the fear that they wouldn't be there when I got home.

"Very well," she said. "I'll see you in an hour." She didn't say goodbye, she just hung up.

That left a phone call to Mario, one that I was going to make with a gurgling stomach and enough fear to last until he let me do it again and again and again. Unless, of course, he'd had it with me.

It was six-fifteen on Thursday night when I made the phone call to him that I was convinced was going to be the last one. *Why can't you just be satisfied that I'm trying to be the best doctor I can be? Why do you have to be such a jackass about it?* Yeah, and I hadn't even told him yet. Jumping the gun? Well, duh.

"Hey, kitten," he said as happily as he always did. "Where are you going to be in two hours?"

"Um, on my way home?" I said sheepishly.

"That means you're meeting a patient in your office in an hour," he said as though he had something on his mind. *Oh, no. He's planning on running off with my kids!* "Mario..." I said as panic began to build. The rest just sputtered and died.

"Hey," he said, his voice still alive and wonderful. "Relax. We'll be fine. Don't worry about us running off. We'll always be in your life., Deal with it, bitch," he said laughing.

No one can call me a bitch and get away with it quite like he can. "Are you sure?" I said. "I worry so much..."

"...and I can't figure out why. I have the best wife, the best kids and the best...um ...person in world." That's a reference to Violet Hatemen. She's a full-blooded Blackfoot Indian and she's adamant. She isn't our housekeeper. She's our friend who just happens to live with us and gets paid a pirate's ransom for the privilege. Her son David is arguably Travis's best friend. Once I tried to accuse Vee of having an affair with Mario and both of them laughed so hard that I thought either of them might need medical attention. She called someone and said, "Can you be here in five minutes?" Well, long story short, the most beautiful man I've ever seen – well, next to Mario – showed up and Vee wrapped herself around him, kissed him and finally said, "Next to Tim, Mario is sloppy seconds." Hell, she didn't even apologize to Mario. She just stuck her tongue down Tim's throat and then took him to her room on the *third floor.* Yeah, I have a big home. Still, we heard them that night. As a sign that Mario isn't running off? Sometimes she hears us.

"Well, give me two hours and I promise I'll be home." Hell, I meant it, too.

"Babe? Don't worry about a thing. We're cool and have been ever since I made you my blood sister."

I turned my palm and looked at the scar. It went back to a time that Aunt Tiffany thought that my Mom didn't want her in the family. She took a knife, cut herself across her palm and then Tiffany did it, too. Then they held the bloodied hands together and Mom swore that Tiff would always be her sister. Mario saw them do it and did it with me. I was six and he was seven. We repeated the ceremony on our honeymoon. He swore to me, "That we will always be together, in this life and the next one." Maybe I should believe him and believe that his words are true. I rolled my hand into a fist and smiled to myself.

"Mario? I'll be home as soon as I finish with my patient." He never asks who it is. He waits for me to tell him. Yeah, patient confidentiality means a lot to me, but not as much as a successful diagnosis does. Sometimes his insight into the process rivals my own and I'm the doctor. "Rebecca Ruth Seer. She was here last night, too."

"Seriously?" he said. "The Voice of God is talking to a pagan?"

Right there. That's a small reason why I love that man. He can boil down a problem faster and more accurately than anyone I ever met. Rebecca Ruth Seer pops up the media every now and again. She comes across as pious, as *literally* being the voice of god and never apologizes for her opinions. She has, over the last few years, come across as someone who would much rather let God – capital letter God – cure whatever is wrong with her than a mere doctor. Again, every now and then someone pops up the media as letting their child die rather than take his or her curable condition to a medical professional. Sometimes that person is prosecuted for whatever crime it represents – and don't ask because I don't care even a little bit about the criminal justice system in this country – and then the public feels better about itself because another nut was put away.

But Mario.

Indeed, why did RRS come to me rather than let God cure her? It would be her way to cure an illness. Beyond that? Why me? There is a hospital right across the parking lot. "Babe?" I said. "You just got free sex."

"Again?" he whined. "Why can't we do something a bit more interactive. Like dinner."

I laughed. "Dinner is more interactive than sex?"

"Well, sure. The way you do it."

"Are you saying that you don't like our sex life?"

Like a little kid pouting, he said, "Well, okay. If I have to."

I laughed again and said, "Yep, and only with old, ugly me."

Maybe I should stop. Why? Because he started telling me in the Sioux language what he thought of my beauty, grace, elegance, style, heart, emotions and so many other things that I could only say, "Mario? I love you so much."

He didn't have to tell me. I knew that he put his fist over his heart when he said, "Evangeline Monica? There is no one but you and never has been. Please, my precious flower, never worry about me and where my heart is because it's with you."

"I'll see you later?" I said choking up.

"That you will," he said. "You take care of that religious bitch and I'll take care of the rest."

"She's a patient and I'll see you later."

But that question? Why me? That one? I wasn't going to ask it, but there would come a time in the very near future when I wished I had. There was a very particular reason why she had come to me in each of the last two nights. But stupid me, I was obsessed about her condition and not about her motive.

I tried to prepare myself for her visit and never came close to the real issue. The issue wasn't so much her condition, but what she did with it.

Lordy.

***

I trust Albert like I trust only God. He has proven his trust and love of me many times. It is possible I don't tell him often enough that I love him. When we walked out to the car to go to see Doctor SixSixSix, I said, "I love you, Albert." It was heartfelt.

He looked at me as he held open the door and said, "Next to God, no one loves you more than me."

It made my heart flutter. I hugged him chastely, Godly and he returned it the same way.

Time means very little to me. Considering there are long stretches of time that I can't remember, I don't pay much attention to time. I didn't know how long it took to get to Doctor SixSixSix's office. There was a chance I wouldn't remember anyway.

I asked Albert, "Are you certain she is qualified?"

"Yes," he said. "She is the most qualified doctor we could see."

"We could go to Spokane," I said.

"We could go to Vatican City and not find a better doctor," he said.

I said nothing because that was his stock reaction to Doctor SixSixSix. He said she was a good doctor and I believed him.

My thoughts went to God thereafter. I prayed silently that Doctor SixSixSix would not want to touch me. The only one who can touch me intimately is God. Therefore, Albert gets a Godly kiss and a chaste hug. He derives a lot of pleasure from it. I don't honestly *know* but I suspect that he has a male orgasm sometimes when I hug him. It is possible that all men experience sex that way. I do not know. Sex has never been explained to me. I have never experienced an orgasm and will never miss it. My first and best relationship is with God. Perhaps those feelings of delight that I get when thinking about Him or hearing His voice are real orgasms. I do not know. I do not care. God takes care of me.

We pulled into a parking lot that I remembered from yesterday. We were here. I had no memory of the trip. I was thinking about God.

"Will you let her examine you?" Albert said. "Please. You are in real pain and I would like to know why. Please?"

I listened for God to tell me what to do. Sometimes He does. This time, He did not. I cannot argue with Him. I accepted that Doctor SixSixSix was going to touch me even if I did not like it. "Albert? Will you not come inside? I would like to do this alone."

He nodded. "Yes, Rebecca I can remained outside. If you need me to help you with whatever she says to you, just ask for me to come inside."

"Okay," I said. Then I went into the office. Albert waited outside.

Doctor SixSixSix was sitting behind the counter. She had her hands folded in front of her. She smiled and looked altogether too evil for my taste. I wanted to leave. I didn't because the pain was getting too great for me to bear. The best solution would be for God to heal me. He hasn't. That means He wants me to look for help. While I don't understand how God could let me suffer like He does, I accept it. I am a sinner. I am guilty.

There was no one else there. I walked up to the counter and said, "I want to know what's wrong with me."

"Will you accompany me to a room?" she asked with a smile.

"Yes," I answered.

She directed me to a doorway that was to her left. I went through it. There was a long hallway with four doors on either side of it. It doglegged to the left at the end. We entered the first room on the right. I was already nervous.

"Please sit," she said indicating the table in the room.

I sat on it and said nothing.

She stood in front of me and said, "Describe what's wrong in as much detail as you can."

"It burns when I urinate," I said.

She wrapped something around my right arm. I think she was going to take my blood pressure. I had that done once a long time ago. It squeezed my arm. It did the same thing this time, too. I was nervous. She said how much it was. The numbers meant nothing to me. Then she put something in my ear. She waited a short time. Then she looked at it and said, "One hundred point one. You're running a slight fever." She looked at me and asked, "Do you itch in any places?"

It was embarrassing. I hesitated to say it. "My...um...legs. On the inside."

She touched herself. She put her hands on her...inner...thighs...*oh, my. I cannot do this.* It was worse than I expected. She was *touching* herself. I didn't even hear what she said. When I didn't answer, she said, "In these places? Does it itch here?"

I couldn't speak. I merely nodded.

"Yes?" she said. "Is that right?"

I nodded again.

She took a thing...what do you call them? The thing you press to someone's...um...chest. Stethoscope? Is that it? I think so. She asked, "Can I listen to your heart?"

It was not a thing I could allow. She was going to touch my...chest area.

I believe she saw my uneasiness. She said, "I will hold one hand behind my back while I press the scope to you. Would take be less stressful for you?"

"I would rather you didn't do it at all," I said.

"It's a precaution that I would prefer to use," she said with that same smile.

"Will you...move it around?"

"Yes, but as little as possible."

Albert would not approve if I did not allow it. God did not intervene. He left it up to me. I squeezed shut my eyes. Then I said, "Please, hurry."

She pressed the...stethoscope?...to my chest. I think I might have made a noise. I was too scared to notice. My hands shook. She moved it to another place just above...my chest area. I almost screamed at her. I did *not* like it. The only thing that could have been worse was if Albert was there. He has never seen me...oh, God...naked. The mere idea of it maddens me.

With my eyes still shut, she said, "Please. I'll wait until you're able."

My hands were still shaking. I felt as though the room was getting smaller. Finally, I said, "Is that all?"

"I would like to examine you," she said.

Oh, Lord. Oh, my God. *Please tell me that it's forbidden.* I waited for God to speak to me. He did not. He was going to let me do this alone. I wanted to scream at her and leave. But the pain returned. I might have made another sound. I know sometimes I do. Albert has told me such. I think God was telling to let her. *I hear and obey.* "What would you like me to do?" I asked.

"To disrobe."

"Is there no other way?"

"No, Mrs. Seer. I need to do this."

"I am a chaste woman," I said. "This is very upsetting to my moral sense."

"I am merely trying to determine what is wrong with you," she said.

But, no. That is not what she was trying to do. She was going to get *familiar* with me. She was going to touch me *in those places*. It was beyond perverted. It was depraved and I could not do it.

I left.

I did not speak to her.

I did not look back at her.

I was right about her.

She was The Devil's Daughter.

God have mercy on her soul.

I wouldn't.

Chapter 6

The door opened at it was just her. The bearded man did not appear. I was sitting at Flo's station where she would greet patients. Rebecca looked nervous, afraid and so completely panic-stricken that I almost expected her to collapse. She was wearing a similar version of clothing to the ones she wore last night. Her shirt was still much too large for her and her pants were so baggy that only a belt cinched tightly about her waist could have kept them up. Well, crap. Or suspenders. I noticed she was wearing hiking boots as though she was about to start a pilgrimage. If I understood the few news reports I ever paid attention to, pilgrimages were things her followers did. She did not. She remained above it all and spoke daily with God. Those were her words. I saw her on a news show one time and that was a direct quote. "I speak with God daily." Worse, her claim has always been that God answers her.

She said, "I want to know what's wrong with me."

Trying to remain upbeat, I smiled and said, "Would you accompany me to a room?"

She said nothing more than, "Yes."

I motioned for her to enter the office and accompanied her to a room. I've seen *a lot* of patients in the last five years, but never one as nervous as she was. Just sitting on the patient's table was unsettling for her. Her hands fluttered like small birds. I said with the same smile, "Describe what's wrong in as much detail as you can."

"It hurts when I urinate," she said. That was it. There no other symptoms offered. It was frustrating, but she isn't the first patient ever to see me that withheld information that would make a diagnosis easier. Yes, I had hoped for more.

The next item was her temperature. She knew what it was and didn't seem too stressed when I took it. I said, "One hundred point one. You're running a slight fever." It rang alarm bells in my head, but her symptoms could mean any of a number of things, so I asked what I knew was going to be a sensitive question. "Do you itch in any places?"

She grew agitated and indicated it "itched" on her inner thighs. Just getting that information was stressing her and I was right, that could make her condition worse. In that case, talking to God on a daily basis was probably helping a bit because it would serve to calm her. When I patted my inner thighs and asked for a confirmation, she got immediately emotional and appeared ready to bolt. To calm her, I smiled and decided to take her blood pressure.

I readied the blood pressure cuff and she looked wary. I smiled, wrapped the cuff around her right arm and took her blood pressure. I assumed it would be high and it was. I suppose I should have been glad she wasn't hyperventilating. I wanted to listen to her heart and knew she would find objections. I showed her the stethoscope and explain it to her and asked for permission to touch her with it. She swallowed hard like she was swallowing a bowling ball. She said she didn't want me to do it and put it bluntly. I offered to hold one hand behind my back and she relented.

I'll say this: *nice rack, ma'am.* No, I never notice stuff like that. Mario says I have the best set in the family, but I know the best rack belongs to my mother and she's nearly sixty. I think I was partially responsible for it, too. She's always been that way, but once about ten or fifteen years ago, she had them reduced for all the reasons you can guess. The first time I saw after she had the procedure done, I couldn't believe it. She looked *smaller* somehow – and I don't mean in her bust. She just looked smaller and I said something like, "Oh, sure, Mom. Cut off your legs, too." She had them "reinflated" because she said she was too vain to look like that. But RRS? While not in my Mom's class, was easily in mine. And *that's* none of your business.

Her heart was hammering hard, but steady. It's not that unusual either. High blood pressure and a heart rate like hers is almost synonymous.

The last part, I k new, was going to be the hardest. I wanted to see the areas that "itched" and I knew I was going to get grief from her. I did. She said something about it "upsetting her moral sense". Look, I've diagnosed some serious diseases and I've never had anyone accuse me of something like that. Even the most devout religious person wanted to get well. Yes, there are some real interesting types that leave God to do everything, but I never see them. RRS was in my office and if I was right, she had a serious disease that needed treatment. Also, if I was right, she had no moral sense. If I was right, then her act before the cameras was just that – an act. Still, I didn't want to judge her, so I told her it was necessary.

Then turned her head toward the ceiling and talked to God. I don't know what He said to her, but I suspected He said nothing because she looked disappointed somehow. Either God did not respond to her or told her something she did not want to hear. That was the moment that I wondered if I was seeing a symptom of something else entirely. No, let me be clear: I thought I was seeing two separate conditions. What are they? Look, I'm going to need more symptoms than I had in order to confirm either one. Christ, I felt lucky to get as far as I had.

In retrospect, I think my biggest mistake with her was when I touched myself trying to confirm where she itched. She looked appalled and unless I was wrong, she felt that way on moral grounds. If could take it back, I would.

Look, I need to make my feeling clear in this case. Patients are not all of a type. They come in all flavors and my job as a doctor is to take what they give me and use that information to make a diagnosis of their condition. Some patients are John Wayne. They don't feel the need to be informative. They are quiet, strong and manly – even if they're females. Then you have the other side of the spectrum, the side that oozes symptoms even if none are present. RRS was an extreme version of the John Wayne type. Maybe a better term is Annie Oakley because she's a female. I say extreme not only because she is fronting religious symptoms and stuffing in all manner of moral reasons why I cannot touch her or examine her symptoms physically. In other words, she was making this harder than it needed to be. But I'm used to that. What I'm not used to is them walking out because she did.

I actually followed her into the parking lot where she got into a car with the bearded man. She was frantic and emphatic with him. She wanted him to leave and was framing her argument in religious terms that included the words "harlot", "Jezebel" and "God's wrath". The man looked at me as though he expected me to have the perfect words to use in order to get her to change her mind. She began shrieking at him and he looked helpless to stop it. It became obvious after a while that she was quoting from a book. Finally, the man shrugged his shoulders, threw up hands to me, backed out of the parking space and left.

It was a personal defeat on a scale rivaled only by Napoleon at Waterloo. As I stood watching the car drive her back to wherever she lived, I began to replay everything that had happened, every word I spoke and every diagnostic trick I had tried. Well, other than a smile, my approach was fairly typical. *Lady? You need help and I mean serious help.* I couldn't say that my diagnosis was firm or that I was even on the right track. If asked to bet, I wouldn't. Still, I thought she had serious trouble and only hoped she would return to me.

All that might have been was interrupted by that *goddamn* man I'm married to. He crawled out of his car – an old Hummer – walked up to me, wrapped his arms around me and said, "Babe? I will *never* walk out on you like that. I mean, not before I get laid anyway." Then he turned, snapped his fingers and *everyone* I knew crawled out of their cars with all the fixings for a great dinner.

Mario always surprises me. Well, maybe he wouldn't if I gave him more thought than I do. I keep telling him that I'm going to be better but I always fail. There are times –like right then – that I wished I wasn't a doctor and didn't have the monomania that went along for the ride.

But.

I said that he surprises me. He kissed me and said, "Rebecca Ruth Seer is your patient? Babe? That woman is as good as cured because you're the best." Then he kissed me again and I completely missed his encore which was, "Babe? This is one of the reasons why I love you. You dedicate yourself to them while making sure we're as good as you can make us."

I was undergoing my own personal Rapture. Well, maybe mine isn't as complete as those who believe that nonsense because I said, "Could you repeat that last part?"

He did.

Dinner was great. Hell, that was a bet I would have lost. What bet? Bet you can't get them all into your office. That bet. Well, we did. We got them all inside and then cleaned up the mess.

Oh, and Wanda was there. Mrs. Wanda Hatemen. She married William-never-Bill Hateman and came dressed in latex leggings that made her ass shine.

Wanda's my best friend.

She was going to prove it, too.

Soon. Very soon.

***

I do not believe I was ever that angry or appalled. Doctor SixSixSix is worse than heathen. She is a witch and no religion suffers them to live. Every time I close my eyes and see her *touching herself* and I have no words for how disgusted I was by her manners. The *only* thing that could have been worse would have been if she had touched her...lady parts.

"God has condemned her," I said.

"What does that mean, Rebecca?" Albert said.

"God does not suffer witches to live. I will condemn her."

He was driving somewhere. He stopped along the side of the road. It was dark. There were no other cars. There were no buildings. We were in the country. He turned to me and said, "Rebecca? Please think about this."

It was too much. I turned to him and screamed, "She touched herself! She put her hands on herself and touched herself! It's beyond perversion! It goes all the way to apostasy! I will condemn her tomorrow in The Temple!"

"Meaning what?" Albert asked.

"That one of our followers should kill her!"

It was simple. I would stand at the pulpit. I would appear relaxed and steady. I would say the words. "Doctor..." and I could not remember her name. It was no matter. I would tell the people there that she must pay for her perversions. They would kill her. They would be following the Word of God and I am His servant.

Albert held his hands level and said, "Can I say something?"

I smiled at him because I love him. "Of course. You have always been Godly."

"If you do that, you will be accused of being an accessory to her murder. You will go to jail."

"I'll be a martyr for the God," I said angrily. Then I took a deep breath and said, "I apologize, Albert. This is not your fault."

He closed his eyes as though trying to be calm. He always was with me. It was another reason I loved him. He said, "And if they take you to jail and God comes back to The Temple, you will not be there. Rebecca? You are predicting this and it will happen. *That* will be a perversion. Rebecca? In the long run, Doctor Six is not worth God."

Yes. He was right. I must be there when God returns. Also, it will not be Jesus, Mohammed or anything of the other saints. Oh, they will be present, but it will be God that ends things. It will be God that determines who will sit at His right hand and who will be thrown in to the dark places. I sighed and said, "Then what must I do? She is beyond wicked."

"Can you give me a few days to think of something? Besides, you are still not well and it grieves me greatly to see you like this, to see you suffer like this."

I was uneasy. "Are you saying that I should see her yet again?"

"Can you honestly tell me that you are not in pain?"

Again, he was right. I am glad he is my husband. He takes care of me. "Yes," I said. "It hurts worse than before whenever I urinate."

He was thinking and I wondered about what. "Tell me, Albert."

"I could take pictures of you and show them to her. You would not need to be present in her office."

Pornography. He was telling to indulge in it. I could not. Then a spasm of pain rolled through my stomach and I curled forward holding back the pain with my bare hands. It was awful.

"See?" Albert said quickly. "She can help! I can show her the areas that I think are infected and you can stay in The Temple and pray. It will help. God will help us."

With God as my witness, I did not want to do this. But it hurt and there were areas that itched and…bothered me. If I allowed this, Albert would see my naked soul for the first time. It unsettled me, but not as much as the pain did. Could I reconcile my beliefs and allow him to take photographs of me? As the pain ebbed, I decided to try. "Albert? I cannot swear I will like it. But I will try."

He got back onto the highway. Then he said, "I am your husband. I will be gentle and will not take advantage of your generosity."

It still made me nervous. I was going to allow him to see me in a way none but God had. I tried not to think of it. I could not. I saw him taking photographs of my lady places and almost lost my stomach to the floorboard.

"Please, Rebecca," he said. "I know you don't want to do this, but it might be an answer for you. You would free of pain and would be able to better talk to God. Is it possible that you do not hear his voice because the pain is too intense?" Then he smiled and said, "You are, after all, human."

I wanted to be strong for God. I thought I had been. Then the pains started. I believe I have been weak thereafter. I should be able to withstand the pain. The other…things…will go away as the illness ends. But what if Albert is right? What if God comes and I am in jail or even unable to hear his commands? What if a little wickedness will make me hear His Word better than I am presently able to hear them?

"Can I ask something that might sound wrong?"

My smile was as wide as I could make it. "You can ask me anything."

"I could photograph you when you're sleeping," he said and winced as though it hurt.

I wrapped my arms around myself. "No," I said shuddering. "You would…touch me."

"Then you will allow me to photograph you?"

I did *not* want to do this. I did not, however, see an alternative. "I will be upset, Albert. You must be patient."

"I have time everlasting for you," he said.

"I will do it," I said. Then I smiled and said, "But not happily."

We were home quickly. At least, that's how it seemed. I've already said I don't have a very good sense of time. God's sense of time is much different than ours. If I am with Him, time seems to pass quickly. That's how it has always been.

Albert asked, "Do you want to do it now and get it over with or wait until tomorrow?"

It was going to take all my resolve to do this. I told him, "Please? Tomorrow?"

"Okay, Rebecca," Albert said. "But, please? I'll be gentle, will not be abusive of your morals or do anything improper. In fact, if you tell me to stop, I will and won't restart until you tell me to. Okay?"

It is easy to love him. He looks out for me. I will ask God if he can be with me for eternity. Since I have been chosen to be His voice, I do not believe there be any problems. Besides, Albert has been wonderful and chastely as I have been.

Still, it hurt to go to the bathroom.

Plus, there were…other…things there, too.

Please, God? Help me to help myself.

I have faith. All will be well.

Faith heals all.

Chapter 7

Doctors are supposed to notice things around them. I think I do. In this case, I noticed that Maddy was curious about the things in our office. She saw the centrifuge that we use for blood work and asked, "Mommy? What's this?" We don't use it much because it's fairly new. The model I bought could be used by a hematologist to study cancer and blood-borne diseases. Of course, I'd have to hire a hematologist first.

I told her, "Well, it could be used for a number of things. For example, if you had cancer, it could be used to help diagnose any number of things that would help me determine how to treat your illness."

She stared at me as though I'd spoke Greek to her. Then she said, "No, Mommy. Really."

She's nine and I wanted her to know everything. Mom? I don't know how you managed with me, but I'll do anything to help her.

"Baby..." I said and then groaned. She had the same issue with me calling her "baby" as I did at her age. I put my hands over my face and said, "I'm sorry, Maddy. I won't do it again."

Then I looked at her and she said, "Uh huh. Just like the last time you promised."

"Five dollars?" I said miserably.

"That was our agreement, Mommy."

My purse was at Flo's station right where I'd left it. I dug out my wallet, found a five dollar bill and handed it to her. Then I asked, "How much does this make?"

"Fifty-five dollars," she said. "I figure I'll have at least a hundred before Travis finds out."

It was my own way to stop calling her "baby". Fifty-five dollars later and I was still doing it. Worse? I only started giving her five dollars for every time I called her that three weeks ago. I figured – stupidly as it turned out – that factoring in money would change my habits. Had I thought about it, I would have laughed because I *never* think about money. In fact, I've considered starting my own medical insurance company for no other reason than to let *anyone* have medical care regardless of their ability to pay. Yeah, and I thought giving my daughter five dollars every time I called her "Baby" would change my habits. Now, if I could only get Mario to see that I have a fat ass, my life would be complete.

She folded up the five-dollar bill, slid it into her pants pocket and said, "Does that thing really help people who are sick?"

"Just like a thermometer reads your temperature," I said.

A brief flash crossed my mind. *Rebecca Ruth Seer had a slightly elevated temperature.* Then I blinked and my daughter had my attention.

"What were you just thinking about, Mommy?" she asked.

"A patient, my last one," I said making good on my vow never to lie to my kids.

"What's wrong with them?" she asked.

I sat in Flo's chair and pulled her onto my lap. Without thinking, I said, "Baby? I don't know. She won't let me examiner her." Then, realizing I'd done it again, I fished in my purse, grabbed another five dollar bill and gave it to her.

She pushed it back at me and said, "That one doesn't count because you were being a doctor."

"But I promised," I said.

"What if something was wrong with me and I didn't like the words you used to tell me? You wouldn't send me away or pay me to see another doctor. You'd help me."

People began to gather around us. Mario knew I was working. Okay, maybe Maddy was my medium, but I was working nonetheless. He said, "Should we leave you alone?" He *knew* who my last patient was. Hell, by now all of them knew who had been here.

"No," I said. I hugged Maddy and said, "I'm with you guys now. Besides, I already have a pretty good idea what's wrong with her."

"But?" Flo said from the crowd.

"I have to be certain, Flo. You know that."

Even Norma said it. "Come on, Evie. We work together. What if she comes in and you're not here? My bet? You haven't opened a case file on her because of who she is. How right am I?"

She was dead-on. I trust these people. I always have and they have never let me down. But something Mom told me *a long* time ago. "Baby? Computers can be hacked. Any computer can. Don't put your faith in them because you'll be sorry." Two things from that conversation: one, while it's possible my wealth came from the same arrangement I had with Maddy because she *still* calls me "baby" and I haven't been one in nearly thirty-five years, I know it isn't because Mom never gave me any money every time she called me that. She gave something far more valuable than money; she gave me symptoms. But two? Norma was right. I hadn't opened a case file on her. She had a certain amount of fame and I did not want someone to hack my system and find out that the most famous religious quack of the century had...well, never mind. I still felt uneasy saying the words unless I had some sort of diagnostic evidence.

"Norma? She's been here twice and she still hasn't allowed me to examine her. I took her temperature, her blood pressure and got an oral admission that she itches in her thighs and genitals. That's it." Then I nodded toward the centrifuge that captivated Maddy and said, "Not even a blood sample. What would you do?"

She smiled. "The same thing you're going to do. Make a house call."

Mario smirked and said, "Saturday, huh? This means I'll have to get mine early."

I held up my hands and said, "I don't even know where she lives. Give me a break."

Norma smiled and said, "You lie, bitch. You know she lives in Arlee. How many temples built to God are there in that place?"

Yeah, true. While I hadn't ironed out my approach to her, I did want to go there. Mario was right, too. I was going to sacrifice time with him and the kids to try to get a definitive diagnosis on Rebecca Ruth Seer. Still, even with the few symptoms I had, Norma – and maybe Flo because she had been married to Doc Pillow for half a millennium – was most likely the only one in the room who could put two-and-two together and have the same suspicions I had. I looked at her and said with a smile, "Blond bitch."

She just said, "Seriously, Evie? You think that's it?"

"I hope not," I said shaking my head sadly. "But the worst part? I have a suspicion about another unrelated condition and only observation will tell me whether I'm right or not."

"What is it?"

"I'll let you know Saturday when I get back. If I have a diagnosis on the first condition, I'll start treating her. But the second? I'm going to need someone who knows a lot more about that subject than I do." I held up my hands again and said, "Saturday. I promise."

We were done with dinner and the clean-up. I hooked my arm inside Mario's elbow and we walked to the car that way. Since each of us had our own vehicle, we weren't driving home together. The only change in seating arrangements was Maddy. She wanted to come with me. I hugged her to my side and then gave Mario the best kiss the circumstances would allow. The bastard still managed to garb my fat butt. I'll probably give him another fifty years to knock that shit off.

There was a small caravan going back to my home. Mario led in his Hummer and I followed in my Pilot. Vee followed in her diesel Dodge pickup. Travis was with David in it.

As an aside? I never check my surroundings. I mean ever. It never dawns on me that someone might be following me. You could lift my wallet out of my purse and I wouldn't even know until I tried to buy something. Considering that I've been assaulted at least three times in my life and raped once, you might think I'd pay better attention to whoever was around me. For example? While no one was following me that night, that wasn't going to be true much longer. And for the record? When it happened? I wasn't going to be very upset. No, let me state that a bit more matter-of-factly. When that happened, my attitude was going to be, "What the fuck took you so long?"

Yeah, yeah. Be patient.

Maddy, I noticed, is a lot like me. She talked all the way home about her friends and how she didn't think she'd like living in Montana, but how "ultra-cool" it is. She started ticking them off on her fingers. First and always is Becky Lansing, Wanda's daughter. Maddy is tall and wants to be petite like Becky and Becky wants to be tall like Maddy. Well, that just figured. Maddy thinks she's going to be ugly because she'll be the tallest girl in the world and Becky thinks she'll be so tiny that no one will notice her. Yeah, opposite sides of the same coin. Friends forever.

Wanda was in the caravan only because she's my best friend and she was going to talk my head off about her new husband, William-never-Bill. That was so cool that it was going to rival my kidnapping.

They should hang a sign around my neck that reads "available for parties" or some such.

Look, had I known what was going to happen, I would never have made plans to go to Arlee on Saturday.

I accused Mom once of being oblivious to her symptoms because "all your blood is in your boobs and not your brain".

Funny, how the apple didn't fall far from the tree.

***

I woke up Friday afternoon and had no idea where Friday morning had gone. Well, that's not true, not exactly. I was with God. God told me so. It happens to me from time-to-time. God wants to talk and the world just goes away. I noticed it when I turned thirteen or so. It took some time before I realized I was with God. After that, I didn't worry about it anymore. Besides, God always told me what we talked about. I'm waiting for Him to announce the date of His return. I get mail from people a lot. Some of them call me charlatan and some of them call me a saint. Both sides are wrong. I am with God on His right hand. There are no words that describe my place in His universe. God talks to me and I relate to anyone who wants to be in heaven with Him what He said. There is no point in lying either. God cannot lie. Therefore, I cannot lie either. Anything I say is Truth.

Albert asked me once if I wanted to start a YouTube channel. I told him no. He asked why. My answer, as always, was succinct. "Did Abraham have a YouTube channel? No. He did not need one. Neither do I." I can use the internet but seldom do. There is literally no point. All the information I need comes from God.

Someone once asked me where I grew and where I went to school. That's easy. I was placed in special schools. I was determined to be a "special needs" child at the age of eleven. They said I was autistic. I know I am not. I am verbal when necessary and can process information as needed. Ask God. He'll tell you. Oh, that's right. Only I talk to God.

I was sitting a front row pew in God's temple. Albert came and sat next to me. I took his hand and risked being called a harlot. He smiled and held it.

"Rebecca?" he said. "We need to take those pictures."

I expected to hear God tell me not to allow it. That didn't happen. God was still letting me find my own way. It disturbed me. Albert didn't have to ask if it did. He knew that it did. It was difficult to sit still. I squirmed because he was going to take pictures, most private pictures. "I know," I said to him. "Now?"

"No time like the present," he said.

"I can't wait until God ends time," I said.

"And word on when that's going to happen?" he asked.

"No. He'll tell me I need to know."

"Of course," he said. "I apologize if I sounded impertinent."

The harlot rose up inside me again and I smiled. "Albert, dear? You are so good for me. What would I do without someone as devoted as you?"

He held my hand and I almost had a physical reaction. I still myself and said, "It is I who am lucky. I could have attracted someone baser than you. Had that happened, maybe none of this would be."

"So?" He said. "Now?"

It violated every sanctity I possessed. However, I knew I had to do it. He was right. What if I did not do this and I was unable to be with God at The End? You must see. You must. It isn't only Doctor SixSixSix and her kind. I cannot kill her even though she is doomed. In that case, Albert made me see her soul and what would happen to it. I do not need to kill her. God will do that.

"You'll be patient?" I asked.

"Yes," he said. "I will take my time and not do anything until you are ready."

We went back to our home. The temple was built for you. It was not built for me. I am with God always. You will feel His presence in The Temple like I feel Him at all times. That is why I did not feel as though I was leaving His presence when I left The Temple.

We went to our bedroom. It is a simple place. Bedrooms should be. Too many people fall prey to heathen desires in them. I do not need...oh, God...sex. God provides my pleasure. I know He does because I can feel it. Even when I experience time loss, I know I have been with Him because I can still feel Him inside me.

Albert had one of those telephones that had a camera in it. He has never used it until now. He held it almost apologetically. He didn't want to do it. He was only doing it to help me. Still, it was going to harrowing. I knew what I had to do. I had to disrobe. I did not want to do it.

"Patience, Albert," I said as he felt the buttons on my blouse.

"I have time," he said.

No, he didn't. None of us do. But I understood what he was saying. I unbutton the top button and froze. I was beyond the level of Jezebel. I had reached the status of The Whore of Babylon. There was no reason not to finish it now. God would forgive me. I unbutton another one and resisted the urge to regurgitate my lunch. I said a prayer for my soul. God would listen and help me. *Please, God. Tell me this is not necessary.* He did not answer. I knew He would not. It was necessary and I knew that as well as God did. I unbuttoned the third button. It was much more difficult than I imagined it would be. There were five more. I closed my eyes and expected to hear God's voice. I did not. I unbuttoned a fourth, fifth and sixth. I was breathing heavily. It was hard to breathe. I sank to my knees and Albert was there.

"Take your time, Rebecca. You don't need to hurry."

"Only one more," I said.

"Whenever you're ready," he said.

I've said it before. I have no judge for time. I do not know how long it took before I stood and unbuttoned the last button and then shrugged out of my shirt. I wear athletic bandages over my...woman parts. I did not need to remove them. My...woman parts...are not ill. It is...everything below my waist.

A spasm made me hunch forward. It hurt. Albert guided me to the bed and I sat upon it. I resisted the urge to scratch myself. It was a heathen desire. I did not fall to its evil temptation.

Finally, I stood and unbuckled my belt. I knew what would happen when I did. My pants would fall. They did. All that was left were my pantaloons. I sat down, untied my boots and kicked then away in a spasm of anger. Then I squeezed shut my eyes and dropped my pantaloons. I was exposed. I was being born. I was in God's Hands. I knew that Albert took pictures. I heard the camera snap. There would have been a flash of light as well. Had I looked, it would have reminded me of creation. I wanted to count the numbers of photographs. I forgot to count them. Maybe it took a week and maybe it took no more than a few moments. But he finished and said with a heartfelt voice, "Thank you, Rebecca. You can dress yourself. I will step out of the bedroom."

I heard the door close. I was alone. No. I was with God. I am never alone. I knelt and pulled up my pantaloons. Then I pulled up my pants and buckled the belt tightly around my waist. The athletic bandages had slipped. I readjusted them to be as tight as possible. Then I put my shirt back on. Then I buttoned the buttons.

Then I ran to the bathroom and puked up my soul.

It was easily the worst thing I had ever done. I prayed for forgiveness. I was convinced God would throw my soul into the fire.

It made me thankful to Albert. He had offered to build a fire pit. I was going to tell him to do it. Doctor SixSixSix was going to be the first one into it. She deserved it. She was going to drool over my nudity. She was going to pretend that she lived in Sodom. Her smiles and debauchery would be swallowed by God.

God in The Highest.
God is All.
I am with Him.
Doctor SixSixSix?
You are doomed.
Not by God.
By Me.
In His Name.

Chapter 8

Friday was a happy day. Well, after my Thursday night it was. I stayed up late with my kids – and that includes David and Becky. Yes, Wanda was there with her shiny pants and kept finding excuses to bend over and pick up some existent piece of flotsam from the floor. William-never-Bill showed up in his uniform and Wanda got so excited that she took him in to the upstairs bathroom "for medical reasons". Never heard it called that before. Mario asked, "We have other bathrooms and we could explore our medical reasons." Well, I resisted – right up until the kids went to bed. Then I excused myself, tugged at Mario's elbow and used foreplay as a reason to say, "Please tell me that you don't think those pants are nice."

He humored me for a few moments and then said, "She's not nice in those pants. She's hotter than a cyclotron at full speed."

Damn. Then, double damn. I mean, we were halfway through the act and I was heating up *very* nicely when Mario just turned himself off, stood from the toilet seat from where we were *engaged* and told me, "Pull up your pants. I need a second opinion."

Well, double damn. How does he do that? I was ready to emulate Mt. St. Helens and he just stops, grabs Wanda, stand her next to me, bends us over and says, "Bill? Choose."

Two things. One, *Bill.* William Hatemen has been adamant ever since I first met him that his name is William. He's even threatened a few people who forgot. Then Mario calls him that and instead of going tribal on his ass, puts his hand to his chin stares at me and my best friend like we were on sale in the New Orleans slave markets and says, "Very difficult, my Puerto Rican friend. But I have regrettably choose my betrothed. Otherwise? I might tap that ass."

And, two; Wanda and I both went ballistic. Well, right up until both of our men kissed us like they meant it. Mario shook Bill's (?) hand and took me back into the bathroom where he finished with me, but didn't finish himself until he knew I had been sated. Bill (?) had to do Wanda again. Poor fool.

Well, and three. Puerto Rican? That makes it okay for Mario to call him Bill? We know there is no Puerto Rican blood in him, so I was going to make an issue of it – right after I calmed down. I hugged him and said, "Please tell me there are colors other than black."

He held me and I felt even better than before. He said, "we aren't going to have this discussion again, are we? The one where you try to tell how misshapen and fat you are? That one?"

I giggled. "Well, you could always refute the evidence like you always do."

He hugged me and said, "Sunshine after a storm, water after wandering in the desert, sunflowers, chocolate ice cream, satin, your facer at waking. All these things and more. Evangeline? You are breathtaking to me and that comes from a man who just emptied his balls."

I giggled harder and said, "Oh, Mario. If you want to me, I will."

"It's not necessary. Wanda worries about Bill. You don't have to worry about me. I will never go away and not just because you are Helen of Troy to me. I will never go away because there is no one else like you in the world. Without you, I would never get that drink of water because I would wander forever in a barren plain."

I smacked his arm and said happily, "Yeah, and who would take care of my children?"

Wanda was standing sternly like an Olympic judge when we exited the bathroom. She was even tapping one of her high heels impatiently. I curled my arm under hers and said, "Mine are going to be red."

Her mouth dropped open and she said, "William? I can have red ones?"

Which naturally started the stupidest fight in our history as best friends. We started squabbling about which of us were going to wear red ones while Mario and Bill (?) stood with their hands on their chins and watched us. Finally, Mario said, "Bill? How could we tell them apart? I mean, with thoroughbreds like these, we could be swayed in either direction. It might be best not to let them wear such things."

"Agreed," he said. "Back to tight skirts."

Yeah, it was pretty stupid. Maybe it's just a measure of how comfortable we are with each other. We hugged and she whispered, "I'll stay with black." I answered with, "And I'll buy red ones." Then we high-fived each other and screamed, "Poker party!" It was almost time for one. If I could just keep my mother from invading it, we'd have fun. Mom has this way of dominating any room in which she finds herself and doesn't have to stoop to latex leggings in order for that to be true.

Yeah, I was tired at work the next day. I had to go across to the hospital to perform a colonoscopy on a patient and found Wanda in the ER wearing her leggings under her smock. Even the interns stared. I laughed with her because she likes William – Bill (?) – to find her irresistible. I try to tell her that it isn't the way the package is wrapped, but what's on the inside and she said, "Well, yeah. You have a fat ass. What else are you going to say?" It was cute and we agreed to do lunch on Saturday. Well, that meant the kids would come with us and so would our husbands, but that was totally cool.

I went back to the office and finished my day with the usual amount of happiness. Everything was fine, there were no more patients in the waiting room – there seldom are anyway because I don't pack my schedule and force my care to be half-assed. It was such a grand day that everyone went home without much fuss. Well, much fuss. Norma, Hannah, Liz, Cindy and Flo wanted to take me over to Sonny's and get me so drunk that even my mother wouldn't claim me, but I backed out of it by saying, "We're buying a condo up at

Whitefish because Mario's decided that he likes to ski. We're leaving Saturday morning."

Both of us ski. Me better than him. Me because I discovered when I was growing up in Maine that I liked the adventure of it, the way I threw myself at the world and tamed it successfully once I hit the bottom of the run. Mario just skied. Maddy skies, too, and she's getting remarkably skilled at it.

But they called my bluff.

Well, Flo did.

"And Whitefish is how far from here and you can rent a lodge for a lot less money than you can buy one for. Evie? What's going on?"

I buried my face in my hands and said, "Mario…"

Cindy said it. "She's horny."

Norma dragged me into a patient room, grabbed a blood pressure cuff and only then did I stop her. "I am not sick!" I said emphatically.

"Well, delusional, maybe," she said. "Since when does going out after work interfere with that sort of stuff. In fact, I have good medical evidence that suggests a drink will lower any inhibitions that might get in the way of a good Friday night."

"One drink?" I said.

"Well, two, or I'll have Flo and Cindy hold you down and force feed you."

Hannah and Liz added, "And we can help."

Well, damn. It looked like I was going to have drinks with them at Sonny's. Hell, dinner, too, Because I am *not* drinking on an empty stomach. We all grabbed our coats and sweaters because it was cool that day. We were all in a good mood when Hannah opened the office door and found the bearded man who'd accompanied Rebecca Ruth Seer reaching for the doorknob. He had a folder in his free hand. Once the door opened in front of him, he stood back until he saw it was just us, the office staff.

It fell to me to ask, "Can I help you?"

He looked at us and said, "My name is Albert Seer and my wife is…"

"Rebecca Ruth," I finished. "Do you need to see me?"

He held out the folder and said, "Please?"

Flo put her nose to mine and hissed, "Wanda's going to be pissed."

I hugged her and said, "I'll be there; just a little late. Start without me."

They all left for Sonny's and that left me alone with Albert Seer. I closed the door behind them and said to him, "In my office or right here?"

He looked agitated and I have the medical degree to support that opinion. Well, maybe not because he began to look more stressed than agitated. Yes, there's a difference, even a medical one. Finally, he said, "Your office? I really need to sit down."

We went back to my office that is at the back of the office complex. I stood behind my desk and motioned for him to sit in of the three chairs that faced it. Predictably, he sat in the center one. I've considered doing a study of people who sit in either of the side chairs instead of the one in the middle. I've never done it and I probably won't in this case either because the patient in front of me cancels out any random curiosity about why he sat in that particular chair. In other words, Albert Seer had my attention.

He leaned forward in the chair and put the folder on the desk in front of me. "It's about Rebecca. I took these pictures of her and wanted you to see them. I realize she's difficult, but she's sick and I want to help her find out what it is." He opened the folder and spread out at least dozen photographs on my desk. "That's what it looks like. I don't know it is, but I figured you would.

He was right. I did know what it was.

I didn't like it.

I didn't like that I was seeing photographs and not Rebecca Ruth Seer.

I bit my tongue and decided to try to do this reasonable. Good frigging luck, doctor.

***

I needed to pray. I needed to pray more than ever before. I went to God's Temple and prayed, *"Please, God. Heal me. Make me whole. Cleanse my spirit, body and soul. Help me because only you can.* I'd never prayed angrily. I realized I just had. It shamed me so much that I rose and ran from His Temple. I ran into the hills behind it. The terrain is rough. The summer makes things dry. Branches twigs and bushes stabbed at me as I ran. All I knew is that I ran uphill. When I could run no farther, I stopped. I knelt, held my hands tightly together and prayed as devoutly as I knew how. *God? I am in your power. You hold me. You shelter me. You protect me from harm. But my body is weak. I lust for Your cleansing power. Make Albert's quest meaningless. Make his vulgarity pointless.* I felt He would honor my request. I felt that if I looked at myself, I would be clean. His power washed over me and I felt so much better. I wanted to dance. I did. I threw my hands at Him in the highest and praised Him as I danced under His warm sun.

Then I stopped because I felt tired. Worse, God had not answered. Still, I felt clean, so unbuckled my pants. Then I slid down my pantaloons and was crestfallen. The sores were still there. This was a disease of the Devil, not of God. Was I not godly enough? Had I not praised Him high enough? Had I expected too much from Him?

I fell to my knees and prayed. Again. I decided that God was not answering because I didn't pray hard enough. So, I prayed until my muscles cramped. I recited an endless stream of exultations. I said aloud until my breath failed. Then I began anew when I felt I could carry on with another long stream of prayer that would show God how sincere I was. I prayed until I was weary and weak. I prayed until I had no more strength and then prayed some more.

No voice.

He did not answer me.

It was becoming dark. The sun was setting. I heard soft sounds around me. Albert told me once there were wolves in the hills. My answer was blunt. "They will not harm me. God will care for me." Now? I wasn't so certain. I was sinning in a fundamental way and couldn't see what it was.

The Temple. God's Temple. He wanted me in it.

I stood and felt so tired. I took a few steps and felt nauseous. I fell to my knees and puked into the dry grass. Despite the attack, I was stronger than that. I rose and staggered down the hill. I could see the grand temple below me. I stopped and stared at it. Yes, I built it, but in God's Good name. The cross at the top of the temple suddenly seemed out-of-place. It indicated Jesus as His chosen and not me. It shamed me. That was why God was not speaking to me. I'd put a cross at the top of His House. He required another symbol. But which one?

My face? No. It would not be worthy of God's House. So, if not that, then what? I sat among the bushes and wondered if my actions would spawn legends. I smiled. *Stupid. God will end this suffering. This is merely a test. He wants you to feel human before He comes back.* It was so simple. I smiled and said aloud, "Thank you, God. Thank you for this insight. I will suffer for You."

I rose and stared at God's Temple. I saw it. Finally. The symbol for God's Temple. A capital R. A very stylized capital R. God would approve. I was His chosen and He would allow this. I had to tell Albert.

Despite my weariness, I ran down the mountain screaming, "Albert! Albert! Albert!"

He did not answer. He wasn't there. Where had he gone?

I was so confused that I retreated to Rebecca's House. I mean, God's Temple. I sank to my knees and asked, "God? My Lord? Where did he go?"

I expected an answer. I did not get one. I tried to think and couldn't. It was only in that moment that I realized how hungry I was. I'd been in the hills above God's Temple without food or sustenance. Was I starting a fast? If so, why? I sank to my knees and decided this was the proper time to find out. "God? What must I eat? What little will You permit me?"

Bread and water.

I knew there were people in the kitchen. They fed the stream of seekers. Pilgrims came everyday looking for Him.

Sometimes I told them that I was His chosen and He spoke to me. I always told them that The End was near. Then the halleluiahs began. They praised me and asked, "When, my Lord? When will He return?" Sometimes I got angry because they expected Jesus. Once I held my fists tightly and screamed, "Why not Mohammed or Buddha? You expect someone and it will be ME!"

But God wanted me to fast. He was going to allow me to eat only bread and water. He was going to tempt me with hunger. That was fine. I could do this.

There were four people in the kitchen feeding a crowd of maybe twelve or so. They could eat. They had traveled far to get here. I asked someone where they kept the bread. A cupboard was opened. I took a slice and then filled a glass with water. I was set. God would be pleased.

I walked to our home. I ate the bread while I walked. I was still hungry. I entered and drank the water. It was enough, but I wondered how long it would be before I would be allowed to eat anything.

I went into the bedroom.

Then it was morning, Saturday. I'd been praying again and lost sense of time. Albert was sleeping next to me. The first thing I realized was that I was not hungry. It made me feel grand! God has sated my thirst and satisfied my hunger! I said aloud, "Thank you, God!"

It woke Albert.

"Um, good morning?" he said a bit sleepily.

"Albert!" I cried out. "God has help me! I feel so wonderful!"

"Um, Rebecca? Can you explain that?"

"God wants me to fast. I ate bread and water last night. I was still hungry when I came in here. I prayed and my prayers were answered! Albert! I feel so wonderful!"

He smiled at me and said, "That's wonderful. It truly is."

He went to the bathroom. I went after he was done. It still hurt. But it was no matter. God confirmed that I was His chosen. I felt better than newborn. I felt as though I'd been given a new life.

I was so happy that I kissed Albert chastely.

He blushed.
Then I giggled.
And wondered if that...if that...was...if that was...what females experience during...sex.
Then I blushed.
Yes. I'd had my first orgasm.
And it came with God.

Chapter 9

I was looking at a severe case of genital herpes. Whoever this female was, she had lesions spread over most of her vagina. My first question was, "And these pictures are of Rebecca Ruth Seer?"

Albert Seer was obviously the man who was asked to leave by Rebecca the first time she came to visit me. His beard was full, but it looked like he kept it trimmed. If I had to guess his age, I'd put it around thirty. He looked strong, too. Well, physically fit maybe. Mostly, though, his eyes looked absolutely alive. They practically danced as he answered, "Yes. Rebecca was not happy when I took them, but she wants to know as well as I do what they are."

Photographs. I'd never diagnosed anyone via photographs. Considering that my mother once told me, "Baby? Never trust a picture. Ever. Or have you never heard of Photoshop? If you don't believe any of this, I have pictures that will prove your father is a biological female." Moreover? She did. "Baby?" she said thus guaranteeing that I would call Maddy by the same name twenty years later, "Never trust a photograph. Period." And now I had the grizzled husband of a woman who was going to tell my children that God was going to kill them that his wife had herpes.

"I need to see her," I said.

"You need to cure," he said.

"There is no cure for herpes," I said. "It can be treated and controlled, but not cured."

"You can't be serious," he said. For what it was worth, that simple throwaway statement was the most basic clue as to what was happening under the roof of God's Temple. Of course, a lot of crap was going to happen until I knew the score. Had I known at that point, it wouldn't have mattered because Rebecca Ruth Seer had issues that needed to be treated. I couldn't have known what was happening to her, but those pictures simply guaranteed that I was going to be involved. I felt the same tugging at my soul that I felt when I thought my mother was dying from aspirin toxicity.

"Mr. Seer?" I said. "I can quote any textbook you like and recommend a dozen websites that will confirm what I just said. I need to see her, though."

He looked away as though thinking. Me? I've learned to read emotions in these settings. I've seen everything from exultation to grief and everything in between. Him? He was thinking of himself and not his wife. That much I thought was obvious. However, knowing the emotions and knowing from whence they came are two different things. I thought he was considering his own exposure to herpes because if his wife had it, then it stood to reason that he did, too.

That led me to ask, "Are you carrying the virus?"

Without thinking of his answer because his mind was so far away, he said, "Me? No." Then he tried to backtrack by saying, "Are you saying she got it from me? I don't have any symptoms like these," he said indicating the pictures.

"Can I take your temperature and ask you a few questions?"

His answer was non-responsive in several ways. "Rebecca Ruth Seer is a virgin," he said. "I've never made love to her. Could she have gotten this in some other way?"

I nodded and said, "Yes, you can get it through other means than sex. There are occasions where kissing could spread it or oral sex with an infected person could spread it. Do any of these sound possible?"

"Kissing?" he said, again thinking furiously. "Like a peck on the lips?"

I squirmed because it was possible. Hell, given the contact RRS had with the public, it could have come from anywhere except for one vital clue. In her, in RRS, the virus was genital. Someone had to have had contact with her in that way for her to have the virus in that area. "Yes," I said as confidently as I could. "That's possible, but then whenever an outbreak occurred, she'd have sores around her mouth. Has she? I don't remember seeing anything like that the two times she was here." Of course, you can have herpes with no symptoms. "A PCR blood test can diagnose whether you have the virus. A culture test would be better."

"I could find out right now?"

"Not on the blood test. A definitive test might take three weeks to run its course," I said. "A culture test? A couple of hours."

Still thinking furiously, he said, "Could she have gotten it by kissing someone else and then by touching herself in that location?"

He was asking if RRS could have gotten type-2 herpes through kissing someone and then transferred the virus to her own genitals by touching herself. Answer? It's possible but not likely. Genital herpes is spread through skin-to-skin contact with another person's genitals or through oral contact with a person who has it. It seemed to me that Albert Seer was trying valiantly to convince himself that his wife got type-2 herpes from a pilgrim who came to the temple she built. The issue is that once that person kissed RRS – no matter how lightly or how suggestively – it became oral herpes not the genital variety that the pictures showed. In the end? Look, anything is possible through skin-to-skin contact. The issue, however, is you have to touch that area with an open blister – and unless RRS had open blisters on her fingers, the answer is no.

"Mr. Seer?" I said. "It is entirely possible that your wife got herpes by kissing someone. That she could spread it to another part of her body is unlikely because she would have to have had open sores on her fingers – or whatever body part she used to touch her genitals. My best answer is that she got the virus through some sort of sexual contact."

I looked at the pictures he'd spread on my desk and seemed to be completely stumped by what to do. Well, I knew what to do. She needed treatment and information on how to act from now on. She needed condoms and caution. She needed to be educated and informed about her condition.

"Do you want a blood test?"

He stood and said, "No."

"Are you sure?"

"Yes." He turned to leave and said, "Is her life in danger?"

"No," I said. "But the symptoms will get worse and keep reappearing unless she gets treatment. Plus, she runs the risk of infecting anyone with whom she makes contact." I stood for no other reason than he was already on his feet. I added, "I could see her. Drive to your place." Almost as an afterthought, I said, "I could do a culture test on her by sampling the sores."

He looked confused. "But, you already know she has it."

"It would be a conformation and nothing else."

"Can I call you?"

I gave him my mobile number. "Mr. Seer? She needs to be diagnosed and told what precautions are available."

"I'll be in touch," he said and left.

I sat back down and began to wonder at what Albert Seer had told me. Not too much of it made any sense. Why? Well, according to the pictures that he showed me, Rebecca Ruth Seer wasn't a virgin like he claimed. Either he's stupid or he thinks I am. Given how she was photographed, that woman was not a virgin which made it possible that they didn't depict her. The media picture of Rebecca Ruth Seer was as he claimed. She's a virgin and not even her husband had had relations with her. So, if all that true, then who was the woman in the photograph? It was a medical mystery and as much as I wanted to believe that I wasn't going to pursue it, I was going to be proved wrong.

I closed up the offices and went to Sonny's. We had fun and even got our SO's involved because Norma is involved with a doctor from the hospital across the parking lot. *Her* name is Kris and no one in our crowd cares even a little. Mario patted my fanny at one point and whispered to me, "The classiest ass in Montana." I whispered back, "And the fattest." He's going to have to live with the fact that his wife has a fat ass.

Well, Kris overheard what I'd said and she said to Mario, "If you tired of that ass, I'll tap it."

Mario laughed and said, "Sorry, but you're going to have to settle for second best."

The night wound down and I went home with my family.

It was the last time that was going to happen for a while.

However, let me emphasize something that I've already mentioned. When I got snatched and it became apparent as to why? I wasn't going to care even a little. In fact, I was going to scream at my captor that I hadn't been snatched long before I had been. I think the phrase I used was, "What sort of inept kidnapper does it long after the need has become apparent?"

My kidnapper would just shuffle his feet and say, "Sorry. I kind of thought..." and then his voice trailed off.

I put my face in that face and s creamed, "Well, next time put some serious thought into it!"

I think I kind of fell outside the FBI profile of kidnap victims.

Like they say...

Practice, practice, practice.

This wasn't first abduction.

Nor my second.

Frigging amateurs

***

I had an orgasm! True, I thought it would be more intense. It left me wondering why people cared so much about them. I've heard of men "getting off", but if mine was how women experienced orgasm, then I wouldn't care if I ever had one again. Still, I felt wonderful, if not a bit feverish.

Albert looked nervous as I woke. I asked, "Are you okay, Albert?"

He answered, "Yes, but that doctor wants to see you."

I forgot. "Oh, my good Lord. You showed him the pictures."

"Yes," he said with a bit nervousness in him.

I understand why most people look nervous. God has already passed judgment on them. They have a right to be nervous. Not Albert. He is among God's Chosen. I know. God told me. So, if not that, then what?

"What did she say?" I asked instead of inquiring about his nervousness.

He ran his hand through his hair. He was worried, not merely nervous. "Rebecca?" he said with all the reverence I was due. "It was more about me than you. But seriously? I'm fine."

I had little choice but to believe him. He does not lie to me. It's possible that Doctor SixSixSix told him that any medical problems between us were his and not mine. God would not allow me to become sick just before His return. Given that I believe everything Albert tells me, I felt that I could better spend my day listening for God to tell of His return. It was imminent. That's all I knew.

To that end, I went to God's Temple. There was a construction there. A team of workmen were digging up an area in front of the pulpit. The pit was maybe ten feet across and maybe that much deep. There were things that looked like nozzles embedded in the dirt floor of the pit. I looked for someone in charge. A man with a patriarchal beard stood directing things. He would know. He looked Godly.

"What is this work?" I said.

"The fiery pit you wanted," he said bowing slightly. He motioned toward the pews and said, "We had to take out four rows of them in order to have enough room for it. It will be done tomorrow."

"How will it work?" I said. I could ask God to make it work. Instead, I felt that God would want me to speak for Him. Any heretics would be burned in it.

He pointed to the pulpit and said, "There will controls there. Dials and switches will regulate the flames and control their intensity. It will all be natural gas."

I couldn't know that Albert had foreseen this need. He would tell me later when about his plans. As I watched, I envisioned Doctor SixSixSix burning in the flames. It would be a just death. She would be sacrificed to God. God would not appear until Doctor SixSixSix was dead. She is Satan's spawn. She has even admitted to marrying her uncle. What more proof does one need of sin?

"Thank you very much, sir," I said to the bearded man.

He clasped his hands together and said, "No, the pleasure of be allowed to do this work is all mine. I thank you for this opportunity to serve you."

I smiled in a Godly and said, "It is being completed much faster than I thought it would be."

"You must thank Brother Albert," he said. "It is his foresight that has enabled us to work this fast. All the gas lines are already installed. The pit itself will be the most difficult piece."

"How so?" I asked. I was truly curious.

He pointed to the middle of the pit and said, "There will be three fireproof poles installed in the middle of the pit. The gas nozzles will ignite flames in a circle around the pole. I imagine dried wood will be placed around the ankles of the victims. Thence, the fires will consume them quickly." Then he pointed to the chapel ceiling above the pit. "Brother Albert foresaw this, too. The stained glass panels will retract and act as a funnel for the smoke caused when the bodies ignite." Then he pointed toward the ceiling over the pews and said, "The masses will be air-conditioned. Panels will be installed between the pews and Lady Rebecca. No one will be harmed except the heathen."

Oh, happiness! Oh, to be alive at such a time! The world will be cleansed of the unbelieving heathen! God's will be done!

"Tomorrow?" you say.

"Yes. It will be done tomorrow evening and ready for its sacrificial saints."

Sacrificial saints! Oh, how Godly perfect! "You have described them perfectly!" I said happily.

He smiled and said, "It is a term that Brother Albert first used."

"I must thank him for this," I said happily.

The man nodded and said, "He will be notified when we are finished."

It was even better than an orgasm. It was positively heavenly! I believe – fervently believe – that God allowed me that one orgasm in order for me to compare it with truly good news.

I found Albert in the kitchen talking with one of the people who worked there. It was a female. I waited with God's own patience as they finished their conversation. Albert looked intently on something. He was probably directing things for the masses who came everyday waiting for God's news. The only words I heard were, "Out of control". Albert said them. He would have a good reason. All I wanted to tell him was how happy I was about the pit.

The girl looked at me and nodded toward Albert. Whatever orders she had received had been understood. She went back to work in the kitchen. I approved of her shapeless smock. Women – like Doctor SixSixSix – who wore tight clothes and advertised themselves were harlots. The girl in the kitchen was one of God's children. Doctor SixSixSix would be tied to center post in the pit.

Albert looked busy. I decided to make myself brief. "I talked to the man in God's Temple. He said the pit will be done tomorrow!" It was all I could do to keep myself from touching him. I was ecstatic like never before. God's enemies were finally going to pay!

"Yes," he said. "Brother Gilroy said he would tell me when it was complete."

I itched. I wanted to scratch but denied myself. God was reminding me that my place in His world was to be completely chaste. I had always been that way. I was not going to fail now. God's return was imminent and I was going to greet Him the way I knew He wanted to be greeted.

I leaned close to him. "Can we capture her? That heathen doctor? I so want her to be the first sacrificial saint." Then I smiled with absolute glee and said, "Brother Gilroy? Is that his name? He told me that was your idea. It's wonderful, Albert!"

He held out his hand to me. I took it and it felt even better than an orgasm. I'm glad I had a point of reference now. I would never again need one. God's work held so much more pleasure. I underscored why God was needed so badly. Human beings are filth. Inject each believer with God's Love and the human race will live forever. Removing evils like Doctor SixSixSix will be a very good thing and it will done at a very good time.

"You might be right," he said. "Give me some time to think on it."

I said, "You have time, but not a lot of it. God's return is imminent."

He nodded and said, "It will be done tonight."

It was too difficult to contain. I was giddy with delight. God's will was going to be done! The mother heathen was going to die.

And I was going to be the one who burned her alive.

God In The Highest?

I hear your words and obey.

The heathen will die.

Chapter 10

Maddy wanted to come with me since it was Saturday and no one was working in my office. We were sitting in the kitchen and I was having a hard time keeping a straight face. She was listing all the reasons she should be allowed to go with me. She gave the first reason with wide eyes, enumerating that it was her first reason by holding down her index finger with her other index finger and straining her neck out as she said, "You never have a 'Take Your Daughter To Work Day' and they do that all the time in school!" Her second reason was with her middle finger held down with her other index finger. She stuck out her neck over the table and said, "How will I ever be able to tell if my own kids are scamming me unless my mother – WHO IS A DOCTOR – shows me how I did it and then shows me real sick people!" The next reason was, "If you don't take me with you, I HAVE TO GO WITH DAD, TRAVIS AND DAVID TO THE DANG LAKE!" The one after that was, "I need ten more dollars to get a cute outfit I saw in the store and I figure you'll call me 'baby' at least twice while we're out." Then she ticked off her thumb with her index finger and said, "And besides. I WANNA GO!"

Mario kissed my forehead and said, "Well, you know where we'll be – and that includes Alex." Then he tossed me a roll of something that turned out to be a roll bound with a rubber-band of fifty five dollar bills.

"Two hundred and fifty dollars? You think I'm that absent-minded?"

He laughed, said, "Yep," and left.

Maddy giggled behind her hands.

I smirked at her, "Not once today, little girl." Then I dropped the roll of money into my purse.

That left Vee. "Where will you be today with everyone gone?"

She has a dazzling smile. I only wish mine was that glorious. She flashed it and said, "Your damn girlfriend, Wanda, wants to teach me how to be a white woman." She's one hundred percent Blackfoot if I haven't mentioned it. She used to joke about scalping me while I slept. Then one day I woke and she had a hunk of hair in her hand. I actually panicked and touched my hair. It was still there. She threw a wig at me and said, "Wanda wants to see you as a redhead." Yeah, it was *red*. Well, in my own defense, I did say that I'd just wakened.

"Become a white woman?" I said. "What's that mean?"

That smile again. Then, "Well, as near as I can tell, it means we're going shopping."

Both of us laughed and it took Maddy with us.

Yep, Maddy was going with me that day.

I hugged Violet and she headed out to be with Wanda. I was jealous as hell because we could have done it together, gone shopping and just be girls. Maddy would have loved it. Crap, she had the money to go shopping, too.

We went out to my Pilot and her first question was, "Are we going to your office?"

I smiled and said, "Nope. We're going to IHOP." There's one just before the hospital. I can't say it's our favorite place, but Maddy likes it. She especially likes their Chocolate Chip Pancakes. Today, she was going to get them.

Her eyes widened and she said, "Can I? Really? Chocolate Chip Pancakes?"

"Yes, baby..." and I never got another word out. I growled into my hands that I had pressed over my face, reached into my purse with my right hand as my left was still pressed to my face, fumbled for the roll and gave it to her.

She took one five dollar bill from the roll and handed it back to me. "I'm not a thief, Mom," she said haughtily. Then she giggled into her hands and said, "It's the cutest outfit, Mom."

"I could just buy it for you," I said miserably.

"Or you could buy me another outfit," she said.

Yep, two outfits and I hadn't even started the car yet. I laughed and said, "You got it."

"Can we do it after you're done today?" she asked eagerly.

"We can go right now," I said.

Well, the dynamics of nine-year-old girls is a bit emphatic. She hit the fan. well, relatively anyway. "Mom!" she said, her voice breaking and squealing. "I want to know what you do and that's what I'm going to do! We can go shopping later!"

Chastised by my daughter. I smiled at her, started the car and said, "Well, everyone should start their day with a full stomach."

Like the people at Sonny's, the folks at IHOP knew me. One of the waitresses, a lady named Norma, said above the crowd, "Doctor Six! Who's your PA today?"

"What's that mean, Mommy?" Maddy said with wide eyes. "What's a PA?"

"Physician's Assistant. You know Norma. She's one."

That caused her to start clapping her hands and saying aloud, "I'm a PA!"

Norma approached us with menus and said, "That you are, little lady."

"Mom still calls me baby," she said happily. "She has to pay me five dollars every time she does."

"And how much has she given you so far?" Norma asked.

"Sixty dollars," she said.

As Maddy slid into the booth opposite me, Norma asked silently, "Doing on purpose, are we?"

"Nope," I said. "Can't break the habit."

"You sly dog," she said and walked away.

Her hair is blacker than mine. I think that was something did well, even if unwittingly. She likes her hair and we spend time together styling each other's. Yeah, it's a pain, but a nice one because I like doing it. We've talked about it, her hair and our efforts together to keep it stylish. We've done it so many times that she said as she read the menu, "Yes, Mom. I like my hair and you can play with it when we get home tonight."

"That obvious, huh?"

"Yep," she said just like I do.

"Question?" I said.

She put down her menu and looked at me. "Um, okay."

"Why, Maddy? Why do you want to spend your day being as bored as I know you're going to be?" For what it's worth? I *knew* she didn't see symptoms in me the way I saw them in my mother. This was something else. I didn't know what it was, but I was going to be as intent as I could possibly if it would help her.

She looked out the window and said, "Do you remember when Woody broke his leg?"

Woody Peterson is another of Travis's friends. If I had to pick between him and David as which one was his best friend, I couldn't – and neither could Travis. But remember? Yes, I did. I felt I was completely at fault for witnessing a suicide and not trying to talk the man out of it. Oh, he was quite the bastard, but my oath as a doctor doesn't count attitudes. I am pledged to help them – whoever they are - and not judge them. Well, I did. No, Maddy never learned of his crimes. She was referring to the incident that brought me back into the world and back to practicing medicine. Woody was hit by a car in front of our home and his leg was broken.

"Yes," I said a bit warily.

"Mom?" she said looking at me with something I'd never seen before. "You knew what was wrong with him just by touching him. You knew what would make him be okay and that someone needed to call 911. I was scared because Woody was in pain and you knew what to do. I want to know what to do if someone around me needs help. Do I have to be a doctor to know stuff like that?" I'd like to say it was reverence, but I think that would be wrong. She was trying to put a human touch on a feat that she saw as magical. I think we live in an age where people are swamped by endless technology and are looking for more human answers. The age of robots that I keep hearing about isn't far off. Kids like Madison Sixkiller-Collins Collins see all those stupid, stupid Twilight movies and wonder what's real and what isn't. Sure, I could be wrong because I tend to be obsessed with medicine and my role as a doctor, but in this case, her case, I don't think I am. In her case, she wants to be aware of her life and how to help others when it gets too heavy for them. While it's way too early to start pigeonholing her into this field or that one, it's never too soon to help your kids be better people. That's what this is about.

"No, baby," I said without even realizing I'd done it yet again. "Life is all around us, but most of us never manage to see its details. A broken leg hurts, but it's not the end of the world. What if Woody was merely crying because someone said something that upset him? That's pain, too. You simply need to know how life works and what to do when it appears to be broken."

She looked confused, but ready to fight through it. "Mom? I don't know what all that means, but I'm here because you know a lot more than I do and I figure you can help me. If I start to bother you, just tell me. Please? And you don't owe me for that last one."

I handed her another five dollar bill and said, "What color is it?"

She began to giggle and said, "Red! I love red stuff!"

And we began our day as girls being girls.

Lord, it felt nice.

It wasn't going to last.

However, I was a mother that day before I was a doctor.

Just don't make us angry.

You will be allowed to regret it.

***

I heard a voice. It said, "This is Sandra and I want out."

I began to panic because I knew that voice. It was completely ungodly and evil. Worse, it wasn't chaste in any sense of that word. It used language that I would describe as heathenish. I have heard in the past. I was about sixteen when I first started hearing that voice. She cursed me for "being in control". She called me names that I cannot repeat. I have asked God to stop her from talking to me, but He has neither responded nor stopped her.

Sandra, I believe, is The Devil. She speaks like The Devil would speak. The only defense I have against her is my stronger will. I seldom respond to her. Today, I had to make an exception.

"Who are you?" I said to the air around me. I was in my bedroom. Albert was gone. He said he was going to check on the work in God's temple. He wanted Brother Gilroy to tell him what still needed to be done.

"Who am I?" Sandra said as though it was obvious.

"Yes," I said with some fear. "You speak to me, but I don't see you."

"Go into the bathroom, you freaking idiot," she said.

"Why?" I said.

"GO INTO THE FREAKING BATHROOM!" she screamed.

I went. I didn't know what to do. "Okay," I said to the air. "What now?"

"Look in the mirror," the voice said.

I did. "Now what?"

"Say, 'Hello, Sandra.'" Then she said, "Oh, and Sappho, Anne Frank and Guinevere are not real. I am. I am you, you total freaking idiot. Now let me out."

Slowly, so slowly, I began to see another person who looked like me, but was inside my head. Her hair was combed into a heathen style and her clothes...Oh, my Lord...her clothes were depraved. The one thing I could not abide was the paint she put on her face. I think they call it makeup. I put my hands to my cheeks and saw my eyelashes. They were longer and darker. And stuff over my eyes. Worse was the...lipstick(?)...I think they call it. It was as red as blood and as depraved as the clothes she wore. Men would call her pretty and copulate...Oh, My Lord...no...with her. Worst of all? She would enjoy that tepid thing I know as orgasm.

"Oh, give me a break," she said. "You didn't have an orgasm. I know what an orgasm feels like and that wasn't it. All you did was kiss the poor fool. If you want an orgasm, all you have to do is…"

And NOOOOOO!

That was enough. I crammed her back into a box and left her there. I saw the image of what she was going to say. It was as disgusting as you might imagine. I strained to hear her voice. I could hear only the softest whines. She was gone and would disappear before too long. She would be dead when God returned. Still, I sat down on the toilet because it scared me. What if she came back and I was not able to withstand her advances? What if my strength wasn't as strong as hers?

Then…a pain. The same type. In my…stomach area. I moaned, leaned over and then stood, raised the toilet seat, dropped my pantaloons and moaned as I urinated. It hurt more than ever. I cleaned myself by rote. I never, ever look. I simply wipe myself and disregard my own flesh. I know that Albert says I have a disease, but I can withstand the pain. God will help me.

I need to find Albert, so I clothed myself again and hurried to God's Temple. Albert would be there. He was. He was talking to Brother Gilroy and pointing to the pit. I waited for him to finish.

As I waited, I wondered what would happen if Sandra got out. She never had, but how would Albert react to her? How would he react to me being *that* person? How would he react if I was as wanton as she was? Maybe it was something I could ask him.

Albert finished with Brother Gilroy and the man went back to work.

He smiled at me when he saw me. "Hi, my lady," he said as happy as he was. "Can I help you?"

"I need to sit somewhere," I said.

He smiled and indicated the rows of pews behind us. "I think I can help you find a place to sit."

I love it here. It was the most perfect place in the world. It will be even more perfect when the pit takes Doctor

SixSixSix. God will win in the end. God always does. But Albert didn't need me to tell him that.

We sat in the front row. The entire altar was in front of us. A worker was finishing the switches at the pulpit. I wanted to touch them to practice with them, to use them. I could smell Doctor SixSixSix's soul burning. I could smell her flesh returning to God. Or to Hell. I didn't care where it wound up. She would be gone and so would everyone else that blasphemed the way she did. Marry your uncle? Oh, Lord. Oh, my sweet God.

Albert sat his usual ten inches from me. That was something He told me long ago. A man must sit that far from his wife. Those instructions are in The Book. Pilgrims to this place have read those lines to me reverently. They clutch The Book to themselves. They close their eyes and recite the lines from memory. I can recite the entire book verbatim.

"Are you okay?" he said, his face showing worry.

"Am I worthy of your love?" I asked timidly.

"Of course," he said as though shocked. "Who would say otherwise?"

Lord, but I wanted to tell him about Sandra. I wanted to ask him if I was…pretty…enough for him. Men like…that…stuff. Men like lipstick. Men like painted faces. Men liked hair like Sandra had. Men liked so much more than I had.

"Can I hold your hand?" he said with love in his voice.

I dislike these things. I dislike being touched. I dislike hugs that aren't chaste and Godly. I cannot imagine how my body became infected with whatever that stuff is. I am stricter with myself that anyone else I know. For example, Albert does handshakes with other people. Well, not just handshakes. With other men, he bumps hips with them. Sometimes, they do what he calls "the man hug". It was those things I wanted to talk about. I wanted him to reassure me that my personal attitudes about life weren't going to cause trouble between us.

When he asked to hold my hand? It was pressure I hadn't felt since…Sandra. I took a deep breath and held out my hand to him. He took it and said nothing. He was waiting for me to say something.

"Albert? I see them. I see those women who come in the buses. I see how they look. Their clothes are tighter. Sometimes they paint themselves. Do you want me to look like them?"

I wasn't looking at him. I couldn't stand it if his answer was yes. Instead, he said, "Please, Rebecca. Look at me."

I did.

"You are entirely the most beautiful woman I have ever seen. I am in love with you and not one of the pilgrims on the bus. Can you believe that?"

He reminds me of Abraham. His beard adds to his charm. Sometimes I slip and allow myself to do things that are outside my beliefs. Such an occasion happened right then. I leaned into him and allowed him to touch me. My...female parts, my...motherly parts...touched him and it felt grand. I almost giggled, but did not. It was what a pervert would do. *Sandra? Take that. That is what an orgasm feels like.*

"Albert?" I said. "You make me so happy.

I didn't hear from Sandra again.

I wonder if she tries to interfere when I am praying and time disappears.

No, God would never allow that.

Sandra?

I will never hear from you again.

I will not allow it.

God tells me so.

Chapter 11

Maddy has been to my office many times. This was, however, the first time she'd ever gotten to see me really work. I had three patients that I wanted to visit. Yes, I make house calls. And, also yes, I could just as easily have done this research from my home. The only reason I did not was because I am trying to be a better wife and mother. I will save medicine for when I am actively practicing it. Like now.

I sat Maddy in my lap and showed her how to navigate to a patient's address area. I showed her how to print the information and even print the diagnosis that I'd made on them.

She pointed to Cassie Burgos's diagnosis and said, "What is..." and she tried to pronounce it. "Strained...lig-a-ments. What's that?"

"Cassie plays soccer on the high school team. Okay?" I said.

"Okay," she said.

I hugged her out of my lap and said, "I'll show you what she did."

I knelt next to her and felt the Achilles tendon on the back of her ankle. "That right there is your Achilles tendon. If you work too strenuously, you can strain it. Cassie did. It isn't serious unless you don't do the things that will heal the tendon. For example, she can't play soccer until it heals. Her coach is aware of her injury. If she's been off her feet and resting the tendon, plus putting compresses on it, she should be able to practice with the team Monday at school. She's our first stop."

"How do you hurt it?" she asked flexing her ankle.

"Well, in her case, she didn't exercise before her game. That helps. She should have done some stretching exercises before she went out to play. She didn't."

"Did her Mommy punish her?"

I smiled. "Baby..." and stopped, reached into my purse, handed her the roll and said, "Take one. And I'm sorry, ba..." and said, "Take two."

She unrolled two fives from the bunch and dropped it back into my purse. "You were telling me that her Mommy was angry at her."

"Nice try...Maddy. No, I didn't. Her mother was simply worried about her, so she brought Cassie to me and I told her it was a mild strain that should be okay with some attention. She was relived and didn't yell at her. In fact, we all hugged."

"Who are the other two?" she asked.

It took me that long to discover that Maddy had dressed in the same clothes as I had. I was wearing a thin, black short sleeve turtleneck with tan pants. Her turtleneck was a bit thicker than mine, but it wasn't warm enough to cause her any discomfort. I touched her sleeve and said, "Hmm, nice outfit."

"Daddy said you would realize it as soon as we got to the office." She handed me back a five and said, "I lost that bet." She was smiling when she said it. It dawned on me that she was having fun. She was smiling, involved and looked as happy as I've ever seen her.

I gave the five back to her and said, "Daddy doesn't need to know."

She looked at it, handed it back and said, "I lost that bet, too."

I hugged her and said, "Thank you, Maddy, for helping me today.

She smiled and said, "The other two patients?"

"Carl Wade and Sarah Bright. Carl is an older gentleman who had a colonoscopy. Do you want to know what that is?"

"Duh, Mom."

"They take a picture of the insides of your intestines. I touched her fanny and said, "Back here."

"Ew, gross," she said. "Why would someone want that done to them?" Then she smacked me and said, "And why would you do that to him?"

That was my first emotion when I read about it when I was...nine. Ew gross. It's cute now, but at the time, I couldn't imagine someone doing to me what the procedure mandated. A camera? In there? Ew, gross. I saved my indignation for Uncle Doctor Morganstern, my grandfather's brother. I put my hands on my non-existent hips and snapped, "A colonoscopy! Are you serious? Do you know what they do to you?"

He was smug, the bastard. Well, no wasn't. He smiled, folded his arms and said, "Colon cancer. Counter that. How would you diagnose colon cancer without a colonoscopy? Plus, there are other reasons to use that procedure."

We were having dinner with my grandfather and grandmother. As aside? Gawd, how I loved my grandmother and her high heel collection. She had these knee boots that when I wore them went up to my crotch. I walked into their living room one day and grandmother almost burst a stay in her corset because she laughed so hard. Yes, my grandmother wore a corset because she knew it drove grandpa crazy.

But, Uncle Doctor Morganstern took the stage that day. He told me all the reasons why a person would *submit* to that procedure and then said, "Unless, of course, the youngest generation finds another way to diagnose those particular conditions without stooping to..." and he stuck his nose in my face and finished with, "having a camera shoved up your ass."

"You're mean," I said to him.

He smirked and said, "And don't ever develop colon cancer or you'll have two reasons to hate me."

And now I was facing the other end...oh, sorry...of that conversation. I sat back against the wall next to my desk and said, "I can name half a dozen different reasons why a person might consent to that procedure." I paused and almost did it again, almost called her baby. But I didn't. "Maddy? It's necessary sometimes. All I want to do is make certain that Carl, Mr. Wade, is okay. That's it."

"And Sarah Bright?"

I sighed and said, "She has a fairly bad contusion on her forehead. She was helping to tear down a shed in her backyard and her husband smacked her accidentally with a board that had three nails in it. Two of them penetrated the skin above her eye and the swelling was considerable. All I want to do is make sure the wound is healing okay."

"Her eye is okay?" she asked.

"So far," I answered. "The only reason it wouldn't be is if the wounds became infected. That's my worry for her."

She printed up the directions, maps and then said, "Mom? I'm glad you're my Mommy. You help people and that's good."

"Well, let's go make sure these people are as healthy as I can make them."

I realized I was having fun, too. My daughter was a truly interesting person. Well, to me she was. Okay, I'm prejudiced because she's my daughter, but it seemed real. She was asking questions that I thought were appropriate to the situation and that indicated interest on her part.

Cassie Burgos lives on the south side of town. Since she lived the farthest from me, the office and the hospital, I decided to see her first and then work my way back toward Stillwater Loop where I live. It was going to take about fifteen minutes to get to her place. The visit would depend on how her strain was healing. Since Cass is a smart girl and wants to play soccer, I think she'll be doing okay. Still, I wanted to check on her to see for myself, give her any help I could and then see both Carl and Sarah.

"What can I do?" Maddy said as I drove south on Main Street. It would change back to Highway 93 when it left the city limits. Cassie lived on Willow Glen Drive behind the Toyota dealer.

"Well, since Cassie is a real nice girl, she'll probably let you feel her ligament. Then you can feel mine and then there will be a test on whether you can tell which one is injured and which one isn't."

"Mom?" she said. "Seriously? A test?"

I laughed because it would take an x-ray to determine the severity of the strain if I thought it was serious. It wasn't. "Well, she might wince if you touch it too hard."

She pulled up her pants leg and said, "Where?"

I pointed near her ankle, toward the back and said, "There. There might be some red streaks, too. You would only see them if Cassie hasn't been following her doctor's orders."

She rolled her eyes and said, "Yeah, and her doctor is so frigging strict."

We both laughed and I held out my hand to her. The best part was when she took it, hugged it to her and smiled at me. Thank god she has Mario's smile. I wouldn't wish my shark teeth on anyone - and, yes, I know that Mario says my smile is special. He could have called it something more romantic, like sunshine or like a spread of chocolate. But special? That beckons images of kids who keep getting into trouble. Okay, okay, okay. When Mario says it, he's smiling, holding his hand to my face and is about to get laid, so I can cut him some slack because there is no longer any blood in his brain. It's all elsewhere.

We stopped at the light where if you make a left you're on Willow Glen and if you make a right you're on Cemetery Road. We made a left and Cassie's house was just ahead.

Funny how things turn out.

We'd never make it to Cassie's house.

They tried to be tough, but once you've been raped anally, you sort of lose the ability to be scared by a gun. All they can do is shoot me – and believe me, that's a lot less invasive than anal copulation.

Maddy was sort of a complication that I hadn't counted upon.

Funny how the apple didn't fall far from the family tree.

***

It hurt and I was losing the ability to control the pain. I fell to my knees, the toilet bowl behind me and prayed. *God?*

Please help me to survive this trial. I heard a voice in the distance. I strained to hear it. God was making my trial tougher and tougher. That is fine. There is nothing God can ask me to do that I cannot. God does not give us trials that we cannot overcome. The voice kept on speaking. It sounded harsh. It sounded judgmental. It sounded altogether Godly. The pain did not stop. I clutched at my stomach even though that is not where it hurt. Worse, it was spreading to my...backside. The voice kept speaking. I tried to understand what it said, but I could not.

I needed to find Albert.

The voice got louder. It was Sandra again. She was getting stronger.

"You idiot," she said. "Let me out or I'll cause serious trouble."

"Go away," I said withstanding the urge to scratch myself. The only reason I did not was the location of the itch. I know what orgasms feel like. They aren't that special.

"You keep believing that stuff and one they'll strap you into a coat with long sleeves. Babe? You're a mess and I'm qualified to say that."

I pressed my hands to my ears and stepped outside my home. It was bright sunshine, God's own. God's Temple was just across the grass. There were pilgrims there. It was Saturday. That much figured. People worked. They had to find time to be here.

"Go on, babe," Sandra said. "Let the masses ogle their messiah. And you think I have a superiority complex. Babe? You're a fucking mess and I'm still qualified to say that. And unless you seek treatment for that itch? You'll wind up with something worse."

Even with my hands pressed over my ears, I could hear her. Who was she? Why did she insist her name was Sandra? My name is Rebecca. Why can't she see that?

I didn't know what to do.

Then I heard it.

God's voice.

I dropped to my knees, clutched my hands together in supplication to Him in the highest. And he spoke, "I will return a week from tomorrow. I will return to the Temple. It will be noon, my time for justice. All will be judged for their worthiness and righteousness. The worthy will accompany me to heaven and the unworthy will turn to ash as I speak. You will find that doctor and bring her to me. You will affix her the stake and send her ashes back to hell. I have spoken."

A crowd had formed around me. Pilgrims looking for an answer. I had it now. Questions began. Many people began asking what was going to happen. I stood and saw Albert coming. I jumped for joy and ignored the sensations from my body. Yes! I was having another orgasm! God's orgasm! It exploded all over me as Albert stood before me and said, "What is it, Rebecca?"

"He spoke to me!" I was as close to God now as I ever was. I felt him! He spoke to me! "He revealed the date to me! A week from tomorrow. Noon. In God's temple. All will be judged!"

Around me, everyone dropped to their knees and started singing hallelujah to Him in the Highest. Hands clasped together, faces were raised to the heavens, voices began to proclaim his coming and more kept coming. It was the happiest day on this sorry world. Throughout it all, Albert was there. He made certain no one injured me. He made sure that no one got close.

"Speak!" the crowd said. "Tell us what will happen!"

I pointed to God's Temple and said, "There! I will speak there!"

I ran to toward it and only knew that Albert would be there. I threw open the doors and startled the workmen. The crowd stream in behind me, but did not take seats in the pews. Instead, they crowded around the pulpit. The workers there melted away. It was my place now. It was my place to tell them what was going to happen.

With my hands clasped in front of me, I looked at the crowd and said, "Oh, joy! Oh, happiness! God has spoken to me! He will be here a week from tomorrow at noon. All will be judged. The righteous ascend to heaven with Him. The others will burn where they stand. There is one exception to this. That person will be brought here and dealt with by God alone." I looked at Albert and said, "Your task is to bring her here."

"Who are they?" became a chant. It started from the fear that *they* weren't among the chosen. I said, "Then repent! Fall on your knees this very moment and repent of your sins! All of you are sinners! There are no exceptions! You have eight days to make yourself right with God. Eight days until Armageddon!" I spread my arms wide and said as loudly as I could, "I am yours, God! Do with me what you will!"

Albert was nervous. "Can we speak in private?" he said.

"Yes," I said happily. "But you know that nothing is private from God?"

He nodded and smiled. "Yes, of course."

There were pilgrims in the pit. They were trying to get closer to me. The irony was probably lost on them. However, even though I was ecstatic, I still did not want to be touched. That knowledge, of which Albert was privy, caused him to lead me through a door at the back of the rectory. From there, we hurried to our home. Most of the people who were streaming toward God's Temple did not recognize me. It was unimportant. We reached the house, the kitchen. Albert said, "Tell me what I must do."

"Bring her here. God will punish her on the morning of Armageddon."

"Doctor Six?" he said as though verification was necessary.

"Doctor SixSixSix, yes. Bring her here. The sooner, the better."

"It will take some time. Will you be okay?"

"Yes. Forever now. No one can harm me."

He smiled and said, "Not even if I hug you?"

Oh, Lord, no. No hugs. Then, I remembered God. All will be judged. "Okay, Albert, but be gentle."

He was, but I almost upchucked anyway.

"I will return as soon as possible with her. What will we do with her until next Sunday?"

I forced bile back down my throat and said, "It is a big house. There are places where no one will see her."

He seemed to consider it. "God will kill her," he said. "Is that right?"

"As He promised."

"I'll hurry," he said.

"I will wait for you," I said.

He left in a great hurry. I wanted to tell him not to bother. There was time everlasting now. I sat at a table in the kitchen. No one else was there. I clasped my hands together and prayed.

Sandra.

"Babe? I wouldn't miss this party for the world. And stop calling me Sandra. You stupid bitch. My name is Sanhedrin. Google it. I am here to judge you, just you. Everyone else will be judged in their time. I am here to judge you and your phony-assed orgasms. I keep telling you. If you want a real orgasm and Albert doesn't ring your bell, then you can always…"

And NO! NO! NO! NO! NO! It is the devil's work! It is profane! I WILL not!

"Babe? That itching you have between your thighs and around your ass? You've been bumping ugly with someone. My guess is that old Albert has been doing some itching and scratching of his own. Not that you'd ever notice. Rebecca? I agree with one thing. Judgment day is coming. But just for you."

I fell to my knees and prayed desperately.

Not like when I was a child and prayed for this and that. That was childish. This was my soul.

I will win.

God will judge her.

Whatever her name is.

I'll still call her Sandra.

Chapter 12

My mother did this shit. While she was out saving Portland, Maine from idiots and assholes, I was trying to find out what was killing her. She scratched her thigh one day and I said to myself, "Aha! Skin cancer because you jog with a sport's bra!" I spent the next three days researching skin cancer and actually threw the book at her. I mean, literally. She caught it with one hand, put it on the kitchen table and said, "What am I dying from now?"

"Skin cancer!" I screamed at her. "I saw you scratch yourself! You can't deny it either!"

Well, short story? She actually dropped her pants around her ankles, showed me that she was lesion free and said, "Nice try, baby. I'm sure you'll find it, though."

Yep, I was *twelve* and she was still calling me baby. Had she given me five dollars for every time she called me that, I'd...well...I'd be even richer than I already was.

But what shit am I referring to?

Well, a black Excursion t-boned us on Willow Glen right where the Toyota lot began. Two men wearing black ski masks pointed guns at us and one of them said, "Out!"

I put my thumb and index finger over the bridge of my nose and said, "I'm too old for this shit." Yeah, I didn't like those movies either, but just like you, I watched them. And now I was quoting lines from them. Dammit.

"Mom? Are we going to get killed?" Maddy said.

"No," I said. "Just stay behind me."

"Okay."

She got out my side.

I walked up to the one that had spoken to me, put the barrel right in the middle of my forehead and said as angrily as I felt, "Either shoot me or so help me god, I'll shove that gun so far up your ass that not even a colonoscopy will find it!"

Maddy giggled behind me.

"Um," he said and I recognized him. "I have a gun, lady."

It was Albert Seer, Rebecca's husband.

"Albert?" I said. "I'd say you really need to get laid, but my guess is that you're getting it regularly. How are your symptoms doing?"

Maddy stood between us and said without regard for the other guy with his gun, "What symptoms?"

"I'm fairly certain he has herpes," I said.

"And what are the symptoms of herpes and what it is that?" Then she turned to the guy behind her and said, "And that's not polite! Point that gun somewhere else." Then she said, "I'd threaten you with a colonoscopy, but I wouldn't do that to my best friend." She turned back to me, then turned back to him and said, "And her name is Becky and she's so small, she could probably do that herself." Then she stood next to me and said, "Really? We're not going to be killed? They look pretty stupid and you can never tell with them."

It was too much. I started to giggle and that caused Albert to rip off his ski mask and say, "Look, you two! You're being kidnapped!"

"Mom?" Maddy said. "Am I going to have to write a book report about this stuff because I hate that stuff."

It was too funny. I laughed, giggled and said, "No. No reports. But you aren't scared?"

She threw up her hands into the air and said, "You aren't! I figure Cassie, Carl and Sarah just got pushed to the back of the line somewhere! And if that guy doesn't drop his gun, I'm going to...well, I don't know what I'm going to do because I've never been," and she turned toward Albert and said, "What word am I looking for?"

"Kidnapped," Albert said right on cue.

"What he said," Maddy said to me.

Maddy has very good verbal skills. Well, thanks to Mario. Hell, half the neighborhood can recite the Gettysburg Address backwards because Mario is so good at teaching people how to do things. My guess is that Alex will start calling signals from a huddle as soon as he's able to talk. And, no, I have no idea what I'd just said. Signals from a huddle? That's football, I think. It might be baseball. I'm never sure about that stuff.

"What now?" I said to Albert.

"Get in my car."

"Up yours," I said. I wanted to say, "fuck you," but my daughter sort of precluded me from being that perverse. I added, "I'll follow you. Just lead the way."

His partner said, "Albert? Is she serious?"

I fronted him and said, "First? Take off that damn mask."

He looked at him and said, "Albert?"

"Just do it," he said with a whole lot of resignation in his voice.

"She'll be able to identify us!" he said.

He put his hands around his face and said, "Duh!"

He peeled off his mask and I was facing another guy with a beard. "Great," I said. "Pete and repeat."

Maddy just flapped her arms to her side and said, "Pete and repeat? I heard that one in the first grade, Mom!"

"Sorry, baby," I said. I groaned, put my hand over my face, reached into my purse and handed her the roll of fives.

Albert's buddy saw the roll and said, "Jesus! Look at the money!"

"It's five dollar bills, idiot," I said. "Plus, if you take any of them, I'm going to perform a procedure that will take a specialist in plumbing to undo."

Maddy took a five and handed the roll back to me. I dropped it into my purse and said, "Maddy. Her name is Maddy."

Albert said, "What gives?"

I moaned and said, "I have to give her a five dollar bill every time I call her baby."

He looked at Maddy and said, "How much?"

"Counting this one?" she said, "Sixty-five dollars. I'm buying an outfit."

He looked at me and said, "Thirteen times? Really? You're just giving her money, huh?"

"Mom!" Maddy said harshly. "Are you?"

Yeah, it wasn't a real good kidnapping. It was so bad that a car turned onto Willow Glen and we moved our cars to the side of the road. Even worse? Maddy stood with the second guy and actually held his hand. After, I asked her what they talked about and she said, "The Rockies. That's baseball, Mom." I actually thanked her. No, Albert didn't have real good handle on our kidnapping.

When we got back to the details, Maddy said, "Are you, Mom? Just giving me money?"

Albert wanted to leave, but I said to him, "A second, please? I trying to convince my daughter that I'm an idiot. So, please? Just wait over there?" Instead, they stood beside us on the roadside.

She was fuming. I said, "Maddy? My mother called me baby until I was fifteen. It made me so mad that I swore up and down that I'd never do it to my kids. No, I'm not just giving you money. If you want me to, I will. I'm trying to stop calling you baby and this doesn't help."

"I want my own cell phone," she said. "Plus the five dollars."

"So, we're negotiating?"

"I don't know what that means."

"No, phone. Ten dollars."

"No money, just the phone."

"I have to talk to your father."

"Ten dollars between now and the time you do."

"Done," I said.

She raised her right hand and Albert smacked it with his. "You go, girl," he said.

"Don't encourage her," I sneered at him.

He laughed and to his partner said, "Artie? I figure we're cool." He looked at me and said, "You ready?"

"This is about your wife, isn't it?"

He sighed and said, "Yeah."

"Were those pictures really of her?"

"Yes."

"Look," I said. "I need to call my husband."

Artie was nearly apoplectic. "You do realize that we could go to jail, Albert?"

I took out my phone and said to Maddy, "Can you handle him while I talk to your father?"

"Albert," he screamed. "She's going to send us to jail. You can't just let her call anyone."

Well, damn. I held my phone to my side and said, "Look, idiot. I'm making a house call. Do you mind? I'll probably be late and he'll worry."

"His wife is going to tie you to a stake and burn you alive," he screamed.

Maddy said, "Ooh, marshmallows."

"That was a threat, Maddy," I said.

She put her index in the barrel of the gun and said, "No, Mom. This is a threat and if you aren't scared of it, then I'm not scared of anything they might say."

Still, I looked at Albert and said, "Could you rerun that part about the fire?"

He looked sad and said, "We're building a pool in the chapel. It will shoot water in different designs and I told her that it was for fire and that the damned would be burned there. I never figured it would get this far. She said that God told her to burn you at the stake."

Auditory hallucinations. Plus, she had herpes. The auditory stuff could mean schizophrenia. There was a possibility of DID, dissociative identity disorder. Since Sybil already admitted her condition was a hoax, I discounted that diagnosis quite a bit. Sybil? Oh, come on now. Sally Field? That movie? Well, the real Sybil admitted it was all a hoax, so you can relax now. Your chances of having DID just went down to almost nothing. Still, I had to keep that particular diagnosis in mind. Though a minor possibility, it still could happen.

"We need to get on the road," Albert said thumbing his fob so that the back of his Excursion went up. He tossed his gun in the back and said to Artie, "Yours, too. They'll follow us." Artie looked perturbed, but tossed his gun inside the vehicle. "Make your call, but be prepared to stay until my wife is better."

"Sure," I said. "Where are we going?"

"Arlee," he said. "About an hour and a half that way," he said pointing south.

Once we got on the road, "Maddy said, "Mom? Thanks for this."

"And what is this?"

"A chance to see what you do."

"You realize they're crazy."

She laughed. "Oh, Mom. Our family is way crazier than theirs."

As time would tell?

No.

***

I stayed indoors because people kept knocking on all of them. I didn't mind talking to them, but only wanted to do it from a distance. *Yes. The upstairs bedroom. There's a balcony up there.* I hurried up the stairs. I was glad there was no maids or anything like that. Albert and I kept our home clean. I washed all the clothes.

Our bedroom is sparsely furnished. God says for it to be that way. The only picture in the room is an abstract one of God. I bought it once several years ago. I don't know who Nikki Six is, but now I wonder if she's related to the doomed doctor. I would have to remember to ask her before God burned her to death. Anyway, it's all the colors of the rainbow plus a few darker ones that made me think of His mysterious powers. If God has a face, that is it. That painting is it.

I could hear the crowd outside the bedroom doors. They were starting a chant. "Ree-bec-ca!" over and over. I scratched myself. Then I rebuked myself for doing it. True, it was an unthinking act, but those count as well. *God? I repent of that. I will repent in any way you wish.* Then I put my hand on the doorknob and readied myself. Someone once criticized me for being a media hound. That was why he said I did the things I do. I remember his face on television. The Devil was telling him to say, "She isn't a messenger from God. She's a self-glorifying person whose only actions are those that summon attention to herself. Besides, who is Rebecca Ruth Seer?"

There have been many attempts and requests for me to go on television and tell God's story. Of course, they always say, "Tell your side." It isn't my side. It's God's. I am doing his commandments – and there is only one commandment. *Do His work.* I wrote that down in The Book. People say that to me as a greeting sometimes. Do His work. Sometimes they say, "I am doing His work."

I opened the balcony door and the crowd cheered. I saw a few television people. They were with their vans. As soon as I opened the door and stepped onto the balcony, the cameras all pointed at me. It made me vow to do this the way God wanted it done. People began chanting, "Do His work! Do His work!" It was wonderful. God approved of them and their efforts.

I clasped my hands together and said, "It is going to happen. God has spoken to me. God will return a week from tomorrow. All your tribulations will be over. Those of you who will be saved, will ascend to Heaven with God. Those of you who will not, will turn to ash. All but one. God knows that name. That person will die in the fire. That person is the devil. That person will not survive." There was no point in telling them. It was between God and the devil. It was between her and I. I would command Albert to bind her to the post and he would do it.

There was no more. I turned and went back into my bedroom. I sat on the bed. I was listening for God again. He would talk to me and I would listen and obey.

"You stupid bitch," Sandra said again. "It isn't bad enough the way you are, but then you do this crap. Then you think I'm god or some such. Oh, no! You think I'm the devil. My hope is that this doctor, whoever she is, can figure this shit out and help us. And stop calling me Sandra. I'm you, stupid. If you were someone else, I'd never even talk to you. But you're me and this really sucks – and I have the credentials to make that statement true. And you fucking know it. Bitch."

Again. It was happening again. The devil talking to me and using my own voice. I know I am not...that word. I am a good holy person who wants to obey her God. That is all. That I am doing His wishes makes me more satisfied than I have ever been.

Ever.

Ever been.

To disprove her words – his words – I summoned pictures of my childhood. It was peaceful. My parents encouraged me to find my own path. I read the Bible one summer. I started with Matthew because I knew the Old Testament was basically old Jewish laws that had little in common with what Christ taught. Christ was a prophet and he taught love. Mohammed taught order. It has been, however, that love and order cannot co-exist. Therefore, God will take everyone in one manner or another. He will begin anew, but none of us will be privy to His decisions.

I wish Albert were here. I wish it was a week from tomorrow because everything would done by now. I wish that evil doctor was here so I could punish her myself.

But, my childhood.

It was serene, lovely really. I remember my father teaching me Bible verses. I remember reciting them for my mother. I remember getting chocolate chip cookies whenever I got one exactly right. I'd get two if I could recite an entire Psalm. Some were quite long. There were times I had to wait until dinner was over before I could finish my recitation. All this means is that I was the perfect person to do this. My parents would accompany me to Heaven.

Albert would not come to our bedroom with the evil doctor. I would have to wait for him in the living room. I went downstairs and sat on our nice couch. It's heavenly blue. The walls are white clouds. Our living room reminds me of heaven. I waited there.

"Everything is someone else's decision. Right bitch? You can't even wipe your ass without making a moral tale out of it. And your vagina..."

NO! I WILL NOT TALK ABOUT SUCH THINGS!

"Your urethra is located at the top of your vagina, bitch. It's biology. It isn't evil. You won't go to hell just because you wiped yourself after pissing. And those rashes all over your thighs? That's you, too. Well, me. I picked a bad partner for us. I apologize for that. I'll have to use condoms from now on. But get God out of your ass. I mean that literally. There's a sentence I never thought I would speak. Rebecca? You have God up your ass."

I wanted to beat my head against the wall. It would stop the voice from taunting me.

But then...

No. A week from tomorrow, I'm going to Heaven.

Doctor SixSixSix is going to hell.

She can resist all she wants to, but I know how things will be.

God speaks to me.

And He has spoken.

Things are going to end for us.

Human beings are history.

God said so.

By His name, praise be.

Chapter 13

Maddy and I talked the whole time we followed Albert and Artie to Arlee. Dang? Doesn't that sound like a Broadway show tune? Albert to Artie to Arlee? I can visualize girls with longer legs than I have kicking up quite a storm to rhythmic music. Anyway, it was precious, this time we had together. I thought she might be scared. I mean, after all, they did have guns. Maybe Mario taught them not to fear them. I don't know.

Then...

CRAP! I forgot to call Mario.

I pulled out my phone and dialed his number. It rang and he answered. "Hey, baby. How's it going?"

I laughed because Mario was responsible for me calling my daughter baby. He called all of us baby. Well, except Travis. He called him babe. I was still laughing when I said, "Oh, not bad. We're being kidnapped. Just thought you should know. I'll probably be late."

Well, trust him. He's been saving my life ever since I was six. For what it's worth? He's the reason it took so much time for me to learn how to defend myself. He'd jump out of a doorway and we'd wind up making out until Mom or, most likely, Aunt Dora caught us. One time, Aunt Dora made me remove my bra because, in her words, she was, "Looking for fingerprints." She made a big show of it and then grumbled, "Next time."

His voice got a couple of octaves higher and he said, "Kidnapped? Seriously? Are you hiding somewhere?"

"Ah, no. We're following them in my car."

"Well, wait. Who kidnapped who?"

"Whom."

"Whatever. What the fuck is going on, Evie?"

"I told you. We're being kidnapped and taken...well, being led...to Arlee by Rebecca Ruth seer's husband and a friend of his." Then I began to panic. "You better not call a cop. This is a nice friendly kidnapping and it's going to stay that way. Nothing like a cop to ruin a perfectly good kidnapping."

"Should I be worried?" Then his voice rose another couple of octaves and he cried, "Maddy's with you!"

"Oh, god, Mario. She's fine. She even high-fived one of them. Don't be such a worry wart or the next time I won't call you."

"Wait a minute," he said. "Is this a practical joke? Is Wanda with you?"

"Um, no," I said trying to be factual. "We're really being kidnapped and we're really going to Arlee. And I haven't seen Wanda since she was wearing those leggings last night. Not only does that bitch have a better ass than me, but now she's broadcasting. I should feed her a couple dozen Hershey bars. But, Mario? Don't you dare ruin the weekend for those boys! If you have to interfere send Wanda and William-never-Bill."

"Evie? I don't know what to do. What would you do if I made a call like this?"

I snorted. The damn man. He pisses me off. Try to keep in contact with him and this is what happens. He turns into a typical man and thinks I need to be rescued or something. "Mario? Grow up. I'm just being kidnapped. It's no big deal. Catch a big catfish and show off for the boys. They need a good role model."

"Look," he said. "I'll worry."

"Yeah, worry about me in a pair of those leggings. That's a fate I wouldn't wish on anyone."

"Um, I'll call William."

"You do that. And make certain Wanda wears those leggings because this is a religious crowd and you know how she feels about them."

"Um, okay," he said. "But I'll worry."

"See you later, babe."

"Um, bye?" he said.

Maddy said, "Were you and Daddy arguing?"

I laughed. "No. We were just talking. He thinks we need help."

"Do we?"

"Um, no. We're just going to see a fairly exotic patient. She doesn't want me to touch her and that's going to make a definitive diagnosis interesting at best."

She rolled her eyes and said, "They *did* have guns, Mom. What if they accidentally shot us?"

I laughed again and said, "Then it's good thing I'm a doctor."

We were about a mile from Arlee when Albert pulled to the side of the road. I followed him to the roadside. He got out, came to my window and said, "We need to talk about my behavior when we get there."

"Masculine asshole?" I said. Then I looked at Maddy and said, "Sorry. I don't usually talk like that."

She giggled.

Albert said, "Well, yeah. Rebecca's going to expect it. Don't overreact or think I'm going to do anything stupid."

I resisted the urge to say, "Too late." What I did say was, "You could always take the bullets out of your guns. That way you could be stupid and no one would get hurt."

He appeared to be considering it. His jaw muscles moved and he looked back at his car, wondering about Artie no doubt. "That's a good idea." Then he looked back at me and said, "I hope you believe that all I want out of this is my wife. She's getting worse and becoming a person I don't know." He looked absent for a moment. I thought it was obvious he was thinking about his wife. "That pool I talked about? The one I told her was a fire pit? There are three posts in its middle. All they do is squirt water in intersecting lines that are supposed to be interesting. They do their purpose which is squirting water, but would never stand up to having a person tied to them. You could pull the entire assembly from its roots if someone was stupid enough to tie you to one of them. She thinks I'm going to tie you to the center post and then burn you to death at it." Then he looked directly into my eyes and said, "Doctor? Please help her. She was wonderful. Now? She's making me afraid for her."

"Who's Artie?" I asked as calmly as I could.

He put his forehead on the doorframe and said, "My stupid brother."

"Will he agree to removing his bullets from the gun?"

"Yeah, or I'll kick his ass." Then he did it, too. He looked past me and said to Maddy, "Sorry about that, kid. I'll do better."

"Hey, Albert?" she said from her side of the car.

"Yeah, kid?"

"If you're serious about not wanting to hurt me, you could always make sure that your family doesn't kill my mother. I love her a whole lot and all she's trying to do is help your wife."

I smiled at her and didn't even care what Albert said in reply. I held out my open hand to her and she pressed hers to mine. We smiled at each other and said, "I love you, Maddy." I think that was our most human moment. In that short span of time, we were as together as we would ever get. I felt I knew her better than I ever had. Okay, I have my own issues with motherhood in that I don't think I'm a very good one. I think I sacrifice motherhood for being a better doctor. But just then? I couldn't imagine being anything other than Madison Sixkiller-Collins Collins' mother.

Artie came out of the car and said something to Albert that I didn't hear. Like I cared. I curled my fingers into hers and we clutched our hands together in another private moment.

Albert intruded, though. "Look, something weird is happening at home. We need to get there as fast as possible. Artie heard something on the radio about Rebecca. She made a prediction or something that God is coming. All hell has broken loose back there."

"Drive," I said, "I'll follow."

As though to underscore his claim, I noted heavier traffic than usual coming from Kalispell and points north. Since Missoula is closer to Arlee from the south than

Kalispell is from the north, there were probably more people coming from there than from Kalispell.

Albert pulled out onto the road and I followed as close as was safe. I turned on the radio and started going through my presets until I hit Kalispell's only local AM radio station. The announcer was calmly describing a scene at Rebecca Ruth Seer's home as one of jubilation. She announced God's coming and the faithful were starting to converge on what she called God's Temple.

Great, I said to myself.

As though she could read my mind, Maddy said, "Are we going die, Mom?"

I laughed and said, "Baby?" Then I moaned, pounded on the steering wheel, reached for my purse and Maddy put her hand over mine. She said, "Just tell me, Mom. You can give me ten next time."

"People have been predicting that the world is going to end ever since people first learned how to write. No, Maddy...Madison...the world is not going to end because God doesn't hate you. God wants you to be the best person you can be and that's all He wants from us."

"Like you, huh?"

I didn't understand what she meant. "Um, what?"

"Mom? You're the best doctor in the world because that's what you want to be. I hope that I can be half as good as your when I decide what I want to do."

It became difficult to drive because my heart was bursting with pride, love and respect for her,, for my daughter. She giggled and said, "Now would be a real bad time to hit a tree, Mom."

"Message received," I said, still feeling that pull toward her.

But she was right in one respect. The closer we got to Arlee, the worse traffic became. But consider: Arlee is a town with less than seven hundred people living in it and half of them are of the Flathead Indian Nation. I can't say that native Americans aren't prone to religious hysteria because I've heard of the Ghost Dance crap back in the late nineteenth century. A guy named Wovoka told anyone who would listen that if they wore the Ghost Shirt and danced with him that Yankee bullets would bounce off of them or some such. All that did was lead to Wounded Knee – and if you need to be told what that is, then why are you even living in this country? All I mean is that for its size, Arlee was experiencing its first traffic jam.

Albert must have known a shortcut because sooner than I thought it would be possible, we were at huge spread of buildings over which an archway proclaimed it to be "The Home Of God's Temple".

The radio was right.

There were a lot of people standing under a balcony listening to someone talk to them.

If you have to be told who that person was, then you haven't been paying attention.

My first thought was prescient. *This isn't going to end well.*

Wow. A prediction that came true.

Go figure.

***

My name is Rebecca Ruth Seer, I said over and over with my hands pressed to my ears. The voice wouldn't stop talking to me. It was The Devil and He was speaking in my name. He was telling me things that I knew weren't true. He was telling me that God's Prediction for next week was as false as I was. I screamed, "STOP IT!"

I heard a cheer from outside. It was different than the one that accompanied my announcement of God's intentions. Despite the devil's clatter, I went to the door and opened it just a bit. I wanted to see what was happening. People were turning toward the long driveway. Someone was coming. I opened the door wider and saw...ALBERT! He was driving slowly through the crowd, another vehicle behind him.

I threw open the door and sprinted toward his car. As it should have, the crowd parted before me. I was God's Messenger. The voice was still screaming at me, but it was easy to ignore. Albert was home. He must have tied up the evil doctor because she was not visible from where I stood. She was probably in the back.

The crowd drew closer around me. I began to get nervous because they were much too close. Albert and his brother, Arthur, got out alone and approached me. I couldn't see who was driving the car that was behind them. I didn't care. I said, "Do you have her?"

"Yes," he said. He stood at a respectful distance from me.

"Where is she?" I could say aloud what I thought. There were too many people. Then, the voice broke through and screamed, Why not? She's the devil! They will listen to you! Tell them who she is! I almost did. The only reason I did not was that God had commanded me to bind her to the inner post and then burn her. If I said anything now, the crowd would have her. That was not allowed.

"Right here," Doctor SixSixSix said as she came from behind Albert and stood next to him.

"Albert?" I said nervously. "Explain this."

He nodded toward the house. 'Sure. Let's go inside."

She had a little girl with her. She probably kidnapped her and forced her to come with her. I would have separate them and save her life. She would be among the chosen. She was a cute little girl. I figured she was maybe ten or so. I was going to have to get her away from the evil one.

"That would be fine," I said. "Let's go inside."

There were television people shouting questions at me. Considering I had the devil doing it ,too, they weren't hard to ignore. The only lapse I suffered was when a blond bimbo stuck a microphone in my face and asked, "Do you really hear God?" I turned to her and snapped, "Yes, and he told me you were not among the saved." I regretted it as soon as I said it. In truth, I did not know anyone's fate but Doctor SixSixSix's. Hers was ordained. She was among the doomed. The television lady might be saved for all I knew. Still, we went to the doors of my home and went inside. It was time to save the little girl.

I don't have children.

Sandra – the devil – started screaming inside my head. "Oh, you frigging-assed liar! Who are John, Joseph and Abigail! Or let me ask it another way! When was the last time you even saw them or thought about them! You leave that child alone!"

It was getting confusing. I sat in my chair. It was opposite our fireplace. Albert sat across from me in his chair. Arthur did not accompany us. He doesn't say much to me. The little girl sat with the evil one.

"Child?" I said to her. "Would you like to sit near me?"

The evil one showed her true side. She put her arm around the little girl and said, "She's with me."

That was clearly impossible. The girl was obviously under some sort of spell. The evil one is crafty and can turn your senses inside out.

"YOU LEAVE THAT CHILD ALONE, YOU FUCKING BICTH!" the evil one said from inside me. That voice, despite its harshness, would be easy to ignore. The danger would come when the evil one would begin to show the little girl things that were not true. Children were highly suggestible. I had no doubt the little girl was under a spell of some sort. I had to get her away from the evil one before her soul was forfeit.

I stared hard at Doctor SixSixSix and said, "That is yet to be determined."

Albert stood between us so that I could not see the child. "Her name is Madison, Rebecca. Please. This isn't about her."

"That is true," I said to him. "This is about the woman."

"She's a doctor," Albert said. "She wants to help you."

The child...Madison?...said something to the evil one that I did not hear. I leaned to my left so I could see the child. "I'm sorry? What did you say?"

"Nothing," she said. Then the stakes for her soul became paramount. She said, "I was talking to my mother."

Her mother! That was clearly impossible! God would never...but then God allowed a lot of things. I was confused and pressed my hands to my ears because the evil one was speaking inside me. He was saying the most dreadful things. Most of them concerned the girl...Madison?...and that I should leave her alone. He even said things that I knew were not true. He said, John, Joseph and Abigail aren't enough! You have to start screwing up her life, too! I have no children. That is something that is physically impossible. I am a virgin. Albert has respected my desire to remain so. Even so, they are innocent in the eyes of the Lord. The Bible doesn't say that. The Book does.

"Child," I said to her. "We will help you escape from bondage."

The evil one stood and took a position next to Albert. She said, "You leave her alone. I'm here to help you and nothing else."

I stood to face Albert. "Do something with her."

He said the one thing that changed my mind.

"The girl can turn her from the dark one. She has already had an impact. Let them go together."

"What will you do with them?"

"Put them in the basement," he said. He was holding his rifle. He patted it. "They will not get away. Not now. Not after all I had to do to capture them."

The little girl held Doctor SixSixSix's hand. Perhaps the change was already underway. I had eight days before God would stop the world.

"Go," I said. "We have time yet."

He nodded. "That we do." Then he patted his gun again. Then he said, "They aren't going anywhere."

I was hopeful. The little girl was a sign from God. Saving Doctor SixSixSix's soul was still possible.

But the evil one is powerful.

I did not have my hopes up.

Albert led them away.

It was a very good start to Armageddon.

Chapter 14

The grounds of Rebecca and Albert's estate were one thing because there were hundreds of people chanting in the road. I didn't recognize the chants, but they were not important to my reason for being here. However, I was about to meet Rebecca Ruth Seer on her own terms. That was quite another thing. Still, had I known what was about to befall me, I wouldn't have changed my mind about being here. That woman needed help and I was doctor. Dammit.

Most of the crowd followed and grouped around Albert's vehicle. A few grouped around mine, but they seemed to be trying to figure out who we were. They did no harm to my Pilot, but even if they had...well...dammit...I have all this money, see, and I can always get another one. Thanks a whole lot, Mom. I'm a rich bitch and I can buy my way around the world.

Maddy said, "Mom? Are we in trouble?"

I smiled. "No. They're just happy."

"Like when the Patriots won the Super Bowl?"

"Like that," I said. I had no earthly idea who the Patriots were. Was The Super Bowl a baseball game and did that mean they won?

She giggled. "It's football, Mom."

"Where do they play?" I said as I drove slowly toward a huge mansion.

"Foxboro, Massachusetts. They're Grandma favorite team. Uncle Alex played for them."

Ah, yes. I remember now. We used to run around the house wearing number thirty-two, his jersey number. I love that man and I named my youngest son after him. Alex Payne? You saved my life. I just hope you don't have to save it this time. Otherwise, I'm dead because you aren't here. Albert parked as near to the front door as he could and I crawled into the nearest space to his that was unoccupied by either cars or people.

Things got a bit weird at that point because RRS came outside. Actually, she was already outside by the time I parked. She was talking to Albert and asking him where I was. I can't say I wasn't worried about Maddy because I was. I wanted her to be safe. But this? The people around us were still chanting and it seemed religious somehow. I didn't recognize the words and not just because I didn't care. I was more worried about my daughter than I was about my soul. Well, that's probably always been true.

I heard RRS say, 'Where is she?"

I stepped up, Maddy under my arm and said, "Right here." I stood next to Albert.

"Explain this," the woman said, her eyes blazing as though she'd just stepped down from Sinai and found everyone else lacking somehow.

"Let's go inside," Albert said.

Well, I'll give her this: my childhood home was better than hers and the home I have on Stillwater Loop is better. Okay, okay, I was getting bitchy and I knew it. It was a nice home. Just nice. Real nice. Okay, okay. I'll stop.

RRS came to a stop in a chair near the fireplace. Okay, it was nice. Real nice. Dammit. I'm trying to be nice. For example, the living room, although Spartan, was comfortable, a nice place for talking. Albert landed directly across from her and Maddy and I sat on a couch just to his left.

I saw trouble ahead as soon as RRS said, "Child? Would you like to sit near me?"

I wrapped my arm around her, pulled her close to me and said, "She's with me."

What began to happen next is difficult to explain mostly because it was weird to watch it happen. First, RRS looked as though someone was talking to her. She tilted her head, let her eyes wander off and that made me say to myself, *Auditory hallucinations.* That's what it seemed like. She was hearing voices. From the way her eyes seemed to be battling back, I'd say the conversation wasn't a peaceful one either.

There had to be a way to get her to talk to me. The more symptoms I catalogued, the better my diagnosis would be.

When her eyes focused, her reply bothered me on so many levels that it took all my self-control to keep from snapping at her. She said, "That is yet to be determined."

Maddy scrunched closer to me and hugged me harder. I wrapped my arm closer around her and said softly, "Don't worry. Nothing is going to happen to you."

As though he'd answered an unasked prayer, Albert stood between us and said to his wife, "Her name is Madison, Rebecca. Please. This isn't about her."

I appreciated his effort all those more because RRS's reply was, "That is true. This is about the woman."

"Mom? Is she crazy?"

For whatever reason, RRS was focusing on Maddy and that was made apparent when she leaned to the side and said to her, "I'm sorry. What did you say?"

As much as I'd wished she didn't say anything, Maddy did. She said, "Nothing. I was talking to my mother."

I can't say that things got out of control at that point because in truth, things already had. RRS was unstable, was listening to voices no one else heard and was proving to be beyond Albert's ability to control her. Hell, from what I heard, she probably always been beyond him. As evidence? I still hadn't gotten an answer from him regarding whether or not he had herpes, too.

I realized that I hadn't been paying much attention to things when Albert patted his gun and began to escort us somewhere else. Maddy held my hand tightly and I wondered where Albert was taking us. As soon as we got beyond RRS's hearing, Albert said, "Downstairs. You can stay down there. You won't be bothered." Then he stopped, looked back through the house and said, "And you better call your husband and get him to pick up your daughter."

"Is she in danger?" I asked.

I've known for a long time that she isn't stupid, just uneducated in the ways of the world. That said, she looked up at me and said, "Mom? What's going on?"

Okay. It was time to stop acting like a doctor and start acting like a mother hen. What's that mean? Well, like I keep saying, *I'm a doctor*, and not an anthropologist. I have no idea what mother hens do, but they seem to want to keep their chicks safe from people that scramble eggs for a living. I hugged her to me and said, "He's right. I have to call your father."

Her eyes bulged and she became my worst nightmare – a nine-year-old daughter on a mission. "No!" she said just loud enough so that RRS wouldn't hear us but she would get her message across loud and clear. She pointed down the long hall and said, "That woman is bat-shit crazy and you're going to help her! Dad already taught me how to protect myself and I'm going to."

Albert nudged her and said, "Hey. That woman is my wife."

She looked at him and said, "And my mother and I are going to help her." Then she actually patted his hand and said, "Don't worry, Al. She's in good hands."

I knelt in front of her and said, "Baby..." and then buried my face in my hands *again.* I wanted to growl and scream, but our circumstances prevented that. "Can I owe you one?" I said into my hands.

"Sure," she said *happily*. Then she said something to Albert while I fumed. "Al, babe? She's never going to stop and I'll have the biggest wardrobe in Montana."

I looked up just in time to see him smile and say, "Babe? Did I hear that right?" Then he looked at me with his serious face and said, "She might be a cute kid, but she needs to get out of here. Call your husband."

I had this way around my mother. I mean, all she ever wanted from me was for me to talk to her. You know, like girls do. She wanted me sit down with her and chatter about the most inane things and I knew it. Oh, it was never about money. It was about the emotional tugging of motherhood. So, every time I wanted something, like going to a friend's house or buying a physician's textbook, I'd sit and make things up with her. Oh, damn,. She always knew, but she always did it. She knew it was important to me, so she sacrificed truth for together time. Once I told her that I was growing a vestigial tail and she said, "Really? Does it curl and wag when you're happy?" I laughed and said, "You knew?" She laughed with me and said, "I even knew that your girlfriend with the perforated tongue was fictional."

All that means is that Maddy began to play me like Stradivarius fiddle. She even told me that Becky told her that Wanda – her mother – was saving up for a boob job because she was jealous of mine. I smirked and said, "Yeah, and her..." and I realized I could tell her that I was jealous of my best friend's...behind. I left it at this, "Maddy? That woman could develop meningitis and that could lead to irrationality that I don't want you exposed to for any reason."

It was Albert's turn to get nervous. "Meningitis? That's..."

"Inflammation of membranes surrounding your brain. If you have herpes, you could have the same exposure she does. Mister? And you have guns."

He looked at Maddy and said, "Lady? Call your husband. I have to go talk to Rebecca."

He left and I thought he was holding his rifle a bit gingerly.

That left Maddy, my sumo wrestler daughter. Well, you would have thought so, too, if you'd seen the way she stood there with her arms crossed and her chin set like a crash wall at the Indianapolis 500. That's a race, right? Otherwise, why would they...never mind.

I dialed Mario.

And did something that I seldom do.

I prayed.

I have more faith in penicillin.

***

Albert came back and that meant they were locked away until Armageddon Noon. Maybe the child could save the doctor. Maybe her real mother would come for her at the end. Children are delivered of God. He will not allow that child to be hurt.

"Rebecca?" he said with a tone in his voice that I did not appreciate. "You need to let that doctor treat you. You could get irrational." It was the last word that made him appear nervous and argumentative.

"What sort of lie did the evil one tell you?"

"That," and he looked at my...lady parts...and continued with, "could lead to meningitis."

"It won't," I said confidently.

He stood before me defiantly. "God didn't give you herpes," he said. "I did."

"I don't have herpes," I said confidently.

"Let her say that. She's a doctor. There's a reason I picked her. There's also a reason a you consented to see her."

This was madness. It was a mistake to see her that one time and I was not going to consent to it again. I was not going to compound one mistake with another. It didn't matter how angry Albert became. It didn't even matter that he ordered me to see her. There was nothing he could do that would compel me.

Albert got in my face. He said harshly, "And, yes, you do. You have herpes because I gave it to you after I got it from Miriam in the kitchen. I'm going to ask the doctor to treat me and you're going with me. If this thing morphs into meningitis, then you could be in real trouble. I'll have to ask her, but I think this stuff can be fatal." Then he put his nose to mine and said, again harshly, "And I will not watch you die, not now, not ever."

What he said was troubling. If his admission was true, then I could no longer be married to him. That wasn't a biblical injunction, that was mine. It came from The Book and was in the first chapter, subset nine. That is where rules of social behavior are written. The first rule is that spouses will remain faithful to each other for the length of their marriage. If one spouse is unfaithful to the other, all the other must do is announce her wishes publicly. As soon as I went outside, I was going to divorce Albert publicly.

"I can see it," he said. "You're going to divorce me by announcing it publicly." Then he got closer and said, "Babe? We signed a pre-nuptial agreement that states you have to vacate the grounds if that happens. When God returns? You won't be here."

That was not...wait. I couldn't remember. Was that true? Was I destined to spend eternity with a man that I wanted to denounce publicly? I think I stuttered because I don't remember exactly. I think is aid, "That is not true."

"Rebecca? You were as poor as dirt when we met. Yes, I loved you then and I love you even more now. But this..." and he waved his hands around my head and said, "Whatever this is? Fucking Miriam wasn't worth all this. If I could? I'd take it back and leave this place. This has been trouble ever since we built it. You don't even remember our children."

That was it. I would not allow anyone – even Albert – say such things. I screamed, "I am a virgin! Before God, I will testify that I have never had relations with you or anyone!"

I can only surmise that being around the evil one made Albert into one of them. He grabbed me, put me over his shoulder and stalked off with me. I was screaming for help, but no one that I saw offered any. Miriam, the she-devil from the kitchen, saw us and bowed away as though submissively retiring. Albert took me up the stairs as I shrieked in Godly pain and humiliation. Not only would I divorce him publicly, but I would denounce him in that matter, too. I tried to bite him, but he merely held me at arm's length once we got to the second floor. Our bedroom is on the first floor. We sleep in twin beds as is proper. It is so written in chapter one, subset nine. "Spouses shall not sleep in the same bed." That is the fifth rule. The sixth rule is just as simple. "Copulation shall be for the purpose of having children. There are no other reasons to indulge in such filth otherwise."

He stood me against the wall next to a door. He said angrily, "You don't remember Johnny, Joey and Abby, do you?" He was daring me to say no. I did. "No, Albert. I know of no such children. I am virginal as you know."

"Rebecca? Those pictures I took of you? They show the female anatomy of a woman who is not a virgin. That's not an opinion. That's a fact. God can't restore it. Medical science could, but hasn't. Rebecca?" he said and threw open the door to the room. "Meet your children." Then he pushed me inside, entered and closed to the door behind him.

It was a huge room. Maybe the size of three bedrooms. The outside wall was ceiling-to-floor windows. The drapes were open on all of them. There were...people there.

"You stupid bitch," Sandra said from somewhere. "These are my kids. Yours, too. If you denounce them, I'm going to make your life hell."

There was a woman there. She had blond hair. She was with three children who were crying. She had them huddled under her arms. She was being a good mother to them. She was probably telling them that they were going to heaven in eight days.

Albert said the most horrific thing. "These are your children, Rebecca. Meet Rachel Harris, the woman we pay to raise them."

The little boy was maybe eight or so. The next youngest maybe six. The little girl was a toddler. The woman said nothing to me, just muttered lowly under her breath. She was probably telling her kids to be polite to me.

The oldest one said the most damnable thing to me, "Hello, Mother."

The woman named Rachel shushed her and gathered him under her arm again.

The three children stared at me with wide eyes.

Albert smiled at Rachel and I knew they had copulated. "Rachel, sweetie? Why don't you go downstairs and get yourself something to eat."

She bowed politely and said, "Yes, Mr. Seer."

She left.

Albert went to where the three odd children stood in front of one of the windows, sat against it and said to the oldest, "When was the last time we went fishing?"

"Last summer," he said respectfully. "All of us went." Then he looked at me and said, "But mom stayed here. Is she okay now?"

So, he'd brainwashed them, too. I wanted to leave and actually turned toward the door, but Albert was there to prevent it. "Rebecca?" he said. "I done with this stuff. We are going to get you cured and you are going to be their mother."

"That is quite impossible," I said. "And you know why. I won't damage the children by subjecting to language they have no part in hearing. But you know my physical condition."

"Rebecca?" he said. "What color is your hair?"

"Red. I have red hair."

"And Joey?"

"Anyone can have red hair, Albert."

He looked at them and smiled. "Kids? I'm going to have to play dirty."

The child named Joseph turned and looked at a desk behind him. Does that mean what I think it does?"

"Yep," Albert said.

"Will she get mad?"

"What do you think?"

And my trip into hell started.

Led by a child.

Damn him to hell.

Chapter 15

I wanted to call Mario, but couldn't bring myself to disturb the weekend he was going to give them.

Maddy giggled. "I know who you're going to call."

"Who, smarty pants?"

"Someone with red hair and really cool leggings."

Yep, Wanda.

I knew she had plans this weekend, but I knew that I needed someone like her to help me.

I said to Maddy, "When she gets here? You're leaving with her."

She giggled again and said, "Just call her."

"Okay," I said. Then I hugged her and said, "You big meanie."

I dialed Wanda's phone number and she answered on the second ring. All that meant was that she and William-never-Bill weren't being intimate. She can't get enough of him and I can't see a reason in the world why that is wrong or should be. The world needs more love and a lot less hate. "Hey, girlfriend. I need a favor."

"No, you can't have William even for a single night. It would just make Mario suicidal."

"Dang," I said. "Never thought of that before. Well, okay. Can I have another favor?"

I love it when she laughs. She has a great one. The world is a better place when she does it. I sound like a tea kettle at boil. Or car tires shrieking around a corner. Or the wicked witch of the west. Take your pick. But Wanda's laugh makes you believe that the world has a better future just because you heard it.

"Sure, pal," she said. "What do you need?"

"I'm in Rebecca Ruth Seer's home and I need you to pick up Maddy and take her home."

Not only does she have a great laugh, but she's smart as all hell, too. She heard the slight hitch in my voice and said, "Well, explain why you would deny your daughter this learning experience. She wanted to go with you and you were all for it. What happened?"

"Well, as near as I can tell, the world is going to end a week from tomorrow and all hell has broken loose around here. There must be thousands of people milling around outside and Rebecca herself is so unstable that I fear for Maddy and anyone else who gets in Rebecca's way."

"Hmm," she said. "So, I'm going to save Maddy. Who's going to save you?"

That damn woman. She thinks she's always a step ahead of me. She makes me so mad. She might be smart but...my boobs are bigger. I started giggling and Maddy looked confused. My giggles caused Wanda to say, "Okay. What now?"

"No matter how smart you are, my boobs will always be bigger than yours."

She laughed and said, "Well, that will only be true until my next birthday. William is getting me new ones. I'll be both smarter and bustier than you. Deal with it bitch. Now answer the question. Who's going to save you?"

"Look," I said seriously. "I'm fine. But I can't do this and worry about Maddy at the same time."

"Well, I could," she said. "And after I get my new boobs? I'm going to start bending sunlight and making bullets go around the corner."

"So, your superpowers are big boobs?" I said.

"Yep. You just have boobs. Mine are special. William said so."

"So, are you going to pick her up?"

"Yeah," she said. "When and where?"

That was just it. I didn't think getting her would be easy. Given the state of the highways that I saw en route here, the police would have to get involved in traffic control if nothing else. Also, while I didn't think RRS would stop people from coming here, I worried about the long-term effect of a crowd that size not having places to sleep, food to eat or sanitary facilities to use. In other words, this place was going to be a fetid swamp in a couple of days. The only way I saw around it other than bringing in a whole bunch of public toilets and sleeping bags was in defusing anything RRS had to say about the hereafter. In my view, the hereafter *always* took care of itself and always had.

"Look," I said to her. "Just call me when you get here. Let me know where you are and I'll get Maddy to you."

There was something else in her voice, but I couldn't place it. You would think that best friends would be able to read each other better than that. Well, in her defense, I'm an open book to her, but I still don't know whether or not she has a bush. You'd think I would know stuff about her. Well, hell. I knew that RRS had a bush because I'd seen pictures of it. But my best friend? I didn't even know what her favorite color was.

"I'll call you," she said. "I'm leaving right now. Don't worry about me."

All that meant was that she was bringing help. Either William-never-Bill or Mario or both. Damn her. She was going to screw up their weekend. "Wanda? I always worry about my friends. Thank you very much."

Well, Maddy looked like Mussolini again which was not a good sign for me. I knew she wanted to stay, but I thought things had the very real possibility of getting seriously out of control before too long. But she had her arms crossed again and I just can't imagine where she learned that. Okay, okay. She got it from me. I looked like that every time I thought Mario didn't think I was pretty. Well, okay. I looked like that every time we had a poker game and Wanda showed me up by dressing in a way that made feel as though I was the homeliest girl at the dance. Well, okay. I looked that way every time Mario tried to buy me something because I'd say something stupid like, "Now you're trying to buy me?" He'd stroke my cheek and thirty minutes later I'd wake up in bed with him and as naked as...well, you can fill in the blanks. Now my daughter was doing it.

"Mom?" she said as though she was standing on a balcony in Rome and being defiant to the world. "I'm not going." Yep, arms crossed and chin outthrust.

I didn't honestly know what to do with her at this point. Why? Well, I wanted to find them, find Albert and his wife. My insistent monomania was screaming full blast at me. If I didn't do something soon, she – and who knows, but maybe Albert, too – would go into full-blown meningitis and that could prove more serious than herpes. While it's rare that people die from it, it can be very serious in people with depressed immune systems. Hell, one of the reasons I wanted Maddy out of here was that viral meningitis is more common among children than adults. While it's true that children under the age of five are at the most risk, I had to try to isolate her because so many people were outside and a lot of them had their families with them. I could be sitting on an epidemic unless I found her – and him, too – and started treatment. Unfortunately, there are no cures for the disease and it usually runs its course in about a week. It's the complications that could arise that worried me.

I had no choice but to keep Maddy with me as I looked for someone that might be able to help me find them. I mean, it was a big house and they could be anywhere in it or outside it.

I found a blond-haired woman coming down the stairs as we came up them from the basement. She looked a bit timid as though someone had yelled at her. Her eyes looked haunted in a way that made me say, "Do you know where Rebecca is?"

She was pretty and looked worried, or maybe frightened. She looked back up the stairs, then back at me. "Who are you?" she asked.

"My name is Doctor..." and I never got out the rest.

Her blue eyes got huge and desperate. "You're her! You're that doctor Albert took her to see!" Then she tried to remember my name and kept getting stuck on, "Doctor Six...something."

I smiled as warmly as my professional self could and said, "Doctor Sixkiller-Collins Collins. Just call me Doctor Six. That's easier to remember. And your name?"

"Rachel," she said. She looked up the stairs and said the most frightening single sentence I'd heard in the last twenty-four hours. "She's with the kids!"

She could have said anything else and I would have simply treated her respectfully and gone on my way. But that? Considering that meningitis hits kids first, hardest and that Rebecca also had a case of herpes just made my wish to find her and help go into overdrive.

Another girl came out of what I assumed was the kitchen. "Miriam?" Rachel said. "Can you help make sure no one goes up there?"

"Sure," the girl said. "What's up?"

"Rebecca is up there with Albert. She's having...difficulty."

The girl called Miriam looked up the stairs, looked at Rachel, looked at Maddy and I and said, "I hope this is that doctor."

"Doctor Six," I said. Then I said, "And my daughter, Madison."

Miriam looked at Maddy and said, "You're a lucky kid, little girl."

And walked away.

That left Rachel. She looked nervous now and I didn't know why. I asked the only question left to me. "You said kids. Whose kids are they?"

"Hers, Mrs. Seer. She doesn't remember them either. It's like she's someone else. There's Johnny, Joey and Abby. Johnny's the oldest. He's ten.

Which only proved to underline one of my fears.

I'll belay saying what it is until I get a better diagnosis than just suspicion.

Either way, those kids could be in trouble.

"Which room?" I said.

"Second floor, first door on the left."

I headed up the stairs, Maddy under my arm.

There seemed to be a lot of that going around.

***

Albert had turned evil. Why God? Why have You allowed this? And why was he insisting that they were my children when that was physically impossible? I am chaste before You. I am all that is Godly in the world. I am as You instructed me to be. They might be good children, but they are not mine. I watched in horror as Albert went to the desk behind them and opened the top drawer of three on its left side. They shared a conspiratorial moment as they removed a photo album from it. The other two children stood waiting for them. They looked scared and they should have. God was about to strike all of them down, not just Albert. The pity is that the children had been infected by him. It wasn't their fault. Still, they were going to burn. Maybe even in God's Temple.

Albert opened the album and showed it to the other children. The oldest child, the one called Johnny, looked at something and smiled. "Do you think she'll remember?" he said. I remember everything. I don't remember them because they were not my children.

Albert looked at me and said, "Please, Rebecca. Humor me. Just look."

I had eight days to humor him. After that? He would die in the flames just like the doctor would die in them. I went to him and he turned the album to me. I looked at the photographs and knew he was of the devil. There were pictures of me holding those children in my arms. I recognized the oldest Child, Johnny, in them. He was smiling and looked happy. But the devil can deceive us. He can make us believe things that are not true.

I looked at Albert and said, "You are with the devil. You have always been with the devil."

"Really?" he said almost happily. "If that's true, then what's this?" he said turning a few pages backwards. Then he held up a picture of me laying in a hospital bed holding a baby. Albert was there, too. He was smiling and looked as happy as I was.

"The devil's work," I said angrily. "These are not my children."

All of them began wailing, even the oldest child. Albert said something to them and hugged all of them. He was conspiring with the devil. He was comforting his progeny. Then he turned to me and said, "What was the name you were born with?"

"That's immaterial here," I said.

"Well, humor me. I mean, I know I'm the devil now but humor me. What name were you born with?"

"I was born Rebecca Ruth Teller. Teller is my maiden name."

His smile was evil. "No, it wasn't. You didn't become Rebecca Ruth Seer until God started talking to you. That was about ten years ago. John was born just before you started hearing voices." Then he held up the picture album again and paged to its front and gave it to me. That's your birth certificate. You were born in Austin, Texas. What name is on it?"

Sandra Marie Peters.

"This is the devil's work," I said.

Sandra started giggling. "You stupid, bitch. You don't hear the truth when people tell you, so why am I not surprised that reading it doesn't affect you either?"

"And why do you do that?" he said. "It's like you're hearing voices that none of the rest of us hear. Are you? Are you hearing voices? If so, my guess is that it isn't god, but you somehow. I'd like you to see that doctor. And by the way, you never acknowledged why we agreed to see her. Don't you remember?"

"I've never seen her before," I said.

He smiled and said, "If that's true and you've never seen her before, then why is she the devil? It seems to me you'd have to have some knowledge of her for that to be true. Or does God tell you that everyone who disagrees with you is the devil?" Then his smile got wider and he said, "But the doctor. Why did we go to her?"

He was insisting that I had gone to her. I hadn't. But his question was valid. If I'd never seen her before, then why was she the devil and why did I want to burn her at the stake in God's temple? "You could always tell me," I said. "Who knows? I might remember her."

"You don't remember Judy and Dan, do you?" he said somewhat angrily.

"No. I don't know anyone by either of those names."

"Dan and Judy Costello. Judy was your best friend. She developed skin cancer and went to Doctor Six who presided over a cure for her. She lives in Kalispell. She recommended her to us and that's why we went. That was only three days ago."

The names – either of them – meant nothing to me. I needed to get out of there. I needed time to think and pray. God would show me the way. I backed up toward the door and said, "Albert? Please. Don't say these things. They are not true and you know it. The children belong to that girl who was here. They are her children and you need to repent of what you said. It was a lie and you know it."

The oldest child, Johnny, came forward and said with tears in his eyes, 'Why are you being this way, Mom? Why are you saying these things? We were going to go to the lake and go fishing this weekend. You told us we were going to be okay."

Albert came to his side. The devil was standing next to one of his children. Albert said, "You like fishing. You always have ever since Lady Bird Lake in Austin. You know more about trout, catfish and other game fish than anyone I ever knew. I thought I knew a lot and then I met you. Sandy? Please come back to me. Please don't be this person. I'm sorry I went along with you. I'm sorry I didn't tell you about Miriam. I'm sorry that I've been such a poor husband to you. But all these things can be fixed. All these issues between us can be worked on, but only if you remember yourself."

I growled at him. "My name is Rebecca Ruth Seer."

"Your name is Sandra Marie Peters," he said calmly. "I will not call you that anymore. I don't believe you talk to God and I don't believe any just God would kill our three children."

I was alone. Somehow I always knew I would be at the end. Well, that was true only for the next eight days. After that, I would be with God. He would take me to him and I would spend eternity at His right side. But I had to get away from that place.

I turned and exited the room.

It could not have been worse.

It was her. It was that woman.

It was that doctor.

God had placed another tribulation upon me. I could do nothing but withstand it. I could...

...and I thought I saw the answer.

It was glorious. I was going to strike a blow for God.

He would not fault me.

He would not blame me.

He would put me at His right hand.

His terrible, swift sword.

Me.

Rebecca Ruth Seer.

Sandra is a devil's name.

Chapter 16

We let Rachel and Miriam watch us go upstairs. No, taking Maddy was not my best idea, but until Wanda could take her from this place, she would be with me.

I can't say the house wasn't nice because it was. It was sparsely furnished for my taste and there were few pictures on the walls. Oddly, there were no pictures of family members or even of friends. Considering what I knew about her family, that she had three kids, I thought it might be an oversight. Considering what my diagnosis was, it was probably deliberate. Still, it made me wonder why Albert didn't hang some pictures of his kids somewhere in the house. Crap, maybe there were some hanging somewhere that I didn't know about. That was likely.

The second floor was long and wide. Any pictures I thought I'd see were conspicuous by their absence. The first door on the left wasn't where I thought it would be either. Well, in my own defense, the rooms on my second floor are all bedrooms and each one has its own door. This one? There were two doors on the entire wall. There were two tables along its length with lamps on them, too. But the doors were widely separated and the first one wasn't where I would have expected it to be. It was at least ten or fifteen feet down the hallway farther than where a door to a bedroom would have been. Well, according to Rachel, if she was here, then that's where she was going to be.

As though to confirm my hunch, the door opened and there she was. Rebecca Ruth Seer. She looked as drab as always. Her blouse was three sizes too big, her pants looked like they belonged to the circus fat man and she wore no makeup that was either obvious or not. Her hair hung limp to her shoulders. In short, she looked the same as I'd seen her two days before. It was her reaction to me that surprised me.

As soon as she recognized me, her eyes bulged and she screamed at the top of her lungs, "It's you! The evil one!"

I could have expected anything at that point except what she did.

She rushed at me screaming and held her fists in...well... a girly fists.

Backtrack just a bit.

Girls don't know how to make a fist. Trust me here. Without someone teaching them how to do it, the fist they make looks completely unthreatening. Mine did when I was sixteen. I've already told the story of how I was raped at that age, but it was everything that followed it that made this particular confrontation into a farce and not a threat. Alex Payne – yes, *that* Alex Payne, the one that dropped *that* intercepted pass in Super Bowl...oh, fuck, I don't remember – taught me how to make a fist and taught me how to deliver a punch. He taught me how to defend myself and then sent Mario on so many seek and destroy missions that it was a wonder I didn't give him my virginity long before I did. I mean, some of those assaults were *nice.* He'd cup my boobie and I'd know exactly who it was and what I was supposed to do to get out of that particular hold. The issue was that most of the time that handhold felt so nice that had he been anyone other than Mario Collins, I'd be dead – or at least raped a second time. And how did I know it was him? Alex was too shy to make that particular garb. He always slid his hands into places that wouldn't hit one of my nicer parts.

So. What's that mean? Well, as soon as I saw Rebecca make that little girly fist, I wasn't scared of being overpowered. I was even glad that I wasn't wearing heels because those things can be deadly. If I hit her just right with those things, I could dislocate a couple of toes and maybe even cause one to detach in a manner that meant the attacker was going to have either three of four toes thereafter. I was glad because I really didn't want to hurt her, just stop her from hurting herself.

She was all enthusiasm and higher purpose. What's that mean? Well, she was screaming for God to guide her through this. She rushed me with those little misshapen fists and then tried to punch me with an overhand jab. I sidestepped her, tripped her and my main worry became that Maddy might get hurt.

"Baby?" I said. "Please stand back."

"That's seventy, Mom."

"I'll give you a hundred if you just stay out of the way."

Rebecca picked herself up and made another charge just as Maddy said, "Mom? It has to be fair and square."

Rebecca tried to stand and punch me but her form was so bad that I just stood there and let her hit me. She tried another punch at my nose and I just caught her hand and held it. "Rebecca?" I said. "What the hell are you doing?"

She screamed, "Sending you back to hell!" Then she yanked her fist back and tried it again.

I did the same thing; I caught it and held it. This time I said, "Unless you stop and listen to me, I'm going to take off your pants and inspect you for herpes right here and now. Understand?"

Well, she did what all good preachers would do. She started sermonizing. She invoked God so many times that I expected to hear a celestial voice boom, "What already! I'm busy here terraforming the Sahara! Make it short!" Well, no voices sounded and eventually I crossed my arms – and, yes, I thought of Maddy and wondered if my pose looked anything like hers – and listened as she invoked God to help her smite the evil one. For a moment, I thought she was talking about a dragon and wondered if she thought of herself as St. George.

Then she tried it again.

Once again, she invoked God to help her "smite" me. My arms were still folded across my chest, but her jabs were so ineffectual that all I did was raise one elbow or the other to fend off her attacks. But you know? I don't believe she even knew how badly she was doing. She was speaking to God and that crap about multi-tasking is just that – crap. A person focused one on task to the exclusion of everything else will accomplish far more than some dimwit who brags that he or she "multitasks". It got so bad that I turned my back on her, bent at the waist and resisted saying, "Kiss my ass." She landed a couple of punches that were so weak that I suppressed a giggle and actually high-fived Maddy who was sitting with her back to the wall.

Well, my patience isn't infinite. I turned back to her, grabbed another punch and said to her as sternly as I could, "You do that one more time and I'm going to pretend that this is a patient's room, take you pants off and examine you right here."

Right. Don't expect logic from a fanatic. She kept screaming – and now I was wondering if she was screaming at me or God – and I decided I would never have a better chance than right then.

Albert had entered the hallway with his kids and stood watching us. I'd call his facial expression one of shock, but I was kind of busy with his wife, so maybe he was high-fiving Maddy and watching a great show.

Fortunately, her pants were so loose that I didn't have much trouble sliding them off. She continued to implore God to stop the evil one. By now, I got it. I was the evil one. Hmm. Never been cast that way before. I'd have to ask Mario if this stuff could be even a little kinky. Crap. I'd don't even know if Wanda's leggings are kinky. I'd call my mother's black corset kinky – but then I'd duck.

Anyway.

Mid-nineteenth century pantaloons. Seriously? We're this far into the twenty-first century and she's wearing something that can easily qualify as bloomers? Seriously? Well, I got them off of her as she kept screaming and flailing those misshapen fists.

Then I pinned her and said, "Rebecca? Mrs. Seer? Just look at this."

The spots were all over her upper thighs and had spread through her pubic hair. It verified that the pictures Albert showed me were of her, his wife.

Well, not just no. She continued to scream and that made me wonder at her mental state because had I been a rapist, she was making it way too easy. I grabbed her face, pinched it and repeated myself. "Look at this! You have a severe case of genital herpes and unless you allow me to start treatment, you could get much sicker!"

Her eyes bulged and she screamed, "No! You are making me see these things because you are the devil!"

"My name is Evangeline Monica Sixkiller-Collins Collins and I was born of a woman named Melodie Chang! She will be your next President! She is a Senator from the state of Maine! I am as human as you are! Now look!"

I heard a child ask somewhere, "Is all that stuff true, Dad?"

I heard Albert say, "I don't know, son. We should ask her when she's done."

I would have felt better had the question been, "Dad? What's herpes?"

I heard another young voice say, "Ew." A girl. Obviously, they'd gotten a beaver shot. A nasty one. Damn. Is that right? A beaver shot? I could never remember that sort of stuff because to me it's not a beaver. It was a vagina. Either way, she was right. Ew.

But she was going to look. I wasn't going to violate every vow I ever took not to hurt, but help and then to let this bitch slip away. I was going to help her. Dammit.

However, even the best laid plans...yada yada. She kicked me, loosened my grip on her, grabbed her pants and...whatever she calls them and fled down the stairs. I laid on the floor staring at the nice light fixtures in the hallway.

Albert Seer towered over me and said, "Does this count as an office visit?"

"Nah," I said. "This is my annual outreach clinic. Free, in other words."

"Well, I'm good for it if it ever becomes an issue."

"I'll have my people talk to yours if that becomes an issue."

He helped me to my feet and said, "Doctor? Maybe you didn't see it, but I did. She saw the lesions or whatever you call them. Maybe it will help."

"God willing," I said.

The only one that laughed was Maddy.

***

Yes! She was here! She dared to come under my roof! I would strike her down and drag her to God's Temple myself! I wouldn't wait eight days for her. God would not punish me either. I was going to smite her and then take her to God's Temple, tie her to a post and burn her as an offering to God. I was, in fact, under strict orders to do it this way. God expected His enemies to die. I was his terrible swift sword. I threw myself at her, my fists formed into hammers from God. I was going to pound her until not even the devil felt sorry for her.

But, no. I discovered that the devil is a crafty one. None of my blows landed true. She kept deflecting them and considering their might and power, the devil was guiding her against me. As a sign of his perversion and of her complicity, she made my pants disappear. They reappeared in the hallway with my pantaloons. One moment I was wearing them snugly and the next they were laying unused. I redoubled my efforts to beat her into submission, but she repulsed my best efforts with an otherworldly ease. The devil was helping her. God was making me do this alone. That was fine. I could beat her any time.

She pinched my face and made me look at my loins. It was such a perversion that I almost threw up. She said something about genital herpes, but that was just the devil talking. I was breaking into a rash because God does not permit such things. To gaze at your genitals is punishable by God. It was obvious what had happened to me. Maybe I peeked when I went to the bathroom to urinate. Maybe I got too personal with myself when I wiped myself with toilet paper. It can only be one or the other. Since I have never had sexual congress with anyone, her words were meaningless.

I fought with her some more and when my efforts proved unsuccessful, I heard God speak to me. *Shoot her.* Yes! It was the best way. Not even the devil could stop a well-placed bullet.

I pushed her away and she said something to the girl that she brought with her. I would save her life and take the devil's. I know she said something about the President, but this rendering unto Caesar was not going to happen. I was going to shoot the devil and win for God in the highest. All glory to Him!"

Albert keeps his guns in a closet in our bedroom on the first floor. He told me once why he keeps them locked, but I know that a good hammer or a good pipe will destroy those doors. I ran into the garage where he keeps his tools. There was a hammer on a shelf there. I took it and ran back toward our bedroom. I had to hurry. Any of them could come and make the issue one that could very easily slip from my control. The devil is a crafty one.

I took the hammer and broke open the door to the cabinet. I grabbed a rifle from the shelf and held it above my head and said, "I am your terrible swift sword! I am your warrior! Guide me to do your bidding! The devil shall not last the day!"

I ran from the house and headed toward God's Temple. There were crowds everywhere. I hailed them and proclaimed God's justice. It was coming and everyone cheered me. I held the gun above my head and cried, "Death to the unbelievers! Death to all those who would deny The Lord is coming! Death to the devil and his hordes!" People cheered me and it heartened me that so many of them understood and were on my side.

The workmen who were preparing the pit were still there. I faced one of them and said with a heart full of love and the expectation that God's love was in this place, "Is it ready?"

He looked a bit hesitant, but said, "Yes, we only have one last water line to hook up and then we can test it."

I wanted to wrap my arms around him, but Godly chastity prevented me from doing so. The water would douse the fires when its work was done. Everything was going as planned. Oh, how I wanted to hug him but that would stoop to the level of the evil one and I would not stoop that low.

People had followed me into the temple. They were waiting for me to speak to them. I held up the rifle and said from the pulpit, "I am going into the hills. Do not follow! Be here when God commands your return!" They began to chant from The Book. Chapter one, subset one. I cheered them. "You are all going to Heaven! You will all be at God's right hand! Be here when he returns! Be here when He speaks to you!"

With that, I turned and left the temple.

It is a short distance from the rear of it to the hills behind it. It was dark, but God guided me. He would not let me fall. I did not. I ran into the hills and knew I had but to wait and then I would see her, see the devil in human form. I would eliminate him from this world and save the little girl that the evil one had captured and forced to be with her. I would turn her over to Rachel because her children seemed to be good ones.

The brush got thicker the higher I went up the hill. I couldn't judge the distance I'd gone, but when I stopped God's Temple looked like a toy in the distance. I knelt in the dirt and prayed that God would show her to me. I would kneel, aim and shoot her. I'd take her dying body in God's Temple, tie it to a post and send her ashes back to hell.

The people looked smaller than I wanted. I had to get closer. I crawled down the hill and saw people pointing up to where I'd come. I didn't recognize any of them. One of them pointed as though he was shooting a rifle. That meant God's Children were helping me. They could help a great deal more if they just stayed away.

It got darker than it had been. The lights in God's Temple were always on, however. Still, I did not see the evil one. From my vantage point on the hill, I would see her if she approached either the temple or anywhere else that led to where I sat watching her.

But it got late.

And later.

And I didn't remember anything after a while.

I vaguely remember someone talking to me, but I don't think it was God.

It could only have the evil one.

That doctor.

She was here.
I woke the next day. It was daylight.
But I hadn't been sleeping.
The devil was afoot.
I was aware.
Very aware.

Chapter 17

I thought my first duty was to Maddy. After Rebecca ran down the stairs, Maddy went to them and said as she looked down their length, "Mom? That woman is as crazy as Travis is when he's singing in the shower."

I stood with her, my arm around her shoulder and said, "You don't like your brother's voice?"

"He scares the cat," she said.

Albert came up behind me and said, "She'll be in the hills behind the temple."

"We need a private room so I can examine you, Mr. Seer."

"My bathroom downstairs," he said.

I looked down at Maddy and said, "You can stay just outside the door. Okay?"

"Sure, Mom," she said hugging me a bit tighter.

"I need to get my kids," he said.

As Maddy and I waited for him, we heard a crash downstairs. The sound of a door slamming shut followed immediately thereafter. I figured it was Rebecca.

Albert came out of the huge room with his three kids in tow and said, "That noise? She probably broke open my gun cabinet. There's an old M1 carbine that she likes. She probably took it."

Great. A nut with a gun. It's not like we don't have a surplus of them in this country. We don't need another one.

I noted that Maddy hit it off immediately with Abby, Albert's youngest. It made me wonder how many friends they had considering their mother's condition. While that was an open question, Albert proved right in one respect. The doors on his locked gun cabinet were smashed and there was a space on a rack for a rifle that was missing. An M1? I don't know what that is, but any gun she took was a complication I didn't need. As upsetting as that was, I decided to stick to medicine.

With that settled, I escorted Albert into his bathroom. I noted the water jets in the shower and wondered how a woman that makes the Puritans look positively libertine thought of them. *Concentrate, idiot.* I went back to work – and that was Albert.

He dropped his pants and I saw no blisters or sores.

"You have no obvious blisters, Mr. Seer. Does that mean you've seen a doctor?"

He sighed and said, "Yes. I took acyclovir that were prescribed by a doctor down in Missoula. Doctor Tremont."

"Gayle?" I asked.

"Vivian," he smirked.

"Just checking." Then I said, "How long ago and why didn't your wife see her if you did?"

"Can I pull up my pants? This would be a real bad time for Rebecca to walk in."

"Yeah," I said and he did.

He sagged onto the closed toilet seat, sighed and said, "Damn. Like six months ago? I got it from Miriam in the kitchen. She got treated by the same doctor. Rebecca? She refused to go even though it was obvious she was having major complications." Then he looked up at me and said, "Things didn't start to get out of control until she insisted that her name was Rebecca. That was easily ten years ago, right around the time Johnny was born. It was like she'd become a completely different person."

He needed to know my preliminary diagnosis. Hell, he might even suspect it. "I think your wife is suffering from one of two conditions. Either paranoid schizophrenia or dissociative identity disorder. The first condition is easier to diagnose than the second. Hell, there are split opinions about it being a real condition anyway. We won't know until we get to talk to her, treat her and watch her reaction to treatment."

His first question was the obvious one. "What's dis..."

I smiled and said, "Think *Sybil*. Maybe you saw the movie or read the book. She claimed to have had several different personalities, then later took it all back and said she made it up. On that basis, that diagnosis will be difficult to prove. Still, the woman I've met is troubled and I can provide several pieces of diagnostic evidence to back that up if you'd like."

He looked as miserable as anyone I'd ever met. He said, "I thought I could control it. This religious stuff? That phony temple over there? All that stuff? I thought if I humored her, I could ride out the storm and help her remember Sandra."

"Sandra?" I said. "Who's that?"

He smiled. "Her married name is Sandra Marie Seer. Her maiden name is Peters. It's fairly well known, too. There are numerous websites that wonder why she changed her name, but no one argues that her real name is Sandra. Crap, she even has me calling her Rebecca. Still, I might be the only one who knows why she changed it."

I smiled. "Because neither Sandra nor Marie are Biblical names, but both Rebecca and Ruth are. How did I do?"

He laughed. "Good. That's it in a nutshell. What say we go and look for her?"

"Is she a danger with that gun?" I asked.

He smiled, but it was more to himself than to anyone else. "I doubt it, but I have to check the cabinet first."

"Well, let's."

Maddy was still paired off with Abby and that left Johnny and Joey to pair off with each other. From what I could see of their behavior, they were used to each other. That was good for our immediate future. How their mother figured into the long-term plans was anyone's guess.

As we descended the stairs, he said, "All that self-defense stuff? That was impressive. Are you one of those self-defense nuts?"

I said just loud enough for him to hear, "I was raped when I was sixteen. My family guaranteed that it would not happen again. It hasn't. Thank you God for my husband and Alex Payne for helping me."

We were on the bottom landing. He stopped and said, "Wait a second. *That* Alex Payne? The one that played for the Patriots? Him? You know him?"

I smiled and said, "Help me end this safely and with your wife in therapy and I'll make sure you meet him."

"Look, I was a kid when he played in Super Bowl…"

And I stopped him by saying, "Look, don't tell me which one it was because I'll never remember. I don't do baseball, football or any of the other 'balls. Please? But, yes. It's him. Between him and my husband, they taught me how not to be picked on, attacked or bullied. I'm not. I haven't been since I was sixteen and he's responsible me being both a doctor and being strong enough to be one."

He smiled, but it was one of self-discovery and a future he was going to make certain he lived to see. That's all it took for him to be a non-believer in the stuff his wife was peddling.

We went into the bedroom and saw a smashed gun cabinet. A space reserved for a rifle was empty. There were other rifles on racks, plus numerous handguns. Rifles and handguns. That's as far as I could go in identifying what they were. If someone asked me to describe an M1 carbine, I'd say something stupid like, "You hold it against your shoulder, pull the trigger and hope you don't shoot off your toe." That went for handguns, too. I hope I never have to become conversant about guns. If I do, it means society took a huge turn for the worse – and I'm not convinced it hasn't anyway.

He came away from the cabinet laughing lowly, like a little kid that discovered a vibrator in her mother's lingerie drawer. Oh, and Mom? I can only apologize for that so many times. Crap, our next president will use a vibrator in the White House. Now, *there's* a mental image that will take a case of good beer to erase.

"What?" I asked as we headed outside.

"I'll let know you when we find her."

It never dawned on me that so many people were drawn to Rebecca/Sandra's message until we left the house through a set of French door's in their bedroom. There were hundreds of people. Crap, maybe thousands. A lot of them recognized Albert. He asked the first one who named him, "Do you know where Rebecca went?"

He pointed into the hills behind the temple and said, "Up there!"

It was darker than...well...hell. The hills were going to be worse. I looked at Albert and said, "I'm not taking my daughter up there."

"Nor I my kids," he said. Then he said, "Wait here. I'll get Rachel. She's very good with them." He went back through the doors after telling his kids, "Wait here. I'll be right back."

"Mom?" Maddy said with the confidence of a sumo wrestler. "You can't stop me."

And I was back at ground zero. My mother could never discipline me. That's what Dad was for. Oh, she tried. And tried and tried, but she never was able to do more than say, "Um, Evie? I...um...think that..." and then she'd hug me. I played out that scenario so many times when I was a kid that I actually ran away from home when I was eleven. Oh, it all worked out, but that acorn that didn't fall far from the tree? Well, Maddy was doing her Mussolini impression again. I knelt in front of her and realized that all three of Albert's kids were watching us. *Come on, Evie. You can do this.*

Long story short? Rachel made sure that all four kids were together as we trudged up into the hills. Maddy held my hand because, in her words, "I know you're afraid of the dark, Mom."

Another long story short?

We found her. Rebecca, I mean. Or is it Sandra? Crap. I'm going to have to settle on one or the other. Sandra it is. Why? Because Wanda's daughter is named Rebecca and I don't want to confuse one for the other.

Oh, and that bitch was here somewhere. Not Becky, but her mother. That bitch was here and when this was over, I was going to...thank her profusely and then let her buy me a pair of red leggings. Take that, Mario, you scum. Try calling my fat ass after I've shoved and squeezed it into a skin-tight leggings, a dream for men everywhere.

Albert giggled when he found her.

And never told me why.

Well, stupid me, I never asked either.

We went back down the hill and kept watch.
He fell asleep, too.
Well, it *was* four in the morning.
I fell asleep ten minutes later.

***

I woke on Sunday morning feeling *wonderful.* God's Day. Sunday is God's Day. We set aside that day every week to proclaim our love for Him. The rifle was still in my arms when I woke. I cradled it tenderly because today was going to be the evil one's last day on this earth, on God's Good Earth. I was going to wait here in the hills until I saw her and then I was going to kill her.

Again, oddly, I wasn't hungry. That was The Lord's doing. He was feeding me with His love. I knelt and said a prayer of thanks. Then I stood and looked at the grounds below me. There were fewer people than yesterday. Then I realized they would all be in God's Temple. Again, I knelt and said a prayer of thanks. Things were going my way. No, I apologize, my Lord. Things are going Your way.

My mission could be accomplished from my position on the hillside. I had spent the night behind a huge boulder. That accounts for no one finding me. Between my appetite being sated by The Lord and my position on the hillside, all I had to do was be patient. She would show herself sooner or later. When I saw her? It would be over until next Sunday.

The day began to become warmer. It was of no import to me. It could snow, it could become hotter than the place of the damned or anything in between and it wouldn't affect me. I was going to do this.

Then I heard a voice.

"This is my place, bitch."

"Who's there?" I said turning to the place from where the voice came.

It moved. From another place, it said, "Leave now. Or suffer. It doesn't matter to me."

It was a woman, a female voice. I trained my gun on the last spot from where the voice spoke. If it spoke again from that place, I would shoot it.

From another place, it said, "Your God can't help you here. This place is mine."

It was the devil! The evil one! It was the doctor! She was doing this!

"I will kill you," I said to the wilderness around me.

"Many have tried," it said. "None have succeeded. You won't either."

I stood, pointed the rifle at that place and said, "I will succeed in God's work! I will kill evil!"

It said. "How do you know I am evil? You could be doing evil in God's name."

I was being tested. I was being tempted.

From another place, it said, "Thou shalt not kill."

I screamed back, "Thou shalt not do murder!"

"In either case, you have sinned against me."

Had I? Was God here in this place? Was my faith being tested? Was killing evil wrong? I took a step up the hill and said, "God battles evil everywhere."

"I form the light, and create darkness: I make peace, and create evil: I the LORD do all these *things*. Isaiah 45, verse 7. The Lord created evil. You cannot kill the Lord."

"That is from The Bible! I have already discredited it!"

"That is from God. You cannot deny God."

What was he saying? She saying? It was still a female. I was getting confused. I sank to my knees and prayed. "God? Dear Lord? Deliver me from this evil. It is confusing me and I need Your help in this time and place. I cannot do wrong with You on my side. I beseech You to help me." I heard nothing.

"Praying to me?" the voice said. "How quaint. Humans do that. When they don't get their way, they throw a tantrum and start asking me to come down on their side and change things. The world is as I want it to be. The universe was created the way I want it to be. You cannot change these things and it is a heinous sin to assume that I will intervene just because someone was mean to you. What's the word? Juvenile. Even your children know better than this."

"I do not have children! I am chaste!"

"The gun in your hands? Is not chaste. Is not of the faithful. Is not of the faith. To assume that I would condemn my own children is worthy of you who already have."

Another voice sounded from inside my head. "I told you, your filthy bitch. I told you that we have children. I do. Now get out and let me make amends to them."

The voice sounded again. It spoke from yet another location. "Do you remember Lot's wife?"

"Yes. She was turned into a pillar of salt for disobeying God."

From yet another place, the voice said, "There are buffalo on these plains. Should you continue to disobey my words, I will turn you into a steaming pillar of buffalo dung. You will spend eternity smelling like shit."

Was I being disrespectful?

"Disrespectful!" a voice screamed inside my head. "You called Albert an evil one! Albert! You married him because you loved him and then you casted him aside as being in league with the devil! What's wrong with you! Us!"

Was prayer no longer worth the effort? Had I so misread the voice of God that even He had turned His back on me? Or was this the evil one?

"You're the devil," I said to the wilderness.

"Ah," it said. "There are bushes all over this mountain. Shall I ignite one and send my voice through it? Would a burning bush convince you that I am God and you are little more than a misguided child?"

From inside my head, the voice said, "Oh, fuck. You're going to burn down the entire mountain and kill how many innocent people down there? Are you fucking serious? Sandra, babe? You're even crazier than that other voice."

I had to do something. I had to decide who was right and who was evil. Had either voice said anything that was even remotely true and of the faith? That was my problem. I couldn't see what to do or how to act. I needed God's advice and He was seemingly humiliating me at every turn.

"I built your house just like you ordered me to do," I said falling into piety.

Sandra again. This time she said, "Yeah, Albert gave you herpes and naturally you thought you were going to die so you conjured up Rebecca Ruth Seer to become the holiest and most devout human being who just happened to have herpes on the planet. Babe? You aren't going anywhere until you can look at your cunt and tell it that it deserves better than you."

Suddenly, there was static inside my head.

I no longer remembered my name.

I no longer remembered where I was.

I no longer felt capable of doing anything.

I dropped the gun not knowing I had done so.

I fell to my knees but not in supplication.

For all intents and purposes, I was dead.

There were no voices in my head.

Mine or anyone else's.

I keeled over and lay in the tall grass.

Chapter 18

My phone rang. I already knew who it was when I answered it. "Hey, bitch," I said to Wanda. "Where you been?"

"Around," she said with her playful voice. "Wanna know where?"

"Yes, you dimwit."

"I'm parked next to a nice Honda Pilot. I'll let you figure out which one."

That meant she was parked in front of Albert's home. I smiled happily because I like that broad. I kissed Maddy and said, "Aunt Wanda's here."

"I'm not leaving, Mom. You can't make me either." Then with an outthrust chin, she said, "Besides. Abby needs me and her brothers are fraidy cats."

Rachel smiled and said, "She'll be safe with me and the kids."

"So there, Mom," Maddy said as though adding punctuation.

Albert added, "Please, doctor. Don't worry about the children. They will be safe. So help me."

Well, as much as I didn't like it, I had to admit that Albert had been dealing with his three kids for their entire lives. Still, I hugged and kissed Maddy, then said, "I'll be right back. You be good."

"I will, Mom," she said happily.

I hurried out the door and down the stairs. Wanda was parked in her Explorer. She wiggled her fingers at me and then made a stupid face. There was a time that I would have told a joke at that point, but that woman is gorgeous. Ever since she met and married William-never-Bill, she's taken to looking like a redheaded Indian that comes complete with braided ponytails.

I got in the passenger side and said, "S'up?"

"Want you to hear something," she said. She handed me a pair of earbuds and said, "Just listen and don't say anything until it's done."

What I heard was a conversation between Wanda and a person I recognized as Rebecca/Sandra. Wanda's voice started with, "This is my place, bitch." What followed was disturbing because every one of Rebecca's answers were predicated on the belief that God was speaking to her and her alone. When Wanda took the place of God in her pantheon of voices, her responses got thinner and thinner. At one point, Wanda summoned the image of the buffalo and told Rebecca that God was going to turn her into a steaming pillar of buffalo shit. Okay, Ew. But the thing that I began to notice were the gaps in the responses. Wanda would say something and several seconds would pass before Rebecca said anything. In fact, the last interplay between them didn't even get a response from Wanda. Rebecca said that she built his house as she was ordered. Then silence.

Wanda knew I was thinking when I held up an index finger. What bothered me were the pauses between Wanda's voice and Rebecca's reply. Sometimes as much as three or four seconds elapsed before Rebecca said anything. *She's hearing voices. Auditory hallucinations.* I looked at Wanda and said, "You noted them, too."

"The lapses? Yes."

"And?"

"Schizophrenia, I figure."

"Not DID?"

"That would take a team of psychologists months if not years to prove," she said. "But you think it is?"

I shook my head and said, "I'd need more time with her before I could even begin to recommend therapy of one type of another."

She smirked and said, "Just making sure you weren't Evie's doppelganger." Then she looked harder and said, "The thing that bothers me is the gun she's carrying up there. I mean, I saw her clearly, but she was so...I don't know...otherworldly...that she never bothered to look for an actual person. She believed she was talking to god and that's a bit frightening because that gives her so much latitude to do anything that it scares me. I mean, now that I have Billy..."

"Hold it," I said almost angrily. "Billy? He won't let anyone call him Bill and you call him Billy?"

She smiled and it was a winner. "Hey, I can call him anything, even shithead and he lets me. That's because I give him the best sex in the western hemisphere." Then she smirked and said, "But don't try that stuff with him or you'll get his crazy wife.'

I pushed her and said, "I already have his crazy wife. So? Rebecca? Did you follow her? Is she still up there?"

"Look," she said seriously. "That gun precluded a lot of stuff."

Which left only one question. "Why, Wanda? What the fuck were you doing up there?"

She leaned back against the seat, sighed and said, "Dammit, Evie. I know how you are. You're freaking Wonder Woman because your mother is going to be President of The United States. It's like you have to prove yourself in everything." Then she sat bolt upright and said to me, "As soon as you told me where you were, I knew exactly what I had to do. That lunatic is telling people that the world is ending next Sunday. Do you have any idea how many people will be here? Do you have any idea what the risks are to them?" She extended her arm toward the temple at the other side of the property and said, "There aren't even any toilets here! The health crisis will be enormous! And I work in an ER! The only way to avert a disaster is to discredit her!"

Well, not just no. "I'd rather help her than discredit her."

She put her face in her hands, growled into them, looked at me, put her face as close to mine as she could and said adamantly, "And if by discrediting her, I help to bring her mind back into the world instead of staying wherever the fuck she is, how is that bad medicine?"

"Unstable people do unstable things," I said to her face which still hovered close. "And like you said; she has a gun.

Wanda? We have to find her, do whatever needs to be done to get her into therapy and find a course of treatment. All without forcing her to use that gun on anyone. That's why I'm here." Then I looked away and said, "Do you really think I compete with my mother?"

"Is water wet?" she said.

"I love her," I said almost sadly. Then I looked at her and said, "Do you think badly of me?"

She put her right hand on my left and said, "I told Billy that when my time comes, that if someone needs to make a decision to pull the plug on me, that I want you to make that decision. There is no one I respect more than you, Evie. You push medical competence to an entirely new level. Babe? We need to find that lunatic and dial down all this angst that she's piled up around here like so much firewood."

I turned my head and looked at the hills that rose behind the temple. "She's still up there, isn't she?"

"Most likely." Then she added, "I'm not going up there either. I came for Maddy and that's it."

I said, "Well, I'm committed, or I should be for being here." Then I said weakly, "Wanda? For the record? This – medicine – is all I've ever wanted to do. Okay, my mother was complicit in my own monomania, but I've never consciously competed with her. Do you believe me?"

We looked at each like the old friends we were and she said, "Look. I'm sorry I said anything. I should know better." Then she giggled and said, "It's just that I've never been invited to the White House before."

"Well, let's go find Albert because I'm not going up there alone."

"Well, I'm not leaving until you do either."

We went back into the house and Wanda said, "A bit Spartan for my taste, but to each his own."

As an aside? There was a picture hanging on the wall in their bedroom that I recognized. If Albert agreed, I was going to buy it from him. In fact, I said, "Just a second. Come with me."

I steered her toward Albert and...Sandra's...bedroom and nodded toward the picture above their bed. "Like it?"

Wanda has a deep streak of Reality in her. Maybe it's from working for too long in an ER. That could be. For example, that stuff about the gun? She's seen too many gunshot wounds because of her job and where she practices it. She knows what a society that has too many guns does to itself. Thus, she's more of a realist than most people I will ever meet.

But that picture?

She knotted her brows together, looked at it and said, "Lord, that's nice and I don't even know why."

I said proudly, "My grandmother painted that. I was maybe ten or so when she did. She called it 'infinity' and between that time and now? I never knew what happened to it. But, my grandmother did that and I want to know if Albert will sell it to me."

From behind me, he said as the kids all grouped behind him and around Rachel, "If you can return Sandy to me, you can have it."

"Oh, Lord, Albert. Do you know how much that picture is worth?"

"Yep," he said with a smile. "But Sandy is worth a whole lot more. You return her to me and, like I said, I'll give it to you."

Well, I can't say that his offer was what spurred me on to do this thing because I would have done it anyway, but it sure didn't hurt. Grandma taught me about how to present myself to the world and I fear that I didn't learn that lesson very well. Mom did. Mom listened to every single word Grandma ever said then acted upon them. Me? I figured that I am still a mostly unfinished work. *Grandma?* I said to myself as I stared at her painting. *I'm trying the best I can. I hope you're not disappointed in me.*

And there it was. Motive. As if I needed any. I fear I am harder on myself than on anyone else around me. You see? My family didn't browbeat us into doing well. They encouraged us to find our voice and start singing. This – medicine – is my voice and I have always tried to sing it as loud and as clear as possible.

I only hoped it was enough.

Sandra? I am a doctor, and as such, I am dedicated to you, your health and your life. I am dedicated to helping you be the best human being possible.

God aside.

***

Fuzzy. I heard fuzzy noises, like static on a radio. I was laying in tall grass and looking at a deep blue sky. The static wouldn't stop. I pressed my hands over my ears and said aloud, "Stop it. Just stop it right now."

Then I realized I didn't know my name. Still lying in the grass, I said, "My name is..." and couldn't fill in the blank. The oddest thing went through my mind at that point. *God will take care of it.* The static kept singing its fuzzy song. I said it again. "My name is..." and nothing came. Another voice sounded, this one from far away. *Don't force it. You will know in a while.* For some reason the name Lot went through my mind. I knew it was a name and also knew that it was not my name. If not, then who was it and why did I think it?

From somewhere deep inside my mind, I heard, *Your name is Rebecca.* From somewhere else, another voice said even more stridently, *No, your name is Sandra. You have three children. Their names are John, Joseph and Abigail.* Is this normal? Am I crazy? How can I not know my name?

I sat up in the grass. There was a huge boulder there. What troubled me more was the gun, the rifle. Why was it here? Was it mine? I struggled to my knees, then stood from behind the boulder and saw...*home.* The place beckoned to me. The voices agreed with me, so that was no help. Instead, I said it again. My name is..." and even squeezed my eyes shut and trusted my brain to fill in the gap. Nothing happened except those same two voices who competed with each other for prominence.

There was a huge church...no, *temple* my mind screamed at me. Again. Neither voice objected to me calling it that. Okay, then. It was a temple and not a church. I looked at the rifle, closed my eyes and let my subconscious tell me what to do with it. *You need to kill evil.* Really? Was I standing in judgment of someone? *The evil doctor.* Oddly, that sounded correct and my mind did not object to it. I stooped, picked up the gun and held it in my hands. It began to feel normal. I held it against my chest and said it again. "My name is...Rebecca Ruth Seer."

I closed my eyes and could hear another voice screaming at me from somewhere. It was insistent and damnably so. It was shouting a warning, but of what I could not say. Should I listen to it? Was it the voice of my conscience? I listened, but heard nothing but vague warnings. I put my finger on the trigger and it felt normal. Yes, I was supposed to kill someone. Did that make me a murderer? If so, should I heed that faint warning voice? Should I drop the gun and handle whatever it represented in another way?

The temple caught my imagination. *It is a place of judgment. It is where God judges us. Have we obeyed His rules? Have we listened to His voice?* My name is...Rebecca Ruth Seer. As I said it, that same faint voice kept screaming for attention. It was telling me something about my soul, about what God expected from me. I looked at the gun, listened to that voice and saw a basic truth. *Both voices are saying the same thing.* But who was the target?

I stood and looked at the wide grounds below me. There were few people about, but lots of cars and media vans. Why would the media be here? I tried to think and almost came up empty. *God? Are you there? Are You still listening to me?* It seemed that God was angry with me. Was the gun why? Had I failed him somehow? Had he commanded me to kill evil and then I hadn't? Or had he told me to stand down and I hadn't? Was God love or hate or both or neither? That distant voice was still screaming. It was like hearing a voice over the noise of a storm. I closed my eyes and tried to listen to whatever I thought was important.

A name.

One popped up in my mind.

Doctor SixSixSix.

I knew her and she was entirely the most evil person I'd ever met. That dim voice screamed even louder. Why? Why was there a voice in my head other than the one I'd been born with? This wasn't normal. On the one hand, God was telling me that the doctor was evil and needed to be killed and on the other, a distant voice was imploring me that such things were beyond human beings. The voice was trying to persuade me to spare her life and just talk to her.

It was time to make a decision. I looked down at the property, saw the temple and my mind filled in that blank. *God's Temple.* Yes, that was right. *There is a fire pit in it. God has instructed you to burn her at the stake at the pulpit down there.* Things were beginning to make sense. That voice, however, would not stop. Like an incessant whisper, it was telling me that God was not talking to me, that the voice I heard as God was a mental condition. It was telling me that Doctor SixSixSix was here to help me. Was that true? Both couldn't be. One voice was lying and the other was telling the truth. If my immortal soul was on the line here, then I had to make the right decision. A voice said, *She is evil. You are correct. You will do as I say.* That was enough. I knew the distant voice was the devil, was Doctor SixSixSix's evil one in disguise. The devil was trying to take my soul and I would not allow that to happen.

However, once again, an image from the Bible sprung to life inside my mind. The picture of a woman – Lot, by my guess – wandering among a herd of buffalo. Why was that? What did it mean? Another voice said, "Isaiah. Chapter 45, verse 7." I knew that part of the Bible. God takes credit for creating evil. Common sense says that good and evil have always co-existed. If so, then was that Bible verse true? Did God create evil and, if so, why?

A bell sounded somewhere.

Of course, the temple bell. The bell in God's Temple.

People began to file out of His house. If I was going to do it, I was going to do it now.

With the rifle cradled in my arms, I headed down the steep slope.

People began to see me. They recognized me. They called out to me.

My course became obvious.

The Bible is wrong.

God did not create evil. God battles evil on a daily basis. His battle to the end of time will be against The Devil himself.

Or, with Doctor SixSixSix in this case.

With God as my ally, I cannot fail.

Oddly, that distant voice, the devil's, was preaching love.

How dare he.

How dare such a mangled creature express the ultimate truth of the universe?

God is love.

It has never been more simple than that.

I will love the doctor to death.

Chapter 19

By the time we got out to the square, his home and the temple, the church bells had rung and people were everywhere. We had to fend off a few people that recognized him and started chanting what sounded like book verses. It was easy for me to ignore them, but Albert had to smile, glad-hand and keep going.

As we neared the temple, I said, "Oh, and before I forget, why did you lie to me about not having herpes? And all those questions you asked me? Doctor Tremont could have told you the same thing if you'd asked." Then I smiled and said, "And knowing her as well as I do, I know she told you what herpes was and how it is spread. So, why lie to me?"

We were in front of the huge temple doors. It was a bad place to talk about herpes, so we pushed through, down the center aisle and into the area behind the pulpit. I'm sure there's a good name for such a place, but I don't know what it is. All I know is that it was private. All I wanted was an answer for his duplicity. I mean, I *know* how herpes gets spread and there was almost no chance she didn't get it from him, not considering her mental state. I mean, if not him, then who could have gotten that close to her?

"I haven't handled this very well," he said to no one. Then to me, he said, "I might be repeating myself, but if I am, so what. I only wanted to help her. She was adamant about sex, about the fact that she was a virgin. For her sake, for the sake of the temple here, I went along with her. But the deeper we got into the lies, the worse she got. Yes, I lied about her condition and mine. Am I sorry? Yes. Will it help to get her off that mountain without that rifle? I hope so."

I hooked his arm, led him toward a rear exit and said, "Relax, Al, baby. I'm not a cop, just a doctor. I want what you want. I want to get her off that mountain without that gun and then I want to help her. That cool with you?"

He stopped at the door, looked at me closely and said, "Doctor? That is all I've wanted throughout this. Please believe me. She won't hurt you."

"Let's hope so," I said and opened the door. The grounds basically ended there. There were sidewalks going to either end of the building, but the hills that turned to mountains started not ten feet from the back of the temple.

The one thing that I hadn't paid any attention to stood to my left at the corner of the temple. Two television cameras and their attendant talent with a microphone. I could have noticed to which networks they belonged, but really didn't care. Both microphones approached us and stuck them in Albert's face. One microphone belonged to a California blond and the other a New England nasal-speaking man with dark hair. Both began asking questions of him, both were different. Albert looked as though he was used to it and merely smiled and said, "No comment," to everything they asked.

The question that bothered me, or at least caught my attention was when the blond nitwit asked, "Your wife was seen going into the hills behind the temple here with a gun. Can you tell us what's going on?"

I loved Albert's answer. "Sure I could tell you, but I won't. Instead, I'm going to better spend my time with her up in the hills."

"Does this have anything to do with her prediction of Armageddon next Sunday?"

He smiled and said simply, "Yep. But I'm going to talk with her before I talk to you."

Then it was my turn.

New England Nasal stuck his microphone in my face and said, "And you are?"

"I am me," I said. "I thought that was obvious."

Then Albert led me up into the hills with him. We got maybe ten feet into them when I stopped and said, "You realize that whatever is going to happen here is going to happen on live television."

Then it was time for my last question of him. "Do you believe what she said is going to happen next Sunday?"

I don't know their past like a lot of people do. In fact, the farthest I get into their pasts are patient histories. Yeah, I've had a few interesting people, a few media types as patients over the years, but it never dawns on me to talk about them with anyone but them. This was a first. This was the first time I'd ever stalked a patient. That's what it felt like. I knew she had a condition or two and I wanted to help her. There were no "buts" either. The media could have her if they wished. I just wanted to help her. My only mea culpa here was that she'd come to me looking for help. But Albert? From what he'd told me, he'd been living with her and whatever condition she had for ten years or so. Could he defend it? Could he defend her?

He took a few steps up the hill, stopped, hung his head and said nothing more than, "No." Then spread his hands at the temple and then spread them toward the entire estate and said, "This temple? Do you have any idea how much it cost to build? And the upkeep? It's not a church to which people belong tithe to. I built it, the house beyond it and the rest of everything. Okay, I have a lot of money, but how many husbands would build stuff like this just to keep his wife happy? And you know? She isn't. She is absolutely the most beautiful woman I ever knew and she sleeps in bloomers! I haven't been allowed to touch her in any way but," and he struggled with the correct word. "Chastely." He rolled his hands in to fists and said, "Do you know how much I hate that word?" He grabbed at his crotch and said, "It led to Miriam and this. I don't fuck around. I love my wife. But after she got to this stage, to the stage where she insisted she was a virgin and that she had no kids, I've been looking for a way out ever since."

"And I'm it," I said. It wasn't a question. It was obvious.

He looked at me as though pleading. "Can you help her?"

"Without her consent and active cooperation? Probably not. Otherwise? There are at least two conditions that describe her symptoms fairly close. Herpes? Can be handled unless it had morphed into something worse." I looked up at him and said, "Mr. Seer? You have to help me help her. If you rely on me, then she'll probably be institutionalized."

He turned and looked up the slope. "When I married her? I said for better or worse. Let's go find her."

He laughed as we trudged up the hill.

"What?" I said.

"It won't help that you're so good-looking."

"Thanks, but I know better."

Well, that had been my refrain ever since my *mother* showed up at one of our poker games in a black corset. Look, she was in her fifties when she pulled that stunt. Wanda still cries when she thinks about it. Her only refrain from that night is, "It isn't fair." She referred to Mom's age and the fact that she could still look like *that.* Next to her? I'm tepid at best.

"Seriously?" he said with a smile. "Are all women as obtuse as you?"

That made me stop. Okay, okay. Mario thinks I'm Helen of Troy or something, but Albert's single statement made bells ring in my head. Maybe I should temper myself. I'm not a psychologist or anything like that. I have no clinical training that would enable me to diagnose someone with mental illness – and that's just what I'd been doing. Okay, okay again. If my preliminary diagnosis about Sandra Seer is correct, then I'll recommend proper treatment from specialists who can better help her than I could or can. But this? Was it even possible? Did women drive themselves so frantic over their beauty that *this* was the result? They have to appear so chaste that God himself would be impressed. But what could lead to this point? What personal catastrophe would cause a woman with…oh, fuck. She has three kids. She's pushed three kids through her body and watched in horror as her body reshaped itself.

I turned to Albert and said, "When was the last time you told her she was beautiful and meant it?"

"I'm not allowed to tell her things like that. She says she is saving herself for God."

Well, naturally. When all else fails, fall back on the one guy in the universe who will think highly of you *if only you apply the rest of your life to him.*

"When we find her," I said. "Forget her instructions. Court her like you used to."

Well, I've been wrong before. Take Mario, for example. When Mom showed up in that black corset? I was wearing a red one. Wanda cried because not only had my mother showed her up, but so had her best friend. Hence, William-never-Bill is going to buy and install new boobies for her. Then? Mom, look out.

But what does that have to do with this?

Well, when Sandra saw me with her husband and saw that we had been...well...*relating* so well, she was going to be pushed to her limit. She was going to be at her wit's end and would try to blame me for what was going to happen.

And what was going to happen?

Well, Armageddon, of course.

A most personal one, but Armageddon nonetheless.

To misquote a song from my childhood, "It's the end of the world and I don't feel fine".

Sandra?

I humbly apologize.

***

I was coming down the mountainside on a diagonal slant. To my horror, Albert was with her, with Doctor SixSixSix. Worse? They were happy, laughing. *He's had carnal knowledge of her.* The voice, God's, was right. God is always right. The devil is always wrong.

The devil.

Her voice started screeching again. She called herself Sandra and kept telling me that was my name. She even implored me to check my birth certificate or my driver's license. "It's your name! You can't do this! She didn't do anything!"

"She...had carnal knowledge of Albert. She must die."

The devil's voice from inside me would not stop. "She's a doctor, not the devil. You hate her because she can prove that you've had carnal knowledge of Albert, too. She can prove with scientific certainty that you had sex with Albert and that he passed the herpes virus to you. She can prove that and doesn't need a Bible or The Book to do it."

"Science is wrong. I do not have herpes. God is punishing me for not being chaste enough."

Her voice changed. Sandra said, "Do you remember William? The goober?"

"Yes," I said hesitantly. He was a boy from my past. He died.

Sandra said, "He didn't die. You killed him. Do you remember Samuel? You killed him, too. Do you remember your mother's restaurant? Do you remember that it burned down? You committed arson. You committed murder. Then you married a man who was a millionaire several times over. Sandra, you poor godless idiot. You belong in jail, not as the founder of a new religion. In fact, any religion you claim to establish is not one I would believe."

I sat down on the hillside and tried to remember those events. Yes, I remembered William. He was goofy, but I did not kill him.

"You went for a walk and he suffered an unfortunate accident. He fell from a cliff that had a wall built in front of it. The police found you at home sleeping. They asked you if you'd been with him that night and you said no. They had no reason to disbelieve you. That had no reason to believe that you dared him to walk on that wall and then pushed him from it. Better police forensics would have found you on that wall. And Samuel? Our father had a manual for every car ever built. You found out where the brake lines were on his parents car and cut the lines. You knew he liked to speed. He hit a freeway stanchion at eighty miles per hour. You wore gloves. You burned them in the oven in the restaurant. Then you burned down the restaurant. Sandra? You belong in jail."

"Mom built another restaurant," I said.

"Sure. She had insurance. But even now, her life is hard."

Was any of this true? I looked at down the hill and saw people down there staring up at me.

"Surrender," Sandra said. "Confess your sins to them."

I needed to pray.

I ran back toward where the boulder could shield me from everyone else and dropped to my knees and prayed. *Oh, Lord? This is Rebecca, your child and most ardent believer. Is this right? Have I committed these grievous sins? Have I sinned against my own mother? Are these things true?* I expected to hear God's golden voice. I expected to hear The Truth. I squeezed shut my eyes and heard...nothing.

Except Sandra.

"Don't you see? It isn't god. It's you. God doesn't need you to speak for him. His voice carries storm clouds and the hottest heat and the deepest snows. He can speak for himself. He doesn't need sinners like you to carry his banner."

This was not true. These things were not true. I would never kill anyone. I would never burn down my mother's restaurant. I love her and always have.

"You damn liar. You refused to work for her and found the first rich guy with money and married him. Okay, I'll stipulate that you love him and let it go at that. But you've turned your back on him and your kids for ten years now. More than that? Each time he makes a point or scores one, you step further out on the ledge. Sandra, you stupid bitch. Come down, confess your sins to the proper people and take your punishment. And next Sunday is just another day. That's an arbitrary deadline that you imposed on yourself. My guess? That's the day you slide into complete catatonia. Where can this end but there?"

But, no. God has chosen me to be his terrible swift sword. God has chosen me to command everyone to take sides at last. God has chosen me to be his trumpet, to call everyone to task.

I stood and looked down the slope to where Albert and the devil in the form of Doctor SixSixSix were coming up toward me. I stood and blocked out all other voices, especially *Sandra's*. My name is Rebecca Ruth Seer and I will watch the ashes of the devil spiral toward the ceiling of God's Temple. I will watch as all the sinners turn to ash and then watch as they spiral down to hell itself where eternity itself will not be long enough for the torments God will inflict on them.

Sandra managed to get in a last word.

"You see? Even you admit it. God is responsible for evil. God created good and evil at the same time and then expects us to choose between them. Sandra? This isn't going to end well."

For her? No. I will never again hear her voice or listen to her godless diatribes against The One True God. I have written His Book, The Book. People will read it and either believe or not. Those that do will join me in heaven. Those who don't will spend eternity with those like Doctor SixSixSix and her lies.

It was time to end her suffering.

I pointed the rifle at them and screamed, "You will not confuse my husband beyond this moment. You will go straight to God's Temple and suffer His wrath."

Albert, to my eternal gratitude, laughed at the evil one. I don't know what he said, but the doctor did not look convinced. I stepped from behind the boulder and headed toward them. Albert spoke to her again, but she was still an unbeliever. That was fine. I did not expect the devil to take sides with God. God will triumph in the end and I will be at His side.

The day was as glorious as God could make it. Bright sunshine, puffy white clouds and a clear path to the evil one and her demise.

I had my finger on the trigger, but did not want to shoot her. I wanted her to burn forever in hell. I was going to send her there.

Albert laughed again and the doctor looked nervous.

Be afraid, bitch. Be very afraid because The Lord is coming for you.

Albert said one last thing to her and she raised her hands. I went down the slope and held my rifle on her. If she bolted? I would shoot her. It was all very simple now. Albert had returned to the Lord's side and helped me capture her.

"Turn around, unbeliever," I screamed. "We are going back inside God's temple where you will see His wrath."

She looked uncertain, but turned toward the doors and headed to her doom.

I followed her, Albert falling in beside me. He said nothing.

We walked back to the pulpit where the pit stood ready.

"Into the pit, heather," I said.

To my surprise, she went.

She even put her arms around the middle post.

Then she smiled and said, "Light me up."

That was not going to be difficult.

I went to the pulpit where the controls were, closed my eyes and said, "Into your hands, I commend this spirit."

I put my finger on the button that would destroy her.

I have never felt this glorious.

Never.

Chapter 20

We saw her coming down the hillside at the same time. She had her rifle pointed at us – and well, at me – and was heading for where we stood.

Albert said quietly. "Please, doctor. She won't hurt you, but you need to do this my way. Remember that pit in there is a fountain, that's all. And that gun? She won't shoot you. Please, don't fear her. I want a long life with her, but I want it free of this crap." Then he laughed said, "Sorry, god.

So, it was in my hands. Me, the girl who was always practical and never ethereal was going to be asked to take Albert Seer on the complete faith that he was exactly what he'd said he was. If I placed that faith in him and he had been flexing *her* muscle, then I was about to die a horrible death. Why? Because of what she said as she marched toward us with her rifle pointed at me.

"You, Doctor SixSixSix, will not confuse my husband beyond this moment. You will go straight to God's Temple and suffer His wrath."

That.

"Please," he said almost mutely. "She won't hurt you. She can't."

So, it fell to me. Again. Albert hadn't convinced me that he wasn't coming down on his wife's side and that he was going to let her burn me to death. But my basic personality was to allow my patients enough room to diagnose themselves if that became necessary. Most times, the symptoms spoke for themselves. True, Sandra/Rebecca had presented me with far more symptoms than most of my patients presented, but few of them ever attacked me with a rifle and a vow from god to burn me to death. Okay, okay, that's just another symptom. It was still going to fall to me to interpret it.

As expected, Albert fell in beside her. While that made me a bit nervous because I *really* didn't want to test the fountain/fire pit, I managed to push my personal worries into the background and fell into watching for symptoms, latent or otherwise.

The first thing she said to me when she came down the slope with her gun aimed at me was a bit off-center, "I am *not* going to confess to sins that I did not commit!"

That.

Okay, okay. She's religious nut and she was referring to sins that someone had told her she'd committed. I mean, right? What else can you confess to? But why lead with that? To me, a doctor, it was just another symptom added to the pile.

She pointed her rifle at the door and said, "Go, Doctor SixSixSix! Walk to your doom!"

Walk. I tried wiggling once for Mario and he laughed so hard that I fell into doctor mode because I thought he'd ruptured something. He hadn't; he just thought my attempted seduction of him was done with a purposeful handful of burlesque. When he realized I was really trying to seduce him, I was so mad that...I let him make love to me. This was not that funny.

I headed toward the door and regretted my inability to see her as I opened it and headed toward my doom – or whatever. I took the time to wonder about why she called me Doctor SixSixSix. Okay, okay. I get the reference. I'm the devil. Talk to Wanda. She'll tell you. Hell, talk to Travis when I tell him it's bedtime. He knows the devil when he sees it. But that appellation troubled me and I couldn't quite say why.

All too soon, we were on the pulpit, the pool/pit in front of us. Whatever was going to happen was going to happen here. Naturally, we were going to have an audience – and television cameras. The pews were full and no one asked any questions. Is this what religion does to people? Does it nail them to their seats while their leader instructs a doomed girl to her death? Okay, okay. Woman. I haven't been a girl since I was raped when I was sixteen. But enough moralizing and pouting. I had a patient and she was broadcasting symptoms like – she was on live TV.

She screamed, "You will stand at the center post and suffer for your sins!"

As an aside? What role does TV play in our society? It seems to me that it is all entertainment. Maybe I was auditioning for the latest reality show – Suffer With God – and I was the star of it. Maybe that's all life is, an audition for a part in the ultimate program.

Well, I played my part. I walked across the shallow pool – because there was water in it now – and took my place on the set. I stood before the center pillar and got wet enough for this to qualify as a wet t-shirt contest. I'm just glad that my back was to the post because I wasn't wearing a bra. This may be reality TV, but I was *not* going to let anyone but Mario see The Ladies.

I can't say that Sandra/Rebecca didn't play her part because she did. She walked up to the pulpit, stood in front of it and gave her role a bit of old testament prophet when she raised her arms, her gun held high and said triumphantly, "God is near! God is here! After we burn the evil one, we need only wait for Him!" Had this been anything other than a church – or temple, sorry – the crowd would have been cheering. It was like the home team hitting a touchdown. Um, scoring a touchdown? Sorry, I don't do sports, so she might even have pitched a touchdown. I just don't know. But the crowd remained respectfully silent as she did everything but read me my rights and then enumerate my various crimes.

She hadn't yet hit the switch that would either burn me alive or turn me in a Tijuana hottie. First, she was going to taunt me. Or try. Trust me, when you've been anally copulated by a guy who told you that he had no choice but to kill you, then can't be taunted by words. Still, she was going to play her part to the hilt. Oh, god. Hilt. Sorry.

She came down from the pulpit and stood at the pool's edge, her rifle held high in her right hand. She spat at me and the gob wound up floating in the water after it rolled down her chin. She really needed rehearsal for that spit.

Then came the sermon. "Doctor SixSixSix is the spawn of the devil!" Well, of course. The Ayatollah could take lessons from her. "She will burn as an offering for God Himself!" and why is God always a man? I thought God was neither and both at the same time? Oh, sorry. I was spoiling her Oscar Moment. "When I burn her here in this place, all that will be left is for God Himself to take us home again!" The TV cameras probably got her in close-up.

But it was time for my own Oscar Moment. She went back to the pulpit which was behind where I was self-bound and pushed the switch. Well, damn. There were water jets ringing the pool, not just in the pillars themselves. What does that mean? Well, my nice light sweater turning neatly transparent and everyone in the crowd saw The Ladies with Their Nipples Erect. Hey, it was chilly in that water.

I swear Sandra/Rebecca started speaking in tongues. Anger? Mad? Mad Cow? None of them describe her mood very well. She began screaming at Albert and then she came after her most obvious target.

Me.

Camera, close-up.

She came to the front of the pool and continued her sermon at me. Yes, screaming. A lot of people call them sermons. She called me Doctor SixSixSix to my face and that was enough,. I was no longer Doctor Evangeline Monica Sixkiller-Collins Collins, the little girl with the big name. I was pissed.

She screamed, "Doctor SixSixSix is going to hell for her sins!"

Okay, okay, I know the allusion. 666. The number of the beast. I don't know all the scholarly and religious claptrap that says the number 666 refers to Nero and that he was the beast. All I know is that my name was mine. I walked up to the edge of the pool and noticed at least three cameras take pictures of my boobies. No matter. They weren't going to heaven. At least not this week. But I was pissed.

I screamed into her face, "My name is Sixkiller! Not only was it my father's name, but I have dedicated my life to ending misery, suffering and death wherever I see it! In that sense? I am a devil-killer! I treat disease, suffering and death like the scourges they are! How dare you accuse me of being in league with that filth!"

Okay, I was arguing with a patient and doing it in a way that assumed her symptoms were not real. Real smart, Six. Well, in my own defense, she assumed that she was going to burn me to death. Okay, okay. That's just another symptom.

Then? Something *very* weird began to happen. She looked up as though someone was talking to her. She said, "I don't remember." I fell into Doctor Mode so fast that had I blinked I would have missed it. Well, no I wouldn't have. I stepped out of the pool and stood directly in front of her. I wanted to see her eyes. Were they dilated? I wanted to hear her words closely and carefully.

"Who are you talking to?" I asked.

"Sandy," she said. "She's crazy. She's saying the most horrid things."

I was on the cusp of something and I knew it.

"What is she saying?"

"That I killed William."

"Who is William?"

Well, without knowing it, I'd stepped into the center of her personality breakdown. Without knowing it, I was about to start to follow a trail that ended at least twenty years before. There were other steps along the way, but when I did not die in flames ignited by her, a cascade began inside her mind that was going to end Sandra/Rebecca in one way or another.

Unless that little speech I gave was meaningless, it was going to fall to me to save her life and make the rest of it worth living and looking forward to.

Hell, I'd strip to the waist if that would help.

I'm just glad that it didn't.

***

Glory be to God!

Doctor SixSixSix stepped up to the pillar, put her arms around it the way she'd been instructed and all that was left for me to do was to burn her. I have been so alone. I have been in the desert looking and listening for God's Holy Instructions. But this was wrong. I pushed the button and water began squirting from the nozzles in the pit. Rather than burn, she got nothing more than wet. In complete frustration, I announced to the faithful, "Doctor SixSixSix is going to hell for her sins!"

But the devil still had a voice. She screamed, "My name is Sixkiller! Not only was it my father's name, but I have dedicated my life to ending misery, suffering and death wherever I see it! In that sense? I am a devil-killer! I treat disease, suffering and death like the scourges they are! How dare you accuse me of being in league with that filth!"

And Sandra was there. Why can't she leave me alone? Why can't she see that I am doing God's work and let me do it?

"What happed to William?" she said hatefully.

"I don't remember."

"You took him up there to that place and pushed him over the edge. He was innocent! He was alive and you killed him! You told him that you liked him and then you killed him!"

A voice said, "Who are you talking to?"

"Sandy," she said. "She's crazy. She's saying the most horrid things."

"What is she saying?"

"That I killed William."

Then...

"Who is William?"

He had such a gentle face. William Frank. I met him in school. He made me crazy and I loved feeling that way when I was with him. We kissed sometimes. It felt wicked and I loved feeling that way, loved that he did those things to me.

But, no.

I was here for God.

Sandy kept at it, kept accusing me of things that...I knew were true.

No, I did not do those things. I am godly.

But things began to get...different.

I saw...

...a young girl and a young boy walking across the greenest grass this side of Ireland. They were holding hands. The boy said something...and static filled the moment...and they kissed but briefly, a peck at lips, a missed moment, giggles and hand holding.

I saw...

...another place, another time, the same young boy and young girl. He's troubled and she senses it. She tries to get him to tell her what's wrong, but he shakes his head and refuses.

I saw...

...that young girl cry at night in her bed. She was pushing him away and that was the reason he was upset. He was upset at her.

I saw...

...no other way to do this.

Then...

...static.

I said, "William? I'm sorry."

Then...

...more static. There was nothing, just gray. I might have fallen. God? Is that you? Are You watching me? How can You not judge me harshly? How can you allow me into heaven after this?

I saw...

...another young boy and that same girl walking hand-in-hand across a lawn somewhere. Was it home? Was it in a park? I couldn't tell. He was telling her something. She was listening and was confused. She thought he was angry at her. She thought she'd done something to him. He cried. She didn't know what to do.

I saw...

...no other way to do it.

Then...

...static and gray. I tried to see details in the static but saw nothing and heard nothing. I think I cried. I think I wanted something. I think I made a mistake.

I saw...

...my mother. She was crying. She was looking at what was left of her restaurant. I remembered. I put something in the oven where Mom cooked pizzas. I was scared. She held my hand. She didn't know.

Then...

...gray. There was nothing more. If my life meant anything, it ended there. I was...what? What had I done.

Then...

...a voice. Mine. I recognized it. Sandy. It was me. No, I would never do those things. I was beyond that sort of stuff. God...was it You? God...tells me things. God...says I'm chaste and beyond sin. I believe Him.

I saw...

...God grow horns. NO! NO! THAT CANNOT BE! I see myself as a young girl. I see myself wondering what to do and not seeing any answers. I ask God at night why William does not like me. I ask God nightly why Samuel doe not like me. I am confused. Why did I do those things? God tells me I am chaste. God tells me things. I see my mother crying. I hear her get angry with me. I see myself telling her that she'll be sorry. I don't remember anymore. I am angry with William. I am angry with Samuel. I am angry at my mother. They will all be sorry.

Then...

...the gray turns black.

There is nothing. I strain to hear any vestige of life and only hear the voice of God telling me I am chaste and should remain that way. Doesn't He know I have always been that way? Doesn't He know? Is He not God?

Then...

...I see God with Horns.

I see myself. What is my name? I cannot remember. I see myself. I have Horns. I am the devil. I am his child. I have done these things. I look at these things and cannot remember them. The devil tells me that I am guilty. The devil says I have done these things. God? God says I am chaste. God says I am beyond these things. God says it is of no matter. God says it is not important.

I see...

...that I do not exist. I see that I want to be right with God. I see that I want to be right with the world. I see the things I have done. I see that I am not right with God. I see that I am not right with the world. I do not see the things I have done.

I see...

...Seer. He says the most amazing things. I tell him I am chaste and he says that is a very good thing. I tell him I will always be that way and he smiles and says the most wonderful things. I tell him that his name is an omen for me. I tell him that he is my seer, my Seer. He will help me find my way. He will be my bulwark against everything that could hurt me.

I see...

...that my life is a lie. I see flames eternal. I see that I have lied to everyone. I see...

...the blackness that will engulf me.

I open my arms to it.

It engulfs me.

I am no more.

I am gone.

I have never existed.

God will have no need to judge me because I have judged myself.

I am gone.

I have never existed.

I am with William and Samuel.

They have forgiven me.

Thank God.

Chapter 21

I have to admit that Albert was right. She couldn't hurt me. I mean, she tried, but when she pointed that gun at me and pulled the trigger? Nothing happened. Click, click, click. Albert murmured, "She never took any ammunition. The box was still full and sealed."

"You could have just told me," I said.

Maybe I should be a bit more exact when I say that she pointed the gun at me. I mean, it was in my general direction, but even if it had fired, the shots would have destroyed some frescoes on the wall behind me. Hell, she wasn't even looking at me or anyone else. Her eyes were glazed over and it appeared that she was either talking to herself or was back with god. Either or both.

However, what got me even more involved than I already was when she collapsed. The entire crowd...um, congregation?...stood noisily, but the only people that crowded the...um, stage?...were the television people. Me? I went to where she lay and saw a woman who'd fallen with her eyes wide open. I felt her carotid artery for her pulse and it was normal, strong and constant. That indicated her heart was strong, but anything else was an educated guess. Okay, okay. Medical humor. Excuse me.

I looked at Albert and said, "We need to get her to a place a lot less public than this."

The TV idiots began peppering me with questions. Trust me. They were easy to ignore. Sandra/Rebecca had my complete attention.

Albert stooped over her and said, "Is she okay to carry to the house?"

"She's healthy enough. More than that? I'll have to examine her."

"Let's go," he said and picked her up and carried her right down the center aisle. She was rigid in his arms as he carried her out the temple and toward his home. The TV idiots followed her and continued showering me with their incessantly stupid questions. I ignored them and felt the pulse in her wrist. It was still strong and steady. Hell, in that moment, her pulse was probably more normal than mine.

I followed him into the house where Wanda had opened the door for him. I'd have to ask her how she knew we were coming. In that moment, she didn't matter as much as…whoever Albert held in his arms. Was it Sandra, Rebecca or neither of them? If someone had asked me to guess, my educated opinion was that it was neither. Without knowing it, it was going to fall to me not only to find the hidden personality but to make certain that it was the right one for her body and for her life.

He carried her to their bedroom and laid her under the picture of Infinity. He immediately asked, "What's wrong with her?"

My first concern was her rigidity. It was a sign of catatonia and could lead to exhaustion if not treated. I lifted her arm and it stayed upright. I was going to fight my urge to have her transported to the hospital in Kalispell – or to the one if Missoula. I crawled onto the bed and squatted next to her. I lowered her arm and checked her pupils. They looked normal, but I knew better. I closed her eyelids and Albert asked why. "Because she's keeping them open and unblinking. They will start to dry out and that's an unnecessary complication." Then I looked at him and said, "Or try keeping your eyes open like she did."

"Okay," he said. "I'm just worried about her."

"So am I," I said.

I didn't see a way around it. I was going to have to have her transported and treated by people who had the means and medications to treat her. For example, muscle relaxers would lessen her rigid pose and would start to show quick results. So, why was I hesitating? And was this in her best interests as a patient? I had a short amount of time before I began to lose it.

I patted her cheek and said, "Sandra? Tell me about William."

Albert was practically hyperventilating. I said to Wanda, "Help him before he faints."

She led him away and he let her.

It was just Sandra and I.

Well, and Maddy.

She didn't say anything, but she stood watching me intently. Me, not Sandra. If I made the wrong choice and Sandra died, then I was doing irreparable harm to her. It was the simple psychology of motherhood. Or of doctors. First, do no harm. Most times, that's easy to prescribe and follow. Here? I might be stepping over landmines or lighting them off for all I knew. Sandra needed a psychologist or a psychiatrist and all she had was a bumbling doctor.

But she spoke.

"Bill? I'm so sorry."

Albert was back. He didn't look any better but at least he was breathing easier.

"Who's Bill?" I said.

"Someone she knew when she was a lot younger."

I turned and screamed at his face, "Who the fuck is Bill!"

"William Frank," he said with annoyance and fear mixed together in equal amounts. "She knew him when she was fifteen or so. All I know is that he died. They were living in Colorado at the time."

What the fuck did it mean? I was practically frantic and if I got any worse, Wanda was going to have to handle my own hyperventilating. I did the only thing left to me. I asked her, "Sandra, honey? Who is William Frank?"

I was holding her hand and as soon as I asked that question, her grip got tighter. "I killed him," she said, her eyes not blank, but focused somewhere else, some when else.

Who would know the details?

"Wanda? I need a phone," I said as my own panic rose.

She rummaged in her purse, pulled out hers and gave it to me wordlessly. I dialed a number from memory and never even worried that I might have remembered it wrong. I hadn't. He answered. I screamed, "Alex! I need information as quickly as you can get it or I might lose a patient!" I'd called Alex Payne.

Bless him, but he didn't miss a beat. "Name?" he said.

"William Frank," I said. "He died about twenty years ago in Colorado. There was a girl named Sandra Peters involved. Can you?"

"Yes, he said. "This number?"

"Yes," I said. "How long?"

Mother used to be a private investigator. She sold her business to him so long ago that I can't remember. All I know is that information is what he does. If he couldn't do this, then I'd call 911 and request transport to Missoula.

"Soon enough," he said. "The impossible we do..."

"Yada, yada," I said. "Just call me back before I'm done talking to you."

"Immediately or sooner," he said. "The apple sure didn't..."

"Yada, yaada," I said. "I have a semi-catatonic woman on my hands and you decide to play word games."

I hung up.

Then I patted Sandra's cheek and said, "Please, honey. Talk to me. Details would help."

She squeezed her eyes shut and said, "Sammy! You, too! And my mom! Then Pastor Kennedy! I did all that stuff! I am going to hell!"

It sounded too much like she was talking to god again. But, no. *This is different. She's talking aloud to herself. She's introspecting.* It gave me some time to think because that showed an active mind, not one shut down by overload. Okay, catatonia can be brought on by something traumatic. Sure, there are other ways to induce catatonia. That aside, it looked to me as though she had written off schizophrenia as a diagnosis all by herself. It looked to me as though I was looking at a case of DID, dissociative identity disorder. At this point, it appeared as though she had created another personality, this one so further morally superior than her own personality that she shrank into the background. But twenty years? Was that possible? Had Rebecca Ruth been created in the aftermath of whoever William Frank was and whatever happened to him?

Take the chance. I looked at her and knew there was no chance she was seeing me. I looked down at her and said with my most commanding voice, "Tell me about William. Tell me what you did to him."

Tears rolled from her eyes. "I killed him. I pushed him from there." Then with sightless eyes, she said, "I'm sorry, Lord. I'm so sorry."

I felt that I was close, but still didn't see the landscape her mind was projecting for her. Okay, I knew that she killed a boy when she was fifteen or so. But if that was true, then why hadn't she ever been arrested? Christ, what were the details?

"Child?" I said with that same commanding voice. "Tell me about Sammy."

"He didn't like me, so I killed him," she said.

I looked at Albert and said, "Tell me you don't know that name. Go on, just try."

"Samuel Hoffman," he said, his eyes looking worried. I think he saw it, too. His wife was confessing to old crimes that were going to haunt her if I ever got her back from the brink of wherever she was.

"What did you do to Samuel?" I said, wondering if she really thought I was the voice of god or if she was just answering the first voice she heard.

"I cut his brake lines," she cried. "He crashed into a bridge support."

I looked at Albert and said, "Does any of this sound familiar?"

He shrugged and said, "All I can tell you is that I know their names and what happened to them. That she's guilty?" He looked at her and worried. "I don't know. This is the first I've heard of this stuff."

The last part was her mother. "What did you do to your mother?"

That issue almost lost her to me forever. She tried to answer and never quite formed the words. Her eyes fixed on a place only she saw and she fell into the bottomless pit again.

Then the phone rang.

It was Alex.

He had information about William Frank.

Oh, yes, he most certainly did.

"Alex, babe? If Mom doesn't make you Director of the CIA, I'm going to tell everyone about the vibrator under her mattress."

"Maybe they should make you director?" he teased.

"Nah, surgeon general," I said. Then, "Nah, I'd rather stay here and help real people."

"Need anything else?"

"Same thing on Samuel Hoffman. Same state."

"What else do I to do but give away freebies?"

But. "Alex? Am I taking advantage of you? I mean, you kept me sane during the worst time in my life. Is this going too far?"

"Bitch," he said. "I'll call you back with whatever there is."

"Thank you, Alex. From the bottom of my heart."

Now the real work started.

***

Not static, but fuzzy. I was dead and wanted to be. But something – someone? – was drawing me back. I did not want to go back there to that place and time. I was guilty and no one would ever feel sorry for me, least of all me. I was the one who deserved that fire. I was the one who...did I kill her? Did I kill that doctor like I had killed both Billy and Sammy? If so? Doctor? I can never tell you how sorry I am that I laid all my anger and guilt on you. Did I hear you right? Is your name really Sixkiller? I hope so because that means you are – were? – a better person than me. I want to be dead.

I tried. Oh, how I tried. I kept going and going and going and did not listen to the intensity of the fuzzy sounds. It was far away and I kept going farther from it. I felt as though I was flying at supersonic speed to a safe harbor where I would be buried for eternity. I deserved it. I was heinous and coldblooded.

But the fuzzy sounds grew louder.

Something touched my neck. I heard the same fuzzy sounds. Was someone talking to me? Was that god? God? Something touched my wrist. Someone? Was someone there? Was it god? God? Oh, how I have begged for forgiveness. Oh, how I have vowed to be the best of Your servants. Oh, how I have failed.

I remember...

...Billy's lack of whiskers and how it bothered him. I think they call it peach fuzz. He wanted a heavy beard and what he got was the lightest of fuzzy whiskers. I thought it was cute.

I remember...

...Sammy liked to drive fast. He said he wanted me to have bigger boobs. I hated it when he called them that. Sometimes we argued. Then, I killed...damn. I let him touch them. I let him pinch my nipples. I didn't like it. It hurt. I asked him not to do anymore and he said he would stop. He didn't. I hated him. I killed...

I remember...

...Mom.

I remember...

...The day Dad left. I hated him but I hated Mom more. She got another guy and I saw them...doing...it. Doing it. Mom liked it. Mom cried out to God and I thought that was the worst thing in the world. I yelled at her and she told me it was none of my business. I told her I wanted Daddy back and she said he could go fu...NO!

I remember...

...watching the restaurant burn while I held her hand. She was crying and saying the most heartrending things. She blamed herself while I knew who really was responsible for it.

I remember...

...not wanting to remember any more. I was digging a deeper and deeper hole and wanted nothing more than to jump into it, pull the dirt onto me from above and remain buried, dead and forgotten for everything I had done.

I remember...

...Mom being angry at me because I did not want to work in her new restaurant. Or her old one. Especially her old one. I remember screaming at her that the only reason she got a man was because she flaunted her...boobies. I told her that she wore tight dresses and that's why that new guy stayed around as much as he did. She told me that they loved each other and that was enough.

I remember...

...Albert. Oh, how wonderful. He never touched me. Is that right? Do I have children? Was I that disgusting that I would spread myself for him? He's a man and he cannot deny himself. But me? How could I tell him one thing and then do another? Did I have children? Did I? I tried hard to think. John. Joseph. Abigail. Yes! John is the oldest. Abigail has the largest vocabulary of a six year old I've ever heard. Joey has a nice voice. Very pleasant.

I remember...

...I will not see them reach to adulthood. I tried to tell them once how depraved I was, but Albert stopped me. He said something about a woman named Rachel and I said that was a nice girl's name. He said that Miriam was nice, too. I told him to find a nice girl. He looked odd when I said that. He asked why. I told him because you can't have too many friends.

I remember...

...Sixkiller. I killed her, too. I kill everyone.

But...

...a voice. Is that you God? Are you taking me home at last? Are You going to throw me into the fire? You should. I have committed the gravest of sins. I have killed people. I have destroyed lives. Everyone I meet tastes death and destruction. You should make me answer for my crimes.

Then...

...a voice asks me to tell Him about Billy. William. There is nothing to tell beyond the fact that I killed him. He was smart, much smarter than me. I could listen to him recite Pi, listen to him describe that nature of the universe and I killed him.

Then...

...God asked about Sammy. That was so much harder because Sammy was so different than Billy. To Sammy, life was simple. The winner goes the fastest and the winner of the race is always first. That was his own story, his own book. As much as I wanted to like him, it was difficult. He said to me once that girls were easy to look at because...and he blushed...they "curve". He tried to tell me what he meant, but I already knew. We were just things to him. What was the phrase? Fuck 'em and forget 'em? I told him that once and he got all embarrassed and upset. He tried to apologize to me but I knew how he felt. I killed him because I didn't want him to pinch me anymore.

Then...

...God said something that made me listen.

Was it you God? Or was it something or someone else?

A voice called me Sandra. Is that my name? I think not. Well, maybe...I don't remember anymore. Again. That voice. God? Is that You?

"God...is...that...you?" I think I said.

"Nope," the voice said. "But I think you should listen anyway. I think you'll find what I have to say as interesting as anything god could tell you."

So. It came to this. I was going to descend into the madness of the world. I have lived there before. I have committed many sins. Maybe this was God telling me that it was time to face up to the things I have done. Maybe this was the voice of man telling me that it was time for me to take my punishment and not to hide behind silly masks any more.

If that was it, then okay.
I was ready for justice.
God's or anyone else's.
Justice often hurts.
I had no illusions.
It was going to hurt.
A lot.

Chapter 22

Alex's news gave me some hope that I could do this without resorting to transporting Sandra to a hospital. Literally, I felt the answer was in my hands when I crouched over her and patted her cheeks. "Honey? Sandy, babe? You didn't kill William Frank."

And I waited.

She'd spent years, a couple of decades actually, building a wall around herself that only God could penetrate. My guess? Even then, the God she constructed in her mind was one that was to her liking. But it was that enormous pile of time that she'd built for herself that I had to allow her to destroy. If she didn't get it on my first attempt, I literally had all day.

Her eyes blinked. "I killed William."

I smiled. "No, babe. You didn't."

"He...climbed...onto...that...wall...and..." and she couldn't finish it. She was there with him and she had constructed a scene that fit her own predilections. If you want to exchange the word "prejudices" for the one I used, that's fine. All I was trying to do was salvage her mind, her personality and let better people than me fill in the blanks because there were going to be some.

"And?" I said smiling down at her. "What happened?"

If her eyes held to a fixed point, I'd know I had a lot more work to do. It was only if she blinked and started to move her eyes around my face that I'd know I'd made a basic connection to her. For what it's worth? They remained fixed and stared over my shoulder at something far away. That was fine because I knew where she was. She was with William that day. Well, her mind was anyway.

"I..." she said as her voice began to break into a million little pieces. "I...I...killed him."

I put my face near to hers and gave her my best smile. "How, babe? How did you kill him?"

"I...pushed...him...him...him...from...the...the...wall."

It was almost too much. She almost retreated behind that Godwall again. To prevent that, I said, "Um, no. That's not what happened to William Frank. Would you like to know how he died?"

If I had to guess, there were two primary personalities inside her who were struggling for predominance. Unless I did this just right, it was possible they could cancel each other out and she would fall into a state of catatonia much deeper than the one I was faced with here and now. If that happened? I would have no alternative but to call 911 and summon help. Literally, it was up to her now.

She blinked, but her eyes did not move. Then she said, "No. You are wrong. I killed him. I deserve to be punished."

"Do you want to know how he died?" I repeated.

"I know how he died," she said, her voice a b it stronger.

"Okay. What day of the week was this?"

"Friday night. Everyone was at the football game. We went for a walk."

"That is incorrect," I said still smiling. I wanted to look happy and energetic and upbeat and willing to face life rather than hide behind it like she'd been doing. "He died on Sunday morning."

She looked at me for the first time. Then she spat, "You don't know! He was on that wall and I pushed him off of it!"

I put my hands on either side of her face and said, "No, he died on Sunday morning when his parents were at church of autoerotic asphyxiation. You had nothing to do with his death." Then I pulled out my one question that would either crash her mind altogether or force her to the surface gasping for air. "Babe? Sandy, babe? You never had sex with him and when you heard what had happened to him, you blamed yourself and constructed a scenario of murder. Sandra Marie Peters? The only thing you were guilty of was loving him. You loved him and wanted to make love to him and you blamed yourself for never doing it."

Then, I began to plead with myself. *Please, baby, please. Don't retreat in to god. We're here for you. You have a life to live with us. You're innocent of these things.*

But, that wall was high.

She looked at me and screamed, "Stop it! Stop it! You're lying to me!"

I kept up my smile and said, "A story ran in the local paper about his death. Little was known of autoerotic asphyxiation then. But William was a smart lad and he knew his physiology. A lot of people called it suicide, but his mother would not allow that. She even called you by name in the article. He said that she knew you cared about her son and felt bad for you. She, his own mother, did not blame you. Why should your opinion of his death mean more than hers?"

She'd spent most of her life blaming herself for his death. A few minutes spent throwing arguments in her defense at her didn't stand much of a chance of denting the self-loathing she'd defended herself with for two decades. In fact, the sheer façade she'd erected to her own sense of putridness was going to take more than just a few factual items culled from the morgues of an old out-of-print newspaper.

If that's true," she said hateful, but said with the hater self-aimed, "then explain Samuel Hoffman! You say I loved William! I didn't love Sammy! When he died? When I killed him? I was glad!"

Alex still hadn't called me regarding Samuel Hoffman's death. Okay, a car accident twenty years ago might be difficult to trace. Still, I needed information on that death and I knew all I had to do was wait for it. However, that didn't mean that Sandra/Rebecca was going to wait.

Her voice got calm and she said, "William? I'm sorry. Sammy? You deserved it."

A double helping of mental dung. She'd piled so much self-loathing upon herself that it was possible the supply was self-correcting. And me? I was a doctor of physical ills, not mental ones. Sure, sometimes the two disciplines overlapped, but the steps were never very far or very major ones. This? A good lawyer in a courtroom could paint me as being so far out of my depth that not even a submersible could find me. Worse? I couldn't make any assumptions that my theories were correct, valid or even in the ballpark. Gawd, I wish I knew more about sports. Ballpark? Football? Basketball? What happened in such a place? Having some context would be nice.

I knew I was playing for time, for the time Alex needed to find whatever there was to find about the death of Samuel Hoffman, when I asked with my smile still wide and constant, "Tell me about Sammy. Why didn't you like him?"

Tears erupted from her eyes. Her voice, already far away, sounded even farther away when she said as it slipped in a monotone that made my fears for her ratchet up, "I hated him. He was always pinching me. My breasts. It always hurt. I always told him that, too." Then, even farther away, she said, "There was this road that led out of town to the east. It was flatland. All the way to Kansas. He could drive eighty, ninety, a hundred miles an hour and no one ever stopped him. I knew it. I knew that he was reckless. So, I cut his brake lines and he crashed. They said he was really messed up when they pulled his body out of the car. I didn't care. I was glad he was dead."

No tears flowed and no one corrected her, least of all me. I needed something solid, some piece of physical evidence to show to her. Having none, all I could do was smile and hope that I hadn't done more damage than she'd done to herself.

My phone...well, okay, okay...Wanda's phone rang. It was Alex. He said he had news of Samuel Hoffman. "Okay," I said. "Tell me." He did. In a real way, it was far worse than the story that revolved around William Frank.

"Alex?"

"Yeah, Evie?"

"My patient's name is Sandra Marie Seer. You might know her as..."

"...Rebecca Ruth Seer. Yeah, me and Ellie are partying up a storm because the world ends next Sunday." Then he said, "Why? What do you need on her?"

I was ashamed of myself. Why? Because I admitted, "Something on her mother. I don't even know her name. She said their restaurant burned down maybe fifteen or twenty years ago. That might be the last thing that turns this one way or the other. Alex? I reaching here. She needs someone with more information than I have. I think I'm screwing this up."

"Evie?" he said. "You realize that I'm alive only because of you and your efforts. If I ever need medical attention and you are in a position to give it, I want you to tend to me. Period. If that woman needs help and you're with her, then she has the best medical help she can get. Dammit, Evie. Stop this shit and help her."

Okay, okay. I got him a heart transplant a few years ago. He did serious steroids when he played football and his heart failed while he was here in Montana. Yeah, I had to pull a few strings, but when your mother is going to be the next president, you get the freedom to do stuff that others wouldn't.

"Ya big bully," I said smiling. "Just get me that information."

"Will do." Then he said, "And all before the world ends next week."

"What a relief," I said.

"You be good."

"Mario says I'm always good, but I don't know what that means."

He laughed. "See ya, Evie."

"Alex? You take care."

"Doctor's advice?"

"Friend's advice."

"Then I don't need a prescription."

"No, you certainly don't."

"See ya in a bit."

I felt so much better when I hung up the phone.

Now, all I had to do was bring back Sandra from the dead.

Almost literally.

***

See! I didn't do that! His own mother found him! I was innocent of murder! I did not kill William!

Then...

...shame. I may as well have killed him. He wanted to have sex with me and I was afraid. I knew it would hurt and I was afraid. I told him we had time. He always agreed with me. Then? His mother found him like that. I could have let him have me and he might not have done that to himself. As much as I wanted to celebrate, I knew the truth behind Sammy. I hated him and I killed him because he wouldn't stop hurting me.

The woman, the doctor got back in my face. I should listen to her. She knew the truth about William. As ashamed as I was, I knew that she was going to tell me the truth.

"Sandy, babe?" she said. I liked it when she called me babe. It was friendly and made me feel better about myself. "Tell me about Sammy."

I did. It was so bad that I heard another voice in the distance. Rebecca was there, was still there. She was cackling like an old woman. I was going to try to ignore her. I knew it was going to be hard to do because of the truth about Sammy.

The doctor said, "Babe? Sammy left a suicide note."

What? I think I blinked and said that. "What?"

She smiled down at me. "Sammy knew you didn't like him, but he liked you. His mother talked to a friend of mine and told him the whole story. He told me. I think you deserve to know the truth after all these years."

Rebecca just disappeared. It was just me now. Of course, there were so many other things that she would not be able to refute that this was mere filler. Still, I wanted to know. I needed to know.

"I...didn't...kill...him?"

"Honey?" she said. "He knew he was hurting you and he said he couldn't stop. He knew he was driving you away from him and he didn't know how to keep from losing you. All that car crap? He did it to impress you. In the end? He knew that it was scaring you and that you weren't going to date him much longer. His mother said that you were always respectable around her and she liked you." Then the doctor smiled down at me and said, "She still does. She doesn't agree with what you said about next weekend, but she said you were always truthful with her and that she appreciated it."

"Why...why...why didn't he talk to me?" I asked.

She looked sad. Doctors have a hard job. Sometimes their patients die. Sometimes their best efforts aren't good enough. Sometimes...and something clicked inside me. Ever since...I burned down my mother's restaurant...didn't I?...ever since I did that, I've let others make decisions for me. Is that true? Did God not tell me that stuff? Is the world not going to end next Sunday? I think I smiled.

"What?" she said ignoring her question.

"God...is...not...coming...next Sunday...He told...me."

"And who am I speaking to?" she asked.

"My name is...Sandra Marie Seer."

She smiled widely down at me and I felt good myself. I listened for Rebecca and could not hear her.

"Why didn't he talk to me?" I asked the doctor. "Why didn't Sammy tell me how upset he was."

Another voice. A man. It was ALBERT! He said, "Doctor? I think I can handle this one."

"Be my guest," the doctor said. She sounded happy. Albert did, too.

"Sandy," he said holding my right hand. "I can entirely commiserate with him. He thought he'd failed you. It isn't more complicated than that. I failed you, too. But Sammy didn't have anything to look forward to. Me? I had to get you better. I decided that rather than run away and hide, run away and drive my car into a freeway overpass, that I'd work to help you. I wish Sammy was here so I could tell him that you don't fail as long as you try."

I looked at him and tried so very hard to speak. "You...never...hurt...me."

He looked, too. Then he said, "Sandy? I gave you herpes."

I tried to point, but my arm was heavy. It shook as I pointed at the doctor and said, "A thing that she can help me with." I tried to laugh, but I don't think it sounded like one. I said, "That was supposed to be funny."

He looked at me with so much worry. "Sandy? Baby? I hope you know how I got it in order to give it to you."

"Miriam," I said. "She's so nice."

The doctor again. "Sandy? Are you going to let me treat you? Rebecca was pretty stubborn that God would heal her."

I was beginning to feel better even though I knew that my mother would never speak to me again. "Can I sit up?" I asked them.

They fixed pillows behind me and helped me to sit up. I still felt heavy. I don't know a better way to express it. I still felt that Rebecca was hovering somewhere. I felt that she was just waiting to take over again. I didn't know how to stop her. "Is Rebecca dead?" I asked the doctor.

She looked like she wanted to say yes, but said, "I don't know, Mrs. Seer. I think you are going to need long-term help before you'll feel normal again."

I looked at my clothes. "Is this what I drove myself to become? Did I become an ascetic because I thought I killed two boyfriends?"

Albert wanted to talk to me, but the doctor took over. "Sandy? Better people than I can answer that with a lot more authority than I have, but I think guilt had a lot to do with it. There are people who can help you sort out what happened and why God spoke to you. Me? I'm just glad I'm talking to Sandra Marie Seer."

With heaviness in my chest, I said, "Rebecca is a downer, right?"

She wanted to laugh, but said, "Rebecca was necessary, I think. She helped you through a very tough time in your life. She stood moral guard over you."

I looked at Albert and began to cry. "I was awful to you."

He squeezed my hand and said, "You gave me three wonderful children. No, Sandy. You were wonderful to me. Now? It can only get better."

"Doctor?" I said. "Do you speak to your mother?"

She laughed. "My mother is Melodie Chang. Yes. I speak to her. Why?"

"Mel..." and my voice dropped. "She is your mother? Will you leave for Washington DC when she's elected?"

"No. I'll stay here. I can't say I won't visit her from time-to-time." Then she asked, "Why?"

I hurt too much. I put my face in my hands and cried. So much of my life was gone and now I find that its biggest piece was missing. Why would she consent to talk to me after what I did to her? I said as I cried, "I ruined her life. She only tried to help me and I ruined it."

They didn't have any answers for that.

I didn't expect them to have any.

I closed my eyes and heard Rebecca far away.

She was coming for me.

Next time?

She was going to win.

I would be gone forever. At best, she would not win either.

Where would that leave me? Would I still exist? Would I be dead? Or would someone like Doctor...Sixkiller (?)...help me to a temporary truce just like this one?

I cried.

Rebecca was coming.

I hate her.

Chapter 23

She was slipping away again. Her eyes began to fixate on a spot on the wall opposite her. I was on the bed patting her face and talking to her when someone knocked on the bedroom door. Rachel stuck her head in the door and said, "Um, Mr. Seer? There's someone out here that says she'd like to see your wife."

"Who?" he asked.

The door open wider and it was a woman about my mother's age. Albert smiled and said, "Mrs. Peters. This is a surprise."

Sandra's mother? Was that possible? Sandy could see her easily from her place on the bed because the door was directly opposite it. While she could do some good here, she could also screw things up royally if what Sandy said about her was true. If she'd burned down her mother's restaurant when she was younger, her mother being here could drive the last nail into Sandra Marie's coffin.

I jumped off the bed with my intent to talk to her outside the bedroom. I hadn't even gotten to where she stood in the doorway when I heard a weak voice from behind me say with warbled imprecision, "Mom? You came?"

Fuck.

I started to cut her off, tried to maneuver her out the bedroom door, but she very gently and very adamantly steered her way past me to confront her daughter. She sat next to her while I began to panic and worry about my patient. Sandy's eyes were wide and ready. Well, I thought she was ready to retreat into deeper madness. I danced around her back like an expectant teenager at her first dance.

Sandy's mother had nice auburn hair that she wore short. Hell, I still didn't even know her name. I went to the other side of the bed, sat on it and leaned over Sandy protectively as I said, "Ma'am? *Please?* Can we talk first?"

She kissed Sandy's forehead and said, "Baby? I'll be right back. I have to talk to the doctor first."

Sandy warbled, "I'm sorry, Mom."

"Don't worry, sweetie. I'll be right back and then we can talk."

Sandy voice wiggled and she managed to say, "Okay, Mom."

We went out to the hallway outside her bedroom door. I kept repeating the mantra, *Smile, baby, smile.* Once the door was closed, I extended my hand to her and said, "I'm Evie, Doctor Six."

Her smile reminded me of cookies and Saturday mornings in the kitchen. Well, *my* Saturday mornings were with Grandma Nikki. My mother *never* baked a batch of cookies in her life. The way she explained it, "I don't want to burn down my home by trying to prove that I'm a good cook."

But the woman extended her hand and said, "I'm Kathleen. If you call me that, I'll assume you're angry at me for some reason. Call me Kathy."

"Great, Kathy," I said pumping her hand like I was trying to blow out a well somewhere in west Texas. "Why are you here? She's very fragile. An hour ago? She was completely comatose and so rigid that I worried about physical damage to her body. Considering what she thinks she did to you, I have to ask you if you're to cause trouble for her."

She sighed and said, "Doctor? Please, don't worry. I've been watching my daughter unravel like a huge ball of string being chased by a cat. When she started calling herself Rebecca? I knew it was going to mean trouble down the road. I mean, she was a fairly normal teenage girl. She listened to the music, went to the dances, got felt up behind the garage and blushed like a ripe tomato every time a boy talked to her. Trust me. I'm not here to cause trouble. I'm here because I need to lay this to rest once and for all."

I was however, a bit confused. I grimaced and said, "How did you hear about this?"

She laughed and suddenly, the world seemed a better place. She has one of *those* laughs, one that makes you want to enjoy a sunny day with a good friend or a book. Well, a medical one anyway. "Doctor?" she said. "I've been here for two days. My restaurant? Is in Missoula. Albert gave me money to open it. I've been paying him back a little each month for the last five years. When I saw her faint outside? I panicked and almost broke down the door. The only reason I didn't were those two girls out here. Miriam and Rachel? They said you were working with her, tending her, treating her. I waited as long as I could."

The girls, Miriam and Rachel, were there listening. They wanted Sandra to be her and not Rebecca. I thought it was obvious. Everyone was on Sandra's side it seemed. But was Sandra ready to face her mother in the final showdown? Sorry. I hate Hollywood, but I can't seem to shake their grip on my subconscious. Anyway, I had to consider Sandy's condition and whether she was healthy and mentally prepared enough to face her final nightmare.

I asked, "I have to know. Did she burn down your restaurant?"

She laughed and said, "Oh, doctor. I'm not here for vengeance. I'm here because that woman in there has suffered long enough. She's kept me away from her for a long time. I have three grandchildren I've never met. This? This could end a lot of one-way angst." Then she held my hands and said, "Don't worry."

Well, I do. I've been worrying about patients ever since I thought my mother had every contagious disease listed in every medical text I ever read. Hell, I thought she had some non-contagious diseases, too. So, worry? It was in my make-up, in my shampoo, in my deodorant, in my underwear, in my skin all the way to my bones. I'd worry until Sandy was healthy and then worry about her every time she crossed the street whether it was against the light or not. Still, we went inside the bedroom together.

Sandy's eyes lit up like the lighthouse on Portland Head. Worried? Ohmygawd. I practically began to hyperventilate. I wanted to throw that woman out of the room and protect

Sandy from whatever harm this was going to do to her. But my mother's voice echoed inside my head. *Treat the symptoms, Evie. So far? I don't have any. Treat someone that does.* Good advice, Mom. That just proves that every mother who ever lived had a bit of doctor in them. Or maybe it was just her. All I knew was that I was going to be there just as closely as Kathy was going to be.

She sat down on the bed next to her daughter. She took her hand as Sandy stared up at her with panic and fear written all over her face. Her eyes were huge, round and the brightest blue. "Mom?" She said. "I'm so sorry. I'm so sorry I..."

And Kathy began what I considered to be the final process of destroying her daughter's mind. By damn, I wanted to scream at her, but her eyes were so gentle.

She interrupted Sandy with a smile and gentle eyes. "Sandy, baby? Please? I came here to tell you something that I should have said with a bit more vinegar in it that I did. Baby? You didn't burn down my restaurant." Then she stopped and smiled at her daughter. "Do you understand that? You didn't do it."

Sandy was breathing hard and clearly did not believe her. She said, "I was mad, Mom. I remember."

Memories. We are cursed to remember. It is the human condition. However, I know better than most people, I suppose, that memories are as fragile as the finest China. Also, what is a memory to me might be a nightmare to you. I didn't even have to guess because that's what I was watching here. By damn, I almost pulled the plug on it. I came *thatclose* to pulling rank on Kathy. Why? Because Sandy was having a complete meltdown.

She started to cry, to wail and to scream over her mother's kind voice. As I almost ended it, I saw something else that I thought might be diagnostically relevant. Catharsis. The definition of that word that I like is an emotional release of tension. That one. There are lots of others. But this? Had Sandy been falling back into a pit from which she would never emerge, her physical symptoms would have been a lot different than they were. For example, she balled her fists and screamed, "I burned down your dream, Mom! I was mad and I wanted you to suffer! I burned down your restaurant and I cannot live with that thought! I loved you and I got mad one day!"

Kathy, though, smiled and said, "Can I tell you my version of what happened?" She held her hands tightly and said, "Please, baby? I'll tell the story and then maybe we can talk about Armageddon." Then she smiled and said, "And maybe have tea."

Sandy was breathing hard, but finally said in the end, "Okay, but we both know what I did. You can't change the past."

Well, Republicans and godless Soviets know that isn't true. Not only can you, but it happens every day in Congress. Good luck, Mom. *Those* people are crazy.

Sandy? Well, as it turned out, not so much.

Her mother took a deep breath, sighed, blew off all the tension and began.

It was quite a story.

It was spellbinding, true and proved to be the perfect antidote to what ailed her daughter.

Hell, even I listened intently.

Well, I had my fingers buried in Sandy's wrist because I wanted to keep track of her blood pressure.

I am, after all, a doctor.

Well, and in that moment, a listener.

***

When Mom went outside with the doctor, Rebecca's voice got louder. Her laughter seemed manic and not just a little frightening. I think I might have said something. Like, maybe, 'Leave me alone." I might have put my hands over my ears. I know, however, that Albert was there in that moment. Rebecca started to call me every filthy name human beings have for women they see as immoral. The issue was that I no longer believed I was immoral, just guilty of a crime against my mother. Albert said soothing things to me as I heard their faint voices outside the door. I knew that they were deciding my future. I knew that Doctor Sixkiller-Collins....and I couldn't remember her exact name. It made feel bad, made me feel unworthy of her help.

Finally, the door opened and they came back into the room. It hurt so bad that I know I screamed and cried. Mom was here at long last to gain her final victory over me. Rebecca would win and at most I'd be mentally dead forever.

She finally said with the same calm voice I remembered from childhood, "Can I tell you my version of what happened?"

Rebecca stood like a moral sentry over my grave. Mom said something about tea. I wanted to add only if it has arsenic in it, but couldn't manage it. Mom was going to recount that night from so long ago. She was going to remind me that I ruined her life and whatever dreams she had for it.

A funny thing began to happen, though. Tears rolled down her face and she said, "Sorry, baby. I promised myself that I was going to be strong, but I guess I'm just as human as you are."

"Mom?" I said and nothing more.

"Baby?" she said. "Do you remember your father?"

"Yes," I said because I did. I hadn't seen him since...

Mom closed her eyes and said with heartbreaking reality, "He left us one night eighteen years ago. He called me vile names and just left. Our home was behind the restaurant." She wiped her eyes and I began to feel horrid for my part in her pain. Rebecca was gleeful and crazy with blood lust. She was going to get mine.

Her tears turned into a torrent. Finally, she managed to say, "You probably don't remember it like I did. You don't get married just to get a divorce. When he left? I felt as bad as anyone ever felt. I felt inadequate, inept and ugly. I couldn't work – especially not in that restaurant." Then she wiped her eyes, looked at me and said with a purposeful intent that I caught, "Baby? You didn't burn down that restaurant. I did. I didn't think you were there. The most likely answer here for us, for you and me, is that you saw me do it and you knew I was hurting anyway. You knew I loved that place, so you decided to take that burden onto yourself. You decided in the deep recesses of your mind that you were an arsonist. Please, baby. Think about this clearly. I poured gasoline over the property, lit a match and then drove away. In truth? I was the worst mother in the world that night because I didn't even know where you were. My guess? You stood in the shadows somewhere watching your home burn to the ground."

Something clicked in my mind. Something that added up to an awful truth, one worse than Armageddon. "You were in jail."

"And you found Albert."

Like recovered film from an old studio, I began to see the scenes of my life in colors I'd never imagined them to be. I was…twenty. Albert made me happy. Then…Mom(?)…burned down the restaurant.

"Baby?" she said gesturing to the home around her. "I'm not surprised that all this morphed in Armageddon because that's exactly what happened to you. I caused Armageddon for both of us. If I had it to do all over again? I'd cry, get drunk as an Irishman and then apologize to you for being a bad example. I lost seven years of my life for doing something that hurt myself a whole lot more than it hurt him. And you? Look what I did to you. I caused a personal Armageddon to cause you to crash your entire life and then try to convince everyone outside that they had a week to live."

I blinked and saw all those old grainy movies from my life. I saw Mom throw gasoline on the grounds and then light a match and torch everything. Everything was burned. I had no clothes, nothing at all.

Albert said, "We went shopping. You lived with me."

"And Mom got arrested because…"

And the doctor finished it. "Because forensics don't lie."

Kathy smiled and said, "The miracle here is that Albert gave me enough money to get started in another restaurant." She smiled at me and said, "I'd really like it if you came to visit and share a meal with me."

I knew that this decision – whether to invite my mother into my life – was the one that was going to determine whether I lived a healthy life or fell into an abyss from which there was no escape. I smiled. "Mom? What's the name of your restaurant?"

She laughed, "The Arsonist."

"Small place?" I asked.

She stifled a laugh and said, "Oh, Lord. No, it's a pretty big place. I even have enough money to buy a place up Kalispell. Sonny's. The guy that owns it is selling it in order to retire. I'm going to be the new chef on the block."

The doctor laughed for a reason she didn't explain. Well, no. I asked, "What's so funny?"

"Oh, Sandy," she said holding her sides because she was laughing so hard. "Sonny's? That's my favorite restaurant in town."

Kathy smiled and laughed, then looked at her daughter and said, "How do you feel about topless waitresses?"

I laughed. "Mom? They won't bother me but they'll cause Rebecca to go catatonic."

"Well, relax. No one is going to be topless, much less your mother with her sagging boobs."

I closed my eyes and wondered about Rebecca. I couldn't hear her any more. I looked at the doctor and said, "Is there any reason I can't see my kids?"

"Nope," she said smiling. "You wait here. I'll get them.

I remembered them now. Johnny was ten, Joey was eight and Abby was six. Johnny had Mom's hair, Joey had my eyes and Abby, thankfully, had Mom's complexion and not mine. Abby was the first to crawl in bed with me. "Arc you okay now, Mommy?" she said with the innocence of a child.

"Yes," I said with a strength of confidence I hadn't felt in…what…fifteen years or so?

"Well, we want to go to play with Maddy at her house. She said she has two brothers, but one of them is just a baby. Can we?"

"Well, that's okay with me, but the person you need to ask is standing right there," I said looking up at the doctor.

Abby crawled over me, stood on the bed and pleaded, "Please, please, please? I really like Maddy and she's my bestest friend in the whole world. Besides, there's no school in the summer. We can play all day."

The doctor said, "Sure. Have Albert call me."

Abby began jumping up and down on the bed. Happy? Oh, lord. There is nothing better than watching your daughter jump up and down in the happy prospect of a new friend. I gathered my kids to me, closed my eyes and listened for the voice of doom. Nothing. Rebecca was gone.

I was feeling pretty good.

I was feeling like I had a chance at last. A lot of my clouds had been driven off by stronger winds that cleared my mind.

Then, to my surprise, the door opened and in walked the last person I ever expected to see again.

I closed my eyes and heard Rebecca.

She was going to make one last run at me.

And I thought she would win this one.

Why?

Well, because of who it was.

Because of what he represented.

The voice, Rebecca's got louder.

She knew she was going to win.

That bitch.

Chapter 24

I didn't think there was anything that would interfere now. Sure, she would need therapy for a while, but I thought it would go well for her. Things looked even better after Kathy told her daughter that she was buying a place in Kalispell. That it was my favorite restaurant in town just made it all that much better. Even Maddy added to my good mood when she handed back her wad of fives and said, "Everyone is calling everyone else either baby or babe. Mom? You win."

I hugged her and said, "Well, I'm still going to try to do what you asked of me. I going to try to call you Maddy. Is that okay, baby?"

Dammit so much.

I actually kicked the wall next to the bed. I plopped down to my knees and looked at her pleadingly. "Maddy? I'm sorry. I'm really sorry. I try so hard. Please, don't be mad at me?"

Damn, but she giggled. "Mom? If you want to keep doing this, I'm cool. Just don't be mad when I tell Abby not to let anyone call her baby because she isn't."

I laughed and said, "Don't worry. I won't be mad."

That was when things got a bit final. Oh, not that I knew it right then, but it was going to be the last act in a play that had gone on for almost twenty years. A man with salt-and-pepper hair walked into the room. Since Sandy was my patient, I got protective of her only because he looked at her. He was wearing a comfortably sport coat and the rest of what went with it. Oh, damn. Comfortable shoes, gray pants, a dress shirt open at the neck and down one button. That sort of stuff. The only thing missing was patches on his elbows. I extended my hand to him and said, "I'm Doctor Sixkiller-Collins Collins. Can I help you?"

Even worse for my tentative prognosis, Sandy was staring at him with evident dread. Her mouth was open and she said with the same horror she used when she discussed William, Samuel and her mother's restaurant. "You're Pastor Kennedy," she said with so much fear in her eyes that I figured it was just a matter of time before something crashed her mind.

He extended his hand to her and said, 'well, no. I'm Doctor Gene Kennedy. I used to be a pastor a long time ago, but that episode ended some years ago." He sat on the bed and said, "Am I speaking to Rebecca or to someone else?"

She said almost regretfully, "Um, Sandy? My name is..."

"...Sandra Marie Seer. Yes, I remember you when your name was Peters."

Hmm. Patterns written in the sands of time. I stood opposite him on the other side of the bed and said, "Let me guess. You're here to correct anything she thinks she did to you...what?...fifteen, sixteen years ago?"

He smiled and it was a winner. Women would love him. "No," he said shaking his head almost sorrowfully. "She probably remembers it just the way it happened." He smiled at her and said, "Ever since your prediction about next Sunday, I knew I had to see you." He waved his hand toward the temple and said, "It's time we sent them home with a better message. Right?"

"What's that mean?" I said. "That she remembers it just the way it happened?"

He laughed and it seemed to be a self-deprecating one. "She was outside a motel room with a camera and caught me...involved...with a woman who was not my wife. It caused quite the stir in the church, got me relieved of my duties and got me delivered of divorce papers from a woman who is now my ex-wife."

Sandy was slipping away. However, Doctor (?) Kennedy saw it, took her hand said, "Child? Don't. The woman you photographed me with was a graduate student in psychology at a local university and she got me involved in it. Not only did I marry her, but followed her degree three years later with one of my own. Sandy? I owe you a big thank you and I'd be honored if you kicked out Rebecca Ruth as being the idiot that she is."

"Idiot?" I said. "Is that a psychological term?"

"In this case, yes. Rebecca Ruth would rather see Armageddon than face her life," he said to me. Then to her, he said, "I would love to introduce you to my wife. I'd love for her to meet the person responsible for our lives."

Kathy started laughing so hard that I worried about internal injuries. She kissed her daughter on the forehead and said, "Little girl? I'd say you completed the circle. You ready to go outside and correct this mess?"

Well, that was my turn. "Folks?" I said. "I think I'm dealing with..."

"...dissociative identity disorder," Kennedy said. "Considering that I owe her so much, I propose two things. One? Any therapy is with me and on me. And two? I'll take care of the crowds outside because I think I'm partially responsible for them."

That left Albert. Well, and their kids. In my medical opinion, Sandy needed rest, therapy and someone to listen to her. Okay, it was fine by me if Kennedy was that person, but Albert had as much say in the matter as anyone besides Sandy herself. When I said to him, "What's your opinion here?" I was gratified that Kennedy agreed with me. He said, "I think the doctor and myself agree that your wife needs therapy and not a hooting crowd. My practice is in Missoula. All that means is that I'll be nearby when she's ready for therapy. But this?" he said nodding his head everywhere. "I can deal with this easily enough by myself."

It left me to ask, "What sort of issues will she be dealing with?"

He looked at her in order to answer my question. "Lots of therapeutic talk between us. Also, antidepressant s which I will prescribe and maybe some hypnosis that will help to identify the underlying causes of the personality disorder. Sandy? It will long-term and potentially emotional for you." Then he looked at Albert and said, "You would have to bring her, but take no part in therapy until and unless I think it becomes necessary." Then he looked at me and said, "More than that, I can't possibly say until we start talking about her issues, the ones that led to Rebecca Ruth."

I nodded and said, "Albert? That sounds like good therapy." Then to Sandy, I said, "And I agree with having Albert take you to and from the sessions with Doctor Kennedy. The sessions will most likely be traumatic and Albert will enable you to get home safely."

Both of them nodded.

That left one more last thing again. "Doctor? Both of them have genital herpes." Then I nodded at Miriam and said, "Her, too. I'd like to treat them all before you start your sessions with Sandy."

Albert said to his wife, "That's a hell of a drive, but I'm willing."

"Um, no," I said. "I'll come here with my assistant," I said nodding at Maddy. "She'll want to consult with her peers. While she's doing that, I can provide treatment for all three of you folks."

I'd like to say that we tied up all the loose ends nicely, but that wouldn't be true. This has always been about Sandra/Rebecca. This entire place exists because of her, not Albert. We were asking her to make a decision about her home and her god, two things that are close to everyone in one way or another. Even disbelievers have to confront that fact. That said, Sandra/Rebecca said, "I need to speak to them."

Well, I wasn't exactly gung-ho for the idea. I didn't think she was strong enough and the issue of her dissociative personality was still front-and-center. She might revert to Rebecca and caused a stampede aimed at us. She might also stand there as though frozen, catatonic to the end. For the record, though, I wasn't worried about myself. Maybe I should have been because I had my daughter with me. My concerns were strictly for my patient and the fact that I didn't think she was strong enough to do this – and I mean strong in every sense of that word as I could. She was just out of the hole she'd put herself in almost two decades ago and I thought it was a bit too soon to confront her ghosts –

even if they did look like god. Hell, even Kennedy took my side.

He said to her, "I think it is premature to go in front of a crowd that will only reinforce your personality disorder."

Albert, however, had more experience than any of us with her. He sat on the bed next to her, took her hand and said, "If anything happens? I'll be there."

That was all she needed.

She looked at him as though she hadn't seen him in...twenty years. She smiled and said, "Why, Albert? Why did you stay all these years?"

His answer was the simplest one possible. Also, the most complex. "Sandra Marie?" he said to her. "It isn't any simpler than that I love you. I fell in love with you on the plains of Texas. This? Is just another hurdle. If you fall? I'll be there to help you up."

"Let's go send everyone home," she said.

Well, damn. Every story needs a good finish.

I was glad I was there to see this one.

As they say in Texas.

Day-yum.

Sandy, babe?

You rock.

***

I don't think Rebecca Ruth was ever scared. Every time the world intruded on her, she looked up at said, "God? You handle this one." In that sense, I don't think she was human, or didn't want to be. Being human, we are given choices and have to choose among them. Rebecca Ruth never chose anything that God didn't officially sanction. She was just a receptacle for his wisdom. But this? Talking to *her* crowd? I knew I was going to have trouble. This is where I was going to bury one of us.

I went hand-in-hand with Albert. The TV cameras were still there. The crowds were still there and the expectations that I put upon them was still immense. Yes, I gave them –

all of them – expectations. Okay, that the world is going to end is not a message that everyone will either believe and/or welcome. I was already labeled a kook by a good portion of the country. That was fine because in the strictest sense of that word, I *was* mental. I could only hope – pray? – that I would be free of mental clouds after I was done talking to them.

They parted like the Red Sea before Moses as I walked toward the temple. Some even bowed. I'll admit to being a bit scared as I walked among them. Doctor Kennedy and Doctor Sixkiller...whatever...accompanied us. Our kids went with us. Her daughter went with us. Her friend that had outfoxed God went with us. Even Rachel and Miriam went with us. I don't know how Miriam and I will treat each other from here, but I hope we can be friends. Why? Well, Rebecca Ruth wasn't wrong about everything. Maybe god isn't coming, but he still wants us to be kind to one another. Or, put another way, let peace begin with me.

The fountain was blooming. Indeed, it was wonderful. Holding geometric shapes and changing colors, it was a testament that there is more to god's universe than we believe is possible.

I took the pulpit. Everyone was arrayed behind me. Well, Albert had to turn off the water. I was as ready as I could be.

A voice, a vestigial one, cried from the wilderness of my mind, "I will always be here. One day, you will fall." Maybe each of us truly does have the power of evil inside us. And was Rebecca Ruth evil? When I look at my children, I wonder why a truly loving god would want to hurt them deliberately. If god could intervene, why not help us rather than kill us?

I stood as straight and as tall as I could. Odd, I thought. I didn't even call this meeting, yet they were here. "People?" I said to them. "Do you not believe it is strange that we are here only because I predicted the end of the world? Do you?" I gripped the sides of the pulpit and leaned forward just a bit. "Imagine what we could do together if these types of meetings were held with the same fervor as Armageddon has been?"

A soft murmur rose from them. Rebecca Ruth cackled. I focused on a man whose eyes looked hard suddenly. "Sir?" I said to him. "Would you like to speak? Have I said something that offends you?"

He spoke from his first-row seat at Armageddon. "Are you saying what I think you're saying?"

I smiled. "And what do you think I'm saying?"

"That you lied. That God isn't coming."

The murmur got louder. Still smiling, I said, "If god was here right now, would you know it?"

That man stood up and yelled, "You said He was coming here and that the righteous would be rewarded!"

Albert came to my side, but I said softly, "It's okay. He just doesn't see. It's going to be up to me to make him see." I looked back at him and said, "Sir? How is god not here right now and how is he not rewarding you right now?" I stepped from the pulpit and walked the few steps toward him. "Or do you require something of him? Or do you make demands of him and require that he bow to you? Is that it? You command and god obeys?"

He took a step forward and said angrily, "I quit my job, lady!"

"Did you even like that job?" I asked.

"It doesn't matter!" he bellowed. "I can't go back!"

"Interesting," I said turning and walked toward the center aisle. There was a little girl with her mother, a little blond-haired girl that looked uncertain about what was going to happen. I pointed to her and said, "That little girl hasn't giggled enough. Also, there are boyfriends in her future and one special boy who will make the human a little happier." Then I turned back to the man without a job and said, "Interesting. You can't go home again. Other than being a terrible novel, it is also wrong. It is the human condition to seek shelter, to seek comfort and to seek it among those we trust. Sir?" I said raising my arms to the multitude, "You came home here. Why not there? Why not leave here with a smile rather than a hate-filled heart?" I took a step toward him and said, "You would deny that little girl her giggles and her blushes and the joy of finding that boy? Would you? Seriously?"

He sank back onto the pew and cried.

I knelt in front of him and said, "We are all friends here." He was Albert's age, maybe a bit older. Unshaven and looking as though he wanted a way out, he cried as I said, "And you unburden yourself on me."

"Amy," he said as tears rolled from his eyes.

"Tell me about her."

"She died. I want her so much."

Movement to my right betrayed the little girl and her mother. The young one, "Mister? That's my name. Amy. We could be friends."

He looked at her, then at me. "I suppose I could talk to Walt and maybe get my job back."

Amy's mother said with a smile, "And my name is Tracy. Maybe we could have lunch and you could tell me about Amy and I could tell you about David."

I stood and said to the crowd, "Will every story have such an ending? Certainly not. But assuming that god will end my misery simply because you are is tragic beyond recall. People? We are here together. And whether the world ends this Sunday or a million years from now, we have time together."

The murmuring continued, but it sounded different. A few people said Amy's name and it sounded complimentary. I knew I could go back to the pulpit, but it would rob me of friends and gain me little but acolytes. Therefore, I decided to walk right down the aisle and speak to them. "Why would I glorify turning someone to ash? Why would you believe I would stop the world simply because you want to get off? People? Anything we do here today will be done without God's interference. If you kill me because you think I lied to you, then that is on your soul as well as mine. Me? I want all the Amy's in the world to have all their giggles and all their blushes. I want to them to look at their mommy's and ask them if that boy likes me. Folks? We all share Armageddon. All of us. One day we will fall to it, but each of us will fall in our time. This? This day is my own personal sunrise at Armageddon." I doubled my right hand into a fist and said, "And I swear that I will live my life to its fullest, so help me god."

And I looked at them and they cheered.

And I closed my eyes and listened for Rebecca Ruth.

But she was gone.

God had taken her.

To her own Armageddon.

Rest In Peace, Rebecca Ruth.

God knows I did not get any rest as long as you ran my life.

It was time to catch up on it.

I have a family to raise.

Chapter 25

Maddy was ecstatic. Well, she'd found a new friend in the unlikeliest of all places. Abby was destined to become one of Maddy's best friends. That was made possible when Albert and Sandy bought a lot within Stillwater Loop, the street where I live. Construction started on the house started three months after Doctor Kennedy and Sandra began their therapy. I started both Sandra and Miriam on acyclovir and both responded well it. Both will continue to have outbreaks, but the more rigidly they take the medication and my recommendation, the better their lives will be. Albert was already taking medication prescribed by Doctor Tremont in Missoula. He handed off Albert to me as a patient only because it made things so much easier.

But why did Albert and Sandra move to Stillwater Loop? Well, Mario and Cayn Wyatt run The Best School from a building right down the road from where we live. The school is run the way Mario thinks best. Period. That means that he talks to every kid every day. Period. And he talks to them separately before he decides on whether or not to accept them as students. Cayn, too. He does the same thing. All that means is that all three of Sandra's kids passed the bar exam to get into their school. They start this fall.

And Kathy? Well, Sonny's does more business than her restaurant down in Missoula, so she hired a manager for it and moved to Kalispell. How much do Kathy and Sandy miss their past? Well, Kathy moved to East Bowman drive, bought a house there. Where is East Bowman drive in relation to Stillwater Loop? Well, Mario can literally throw a baseball that will literally land in Kathy's front yard on the fly. It's just to the west of our home.

But I have to admit that Sandy's recovery proceeded at a far faster rate than I would have thought. Her herpes outbreak responded to treatment and that made her happy.

But her therapy with Doctor Kennedy went even better. There were no signs of Rebecca Ruth. Doctor Kennedy tried calling her a few times, but never got a response. Sandy was completely delirious with joy that not only did Rebecca Ruth not reply to Doctor Kennedy, but she didn't appear whenever Sandy tried to summon her either.

The only trouble that ever appeared were a few of the people who showed up and were angry that Rebecca Ruth lied to them. Each time it happened, Sandy went out to talk to them. Each time it happened, the people came inside and shared a cup of coffee with her and they basically became friends. Sandy told me once, "Doctor Six? That wasn't another person. Rebecca Ruth was never someone else That I replaced. She was me. She was the person I hid behind. She was the person who decided to let god make all her decisions for her. In that sense, she can return anytime she wants. My only defense against her is to be the person I see behind my eyes. That person wants to be responsible for her life and everything she does in it." Damn that was nice to hear.

I still have a fat ass, though.

Oh, please. A woman knows this stuff. Black latex on a fat ass doesn't hide the fat ass, just makes it easier to look at. Oh, sure. Mario says I'm fine and says it the way all men do. Hell, even gay old Cayn Wyatt can say it. Of course, when he says it, he's not saying it to me, or to anyone of my sex. Still, he can say it. Me? Whenever Mario says it – "Oh, damn, you look fine" – I roll my eyes, take off the leggings and try to throw them away. I think I've thrown them away at least half a dozen times, but they keep showing up in my closet. No one will take credit for it, but Maddy giggles every time I come downstairs holding them in my hands.

Oh, and I'm still giving her five dollars whenever I call her baby. The pot is one hundred and five dollars. It got so bad that Travis started whimpering one day when I called him "son" instead of Travis. I snorted, "Look, Travis. You're my son. That doesn't count any more than me calling Maddy daughter does."

"But, it makes me sad," he said because I won't and never have called him "babe".

"Deal with it, babe," I said and then wadded up a five dollar bill and tossed it to him.

It was the last one he ever got from me for that reason, but we started a pool for him when one day I called him "Grandma's boy". He actually started to cry. Oh, no. He loves my mother. But he's a male and those types don't emote and will *never* allow you to call them that in front of other friends. I gave him five and had to call him "Grandma's boy" on purpose a few times just to think I was being as airheaded with him as I was with his sister. In truth? I have *no idea* why I have such a hard time with Maddy and calling her "baby". I still do and still give her five dollars every time I call her that. I don't even think Maddy is angry at me anymore for calling her "baby". I think she likes it. But a deal is a deal. My fear is that she'll have so many cute outfits that we'll have to build her a walk-in closet far sooner than we plan to.

But, damn, life is good. Oh, I still work myself to exhaustion. Hell, both of us do. But we balance the exhaustion with semi-regular poker games. Imagine my surprise when Sandy showed up with her mother and both of them were wearing black latex leggings that looked better on them than they did on me. Oh, and that bitch best friend of mine? She showed up a in a frigging catsuit. You know, the kind Michelle Pfeiffer wore in "Batman Returns". Worse? She had *boobs.* Even worse? Her and William-never-Bill had to excuse themselves to use the bathroom on the *third frigging floor* and were gone for nearly forty-five minutes. When she got back? She looked at me and all she said was, "Meow."

But damn, we had fun.

But who had the most?

Sandy.

Oh, Lord, she laughed until she cried and then laughed some more. Her best laugh was when she arranged a "beauty pageant" for me, Wanda and Kris Tice. She's a trauma surgeon over at the hospital. Wanda preened like a queen and then the men chose me as the prettiest. Sandy laughed until she cried, but so did a few other people. Well, Wanda just cried because, and in her words, "I'm never going to be prettier than you, you bitch." Then she felt her new boobies and said, "Five grand down the drain".

William-never-Bill just closed his eyes and said, "Um, no. Not true."

Mario had a mouthful of beer when he said it and it caused us to find another poker table when he spit all over it. At least Wanda's feelings were assuaged.

At least my mother didn't show up in her damn black corset again.

How does she do it anyway? I mean, how does she find out about a poker game that is basically last-minute and manage to come looking like that?

This time?

Platform boots and a body stocking. Oh, *gawd*. And she played server all night long. She'd dip over your shoulder, give you a generous view of a nice boobie and then work her way around the table. If this is how she's going to win the next election, then fine.

Mom?

Seriously?

Thank you for this, for letting me work out my future on my terms and helping me toward it. And thank you for being active in my life and showing up in a body stocking that will only add to my growing list of nice memories.

Mom?

Everyone should have a mother like you.

And now, John, Joseph and Abigail do.

God bless you, Sandra Marie Peters and god bless Albert, too.

The world needs more people like you than not.

And, yes, I think you know what I'm saying.

My own theology goes like this: If god is coming for me, he's coming for *me* and not *us*. It would be my failing and not ours. God doesn't want my soul until I'm done with it.

And trust me, I'm not.

Not yet.

Not by a long shot.

***

We sold the grounds, temple and all, to a seminary. Oh, we took a horrendous loss on everything, but neither of us really cared all that much. We were tentatively planning on moving back to Amarillo when Mom showed up one day and showed me a photograph of a nice home. "It's going to be my new home." We spent nearly an hour talking about her deal with Albert, how grateful she was, how much she'd managed to pay back when I said, "Exactly where is it?"

She pulled out a map, I mean an old-fashioned map like you buy in gas stations. It was a map of Kalispell and she scrolled to a point north of downtown and said, "It's right here. East Bowman Drive," she said happily. Then she traced the route she would take to Sonny's her new top-of-the-chain restaurant and said, "See? It's not that far."

Well, I was happy for her. She had a nice place, a nice life and I only wished I could be part of it. Then she pointed to a street named Stillwater Loop. "It's named after the stream behind it. The Stillwater River." Then she pointed a spot inside the loop and said, "Guess who lives right here?"

I thought she was going to say, "Your father."

Not exactly.

"Who?" I said truly curious.

"Some doctor. Sixkiller...something."

My eyes widened and I said, 'Really? You're going to be practically neighbors?"

Then she pointed to a spot just outside the loop and closer to the river. "This lot right here?"

"Yeah?" I said.

"Is for sale."

My eyes widened and my mouth dropped. Albert spoke for me. "Who do I call?"

Mom gave him a business card and said, "Her."

It'll be Christmas before we move in over there. Well, we have to design and build a home over there before we can live in it. We're renting a house nearby in the meantime. And by nearby, I mean close enough so that Maddy and Abby can be friends. It doesn't hurt that Johnny and Joey discovered Travis and Woody and hit it off with them.

But everything that happened to me since William has taught me that life is far more precious than I thought. You tend to think that you have time everlasting – and while that might be true in a religious sense, it is not true at all in the here-and-now. For example, I like Evie's friend Wanda. Oh, not that she's a trauma nurse over in the ER, but because she tries so hard to be prettier than Evie. God alone knows they're both beautiful, but each in their own way. Maybe Wanda will never figure it that she needs to stop competing with Evie. Maybe Evie will never figure it out that she's gorgeous and that she needs to deal with it. Heck, maybe I'll never figure out Albert's attraction to me either. Maybe that's why all of us girls do lunch at least once a week. And Kris? Ohmygawd. She's a lesbian. If that alone doesn't summon Rebecca Ruth, then I think I'm safe for the rest of my life.

Oh, and Norma? From Evie's office? she keep cupping her hand to her ear and saying, "Are those celestial trumpets I hear? Is that God?"

Well, I say with complete tongue-in-cheek truth that, "Yep, and he's coming for you and not because you lap up every last bit of Kris's affection, but because he doesn't like you."

Yep, Kris and Norma are an item, an exclusive item.

And does the fact that they're lesbians bother me at all? No. Not a bit. More to the point, should it? As long as they behave themselves the same way anyone else would, then they're okay as far as I'm concerned.

But in the end, my past will continue to haunt me only because it is attached to me. I told all those people that God was going to kill most of the human race *because I said they didn't conform to god's law*. Every now and then I get The Book thrown at me. Funny, huh? Well, no it isn't. The issue for those that throw them at me is that they believed me. Maybe they believe that god – or God – needs to sort out the messes we create for ourselves. Maybe there are those that can't bring themselves to agree with anyone other than themselves. If so? Then the human race can do without them and they can squabble among themselves. But I can't take that back, the fact that I said that particular thing and that people believed me.

Those cameras that were there that day? The TV ones, I mean? Well, that film has been shown and reshown so many times since that day that when god really does come for me, he'll hold against my soul. I was a coward, acted that way and tried to make GOD be the arbiter of everything. I got to a point where I didn't make any decisions. I let GOD do everything. For me? I can never be that person again. Okay, I'll admit that God is a good influence. There is, however, so much written about god that you can literally take your pick about what you choose to believe about him. Her. It. Me? I will never recover from that time in my life. It will haunt me because I let it happen to me and I caused a lot of people pain.

When we sold the property to the seminary and left for the last time? I wished that I could have said goodbye to that period of my life. But I did those things and I cannot deny them, even though Doctor Kennedy said I was sick. Well, literally out of my mind. The fact is, I put myself in that position. I chose to hear god and to attribute to him all the things that were wrong with the world. Okay, child slavery exists in Africa. Is that not wrong? Hell, it existed in this country for over two hundred years. Was that not wrong? Should not god have returned and righted all those wrongs? And if not, then what was his excuse for being silent during The Holocaust? My point? It is a matter of my personal belief that god isn't coming back. Period. He created us and set us free to do as we will. The afterlife is where wrongs are righted. And you can read into that whatever you wish. When someone throws The Book at me? I know that there is another book somewhen into which all those wrongs have been written. What will happen to my soul when my times runs out is personal. You don't need to know.

Is forgiveness real? There are times that I don't think so , especially when someone throws The Book at me. But so many people who were there that day have spoken both kindly to me and kindly of me since then that I believe forgiveness isn't doctrinal, but personal. Being cleansed in the River of Forgetfulness is a thing each of us can do – and should.

Doctor Six? You were a godsend to me. Your singular efforts to help me is the reason I am still alive and not catatonic in a mental hospital somewhere. Yes, I know you felt that you were out of your depth with my condition, but I am here to say that you saved my life, gave my husband a wife and my kids a mother. How does one repay a debt like that? One way is to be a good friend and I will be yours for the rest of my life.

And Doctor Kennedy? Thank you for helping me the way you did. Thank you for concerned about me enough to find me.

Last of all? Thank you, god, for allowing these people into my life. And thank you for making my evil as benign as you did. It could have been a lot worse.

I could have used god as an excuse to kill as many people as possible.

But that is done too much in your good name to make me comfortable.

I will not tread that ground or swim in those waters.

God is peace and love and anyone that says different can kiss my fat ass.

Sorry, Evie. Yours is a lot better than mine.

Oh, damn.

I just had a fit of giggles because Albert doesn't agree.

Bless him.

www.ingramcontent.com/pod-product-compliance
Lightning Source LLC
LaVergne TN
LVHW010203070526
838199LV00062B/4477